SCHOOLED IN LIES

A Kendra Clayton Novel

D1599007

SCHOOLED IN LIES: A Kendra Clayton Novel
ISBN-13: 978-0-615-33432-5

Cover Image: Eka Panova/Shutterstock.com
Cover Design: Angela Henry

SCHOOLED IN LIES

A Kendra Clayton Novel

by Angela Henry

Boulevard West Press

Praise for Angela Henry's Kendra Clayton Series

THE COMPANY YOU KEEP
"A tightly woven mystery..."
—Ebony Magazine

"This debut mystery features an exciting new African-American heroine... Highly recommended."
—Library Journal

TANGLED ROOTS
"Smart, witty, and fast-paced, this second Kendra Clayton novel is as likeable as the first."
—CrimeSpree Magazine

"...appealing characters...witty dialogue...an enjoyable read." 4 Stars
—Romantic Times Magazine

DIVA'S LAST CURTAIN CALL
"It's the perfect script for a great summer read."
—Broward Times

"...this series is made of inventive storytelling, crackling wit and that rarity of rarities in American publishing: an authentic, down-to-earth slice of Black life."
—Insight News

This book is for all the people who love reading about Kendra as much I love writing about her.

Also by Angela Henry

The Company You Keep
Tangled Roots
Diva's Last Curtain Call
Schooled In Lies
Sly, Slick & Wicked

The Paris Secret

Knight's Fall: A Xavier Knight Novel

Prologue

Summer 1996

JULIAN SPICER HAD BEEN pounding away at the same nail long after he'd driven into the loose roofing tile. He imagined the nail was the face of his idiot secretary. He still remembered the pathetic excuses and the tears as she tried to explain why she hadn't given him the phone message that had come four days ago. Four days ago! How hard was it to give someone a phone message? It wasn't rocket science. Not that it mattered now. By the time he'd found out about the missed message, it was already too late. He'd lost out on a major client account, an account that would have put his struggling business in the black. But Julian quickly came up with a way to save himself a lot of money. He'd fired his secretary on the spot.

He shouldn't have hired her in the first place. He'd let himself be talked into it by someone he never should have trusted in a million years. Someone he thought he knew. He'd been wrong. But Julian had ended that association as well, just as quickly as he'd fired his secretary. Still, he felt like a fool every time he thought about the phone call that he'd received two days earlier informing him of a truth he had no idea even existed. Surely the caller had been lying. He found out all too painfully that it wasn't a lie. He was being used. No big surprise. He'd always been a sucker for anyone with a problem. A *soft touch* is what his Aunt Emma always called him. Julian liked to think of himself as a fixer, someone who always knew what to do and how to do it, always full of answers and solutions. But what had that kind of attitude gotten him?

He turned his attention to another loose tile hammering away at it trying uselessly to pound away his hurt and frustration. By the time the nail was well beyond being hammered into place, he had found a new resolve: No more Mr. Nice Guy. From now on he would be all about his own business, his own needs, and his own ambitions and to hell with everybody else's. Julian stood and ran a forearm across his brow to wipe away the sweat that threatened to run into his eyes. He was carefully edging his way across the slanted roof, toward the ladder propped against the side of the house, when he thought he heard a noise down below.

"Anybody down there?" he called out then waited for a response. Nothing. He was almost to the ladder when he heard the sound again. This time he recognized the unmistakable sound of footsteps on the gravel below. Figuring he probably knew who it was, and pissed that this person would have the nerve to show up at his house, Julian stopped in his tracks and angrily called out again.

"Who the hell is down there?" This time he was answered by a hard blow to the back of his head that knocked him unconscious and sent him tumbling off the roof onto the spikes of the wrought iron fence below.

One Year Later

She woke up in the dark. Confused and disoriented, she lay still for a few seconds and tried to get her bearings and figure out where she was. She tasted blood in her mouth. Tentatively, she touched her lower lip and discovered it was split. There was also an egg-sized knot on the back of her head, causing pounding that made even thinking painful. Curled into a fetal position on her side, she slowly turned onto her back and reached out a hand hitting something hard and unyielding mere inches from her face. She tried to straighten out her cramped legs but couldn't. Where the hell was she and why was it so dark? Then another sensation cut its way through the mind-numbing pain in her head. Movement. She was moving.

A familiar smell filled her nose. Exhaust fumes. Car exhaust fumes. She was in a moving car. Judging by the enclosed space she was in, she quickly realized she was in the trunk. Panic welled up inside her and she started screaming and frantically beating on the inside of the trunk. But the car didn't stop and after a few minutes both her throat and hands were sore. She was feeling around the trunk for something to pry open the lock with when the car came to an abrupt stop. She heard the opening and closing of the car door and footsteps crunching on gravel.

Fumbling around in the dark, her hand came to rest on a hard, round, plastic cylinder. A flashlight. She felt for the switch to the sound of a key being inserted into the trunk lock. When the trunk flew open, she flashed the light into her captor's face. When she saw who it was, memories suddenly came flooding into her head, jolting her back in time, making her remember how she came to be in the trunk of a car with a murderer staring down at her.

Chapter One

Two weeks earlier

THERE WAS A TIME when sitting at the big round table in the middle of the cafeteria meant something. Sitting at that table was a status symbol. It was the table that separated the some- bodies from the nobodies. It was prime real estate and if you were lucky enough to sit there, everyone knew your name. I am, of course, talking about my high school days. A time when popularity was at a premium and only a chosen few achieved it, leaving the rest of us geeks, freaks, and loners to survive high school as best we could. But, now, eleven years later, looking around that same round table at the receding hairlines, beer bellies, the beginnings of crows-feet, and the overall world weariness caused by disappointment and unfulfilled dreams, all I could think was, *Oh, how the mighty have fallen.*

I was sitting in the cafeteria of Springmont High School at the committee meeting for the class of '86's eleven-year high school reunion at the table used by the popular kids all those years ago. A table I would have gnawed my own arm off to be invited to sit at a decade ago. Not anymore. I didn't want to be there and was having a hard time hiding it. I'd been roped into serving on the committee by Gigi Gregory, a former classmate and soon to be ex-friend, who was in desperate need of finding someone to take her place on the committee when her husband had surgery and she needed to take care of him, or so she claimed.

I should have smelled a rat when I'd asked Gigi what kind of surgery her husband was having. She looked distraught enough but never really got around to answering me. So, I imagined it was something serious like open heart surgery or brain surgery. It wasn't until a week later, after I'd already agreed to take her place on the damned committee, that I'd seen Gigi and her husband, Mitch, out to dinner at the Red Dragon. I watched as Gigi delicately placed a rubber doughnut shaped cushion down on the seat for her husband, Mitch, to sit on and saw the grimace of pain as he gingerly lowered his bottom onto the chair. Being my grandmother's granddaughter, and nosy to boot, I went over to say hello. It was then that I discovered that Gigi's husband was recovering not from open heart or brain surgery but hemorrhoid removal. Basically, I'd been roped into serving on the committee because of an itchy, inflamed ass. How fitting. That's exactly how I could describe my high school years, a pain in my ass.

The meeting had been going on for more than an hour and so far the only thing we'd been able to agree on was that we hated each other's ideas. After watching my idea of an eighties themed reunion complete with a Prince and the Revolution cover band go down in flames, I'd settled into a funk and cast silent death stares all around the table.

"How about a circus theme? That way we could bring our kids," exclaimed Audrey Grant, formerly Fry, the perky ex-cheerleading Queen Bee of the class of '86.

Back in high school Audrey's pouffy blonde mall hair and banging bod were only rivaled by her extreme flexibility. She could cross her legs behind her head, which, if you believed the rumors back in high school, she did with regularity. Audrey was now a married, stay-at-home mom to five kids under the age of six. Her blonde hair was now styled in a sleek chin-length bob and her once slim figure was filling out a white size sixteen blouse quite nicely while her once flexible legs were slightly chunky and encased in black stirrup pants. Audrey's slim figure wasn't the only thing MIA from our high school days. Her saccharine perkiness had been replaced by a perpetual worried expression that had etched fine lines into her forehead and tightly pinched lips that made her look like a laxative would do her a world of good. However, eleven years and sixty odd pounds had done nothing to lessen Audrey's sense of self-importance and she only spoke to other committee members who shared in her level of former fabulousness, which obviously did not include me.

"The last thing I want to be bothered with at my high school reunion is a bunch of damned ankle biters," replied Dennis Kirby. "All I want to do is party. Am I right, guys?" Dennis looked around the table for affirmation and laughed loudly when Audrey rolled her eyes and turned up her nose.

In high school, Dennis had been popular, in part, due to his resemblance to Sean Penn, a resemblance he *never* got tired of hearing about. He'd also been the star pitcher of our baseball team as well as a wrestling standout. However, with his glory days a distant memory, the muscular body of his teen years had turned to fat and Dennis now looked like Sean Penn would look if he'd eaten Cleveland. He was also still wearing his thick black hair in the same modified mullet from high school and was sporting a cheesy looking goatee that made him look like a pirate reject. He'd been voted class clown of our graduating class, even though most of his humor had been at the expense of dweebs like me.

I still remembered vividly one day during my sophomore year when Dennis had told me his friend Teddy had a crush on me and asked if I wanted to meet him. I, being supremely naive and thinking he was referring to Ted Johnston, the gorgeous star basketball player of our high school who looked like he'd been chiseled out of a chunk of semi-dark chocolate, said, yes, of course I wanted to meet Ted. Dennis pulled out a stuffed teddy bear and threw it at me nailing me right in the forehead. It wasn't for nothing that he was the pitcher of our baseball team. Everyone laughed hysterically and I spent the rest of that year being referred to as Teddy's girlfriend or being asked where my man Teddy was. Dennis had recently moved back to Willow and apparently still thought he was a walking laugh factory. Only the threat of me shoving my size eight running shoe up his ass kept him from asking me about Teddy when I'd arrived for the meeting.

"Spoken like a man who doesn't have any kids. Some of us have families now, man," replied Gerald Tate, former class president of the class of '86, and I suspected, the real reason Gigi Gregory didn't want to serve on the reunion committee.

Gerald was her ex-high school sweetheart, a relationship that had started freshman year in high school and lasted up until freshman year at college where upon he promptly dumped her for a hard partying waitress at the campus IHOP who was a decade his senior. Gigi's still a tad bitter. Gerald was still a good-looking guy, tall, and with the exception of a beer gut, still in decent shape with hardly a blemish in his smooth brown skin, though his hairline looked like it was starting it's midlife erosion a full ten years ahead of schedule. And I didn't remember his eyes being quite so beady back in high school. Gerald was a financial consultant. I had no idea exactly what that meant beyond him having to wear a suit to work but I assumed he was more successful at it than being married. His third wife, and the mother of the last of his four children, had recently kicked Gerald to the curb. His first wife had been the infamous IHOP waitress.

"Hey, look, I like kids as much as the next person. I just don't want them at the reunion. No offense, but I didn't go to high school with you guys' kids. Hell, one day they'll have their own high school reunion. All I'm saying is let us have ours, " shot back Dennis. Everyone else in the room including Gerald murmured in agreement.

Audrey conceded defeat and gave a small tight smile. Dennis slapped her on the back in what was probably supposed to be a friendly pat. But Audrey's face turned bright red and she looked like she swallowed her tongue.

"Shouldn't we have a tribute?" asked a small voice that almost got drowned out by Dennis's big mouth. We all turned to stare at Cherisse Craig.

Back in high school Cherisse had been even lower on the nerd totem pole than I was, if that was possible. Small for her age, made by her parents to wear clothes that made nuns look conservative, and extremely shy to boot, Cherisse caught all kinds of hell in school. Dennis Kirby, and the other kids of the round table, may have had a bit of fun at my expense now and then, but they turned torturing poor Cherisse into an art form. The worst time being when they instructed everyone in homeroom to mouth their words instead of speaking out loud until Cherisse ran screaming from the classroom because she thought she'd gone deaf.

If it weren't for Cherisse's closeness with her twin sister, Serena, who was the complete opposite of her persecuted twin and took no shit from anybody, Cherisse's life would have been an utter misery. Serena left home right before graduation. I wondered whatever became of her. Knowing how horrible everyone at the table had made Cherisse's high school years, I was stunned to see that she was a part of the reunion committee and even more surprised to see how much nicer she looked these days in her fashionable clothes and funky blonde dreadlocks. She was probably just as shocked to see me there as well.

"What did you say, Cherry?" asked Dennis Kirby,

snickering. Cherry had been his crude nickname for Cherisse. His joke being that she'd probably never lose hers. Cherisse looked down at her lap before answering. Eleven years, new clothes, and a bold new hairdo obviously hadn't eradicated her shyness.

"Well, I think we should do a tribute to Julian," she replied, looking down at her lap again. "And my name's Cherisse, fat ass," she added, tossing a venomous look at Dennis. She'd grown some balls after all. Good for her. Dennis just snickered but I noticed he turned bright red, indicating that Cherisse's barb had hit home.

Cherisse's suggestion was met by cold silence by my fellow committee members. Having a tribute for Julian Spicer, the former head of the reunion committee killed in a freak accident while working on the roof of his house last summer, seemed like an excellent idea to me. Besides, Julian hadn't just been a member of the round table gang along with Dennis, Audrey, and Gerald; he'd been their king. Fine as hell, athletic, and smart, Julian had been homecoming and prom king and was voted most likely to succeed. He'd been Audrey's high school sweetheart. Plus, he was Dennis's first cousin and probably the main reason the loudmouthed asshole was even in the round table clique. He'd also been in charge of the ten-year reunion. After his tragic death, the reunion was cancelled.

Not only would no one comment on the tribute idea, but their eyes were all shooting daggers at Cherisse, who in turn looked like she was about to cry. Why wouldn't they want a tribute to Julian? I opened my mouth to ask what the hell was wrong with everyone when the new head of the committee finally spoke up.

"I think on that note we should wrap things up, guys. We'll meet here same time next week, okay." Ivy Flack cast a cool but not unkind look in Cherisse's direction.

Ivy Flack wasn't a member of the class of '86. She'd been a high school guidance counselor back in the day and was currently the principal of Springmont High. Ivy Flack was the reason I'd decided to major in English at college. She'd been my guidance counselor and had been able to get the unmotivated and unenthusiastic teenager that I once was excited about going to college. Though she was now at least in her mid-forties, she didn't look much different then when we were in school and still wore her dark hair long and layered.

Always dressed to perfection in the most up-to-date styles, Ms. Flack was the woman many of my female peers tried to emulate back in high school. She also had political aspirations and was running for mayor of Willow in the fall. She'd initially volunteered to help the reunion committee temporarily when she saw how few people we had. But since none of us wanted to be in charge, Ms. Flack became the head of the committee, by default, though I suspect in exchange for helping us, she was going to expect us all to volunteer for her campaign. Judging by the success of the meeting we'd just had, I'd say we needed all the help we could get.

"We need to keep it simple, guys. I doubt the reunion budget will allow for much more than a catered dinner and a DJ. I'm afraid if we get too fancy we'll have to charge a high price for tickets and we won't get a big turnout. We'll talk more about it next week. Be thinking about some affordable venues that we can rent," continued Ms. Flack.

We all murmured our half-hearted agreements and got up to leave. Cherisse quickly jumped up, grabbed her purse, and rushed off without a word. Gerald, Audrey, and Dennis watched her go and I saw a look pass among them that took me straight back to high school and sent a chill down my spine. It was a look I'd been on the receiving end of on more than one occasion. It was a condescending smirk accompanied by a raised eyebrow and a slight shake of the head. It was a look that screamed *loser*.

This was *not* going to be fun.

Chapter Two

WORK THE NEXT DAY wasn't much better, though for a different reason. I thought spending time with my former classmates was a nightmare. Little did I know I was about to become a student again myself.

"There's just no way around this, Kendra," said Dorothy Burgess my boss at Clark Literacy Center. "I told you that you needed to take care of this last year and you never did. If your teaching certificate isn't renewed by the time classes start in September, you won't be able to teach and I'll have to hire someone to take your place."

We were sitting in her office with the door closed. Dorothy was seated behind her big pine desk strewn with folders, barely organized piles of paper, empty Styrofoam cups, an ancient PC with a kitty screen saver, and pictures of grandchildren that looked like miniature clones of her with their strawberry blonde helmet hair and round chubby faces. Dorothy was a robust size fourteen who managed to stuff herself into size twelve clothing with frightening results. I knew I should have been concentrating on what she was saying but all I could do was stare at the center button of her very tight blue blouse that was in danger of popping and putting out my eye.

"Are you listening to me?" she asked, visibly annoyed. I wasn't in a much better mood myself but managed to suppress a smart-assed reply.

"Sorry. I have to take a class to renew my certificate. Got it." I was still eyeing the button.

"Well, since it's already the middle of the summer, you only have two choices. You can take a six week creative teaching methods workshop meeting on Saturday mornings at the community college, or you can take a six week education theory class meeting two evenings a week at Kingford. It's your choice. Just make sure you pick one of them, okay?"

Neither choice sounded especially appealing, but I nodded my agreement and she turned her attention back to her paperwork indicating that our meeting was over. I wasn't about to give up a second of my Saturdays for something that wasn't going to put extra money in my pocket. So the education theory class that met twice a week at Kingford would just have to do. Since today was the last day to register for it, I happily walked out the door early to head over to the registrar's office at Kingford College.

It was mid July and hot outside, too hot, in my

opinion, to walk the four blocks from the literacy center to Kingford's campus. I hopped into my silver Toyota Celica, popped in a Luther Vandross CD, cranked up the AC, and headed out. Luther's melodic voice started skipping halfway through "The Power of Love" making me desperately miss my old raggedy blue Nova with its outdated cassette player. A crazy woman, who thought I was after the object of her affection, had trashed the Nova back in the spring. It now resided at Boo Boo's junkyard on the outskirts of town. My new car was the nicest one I'd ever owned and everything on it worked, most of the time. But I still missed the little blue piece of crap that I'd driven since graduating from college, like a long lost love.

Kingford College was a small liberal arts college with an enrollment of about fifteen hundred students. The records office, where I was headed, was located in Tyler Hall, a gray three-story stone building that used to be the college president's house back in the thirties. It now housed the records, counseling, and cashier's offices. I found a parking spot with no problem and was headed towards the building's wide front steps when I heard someone call my name. It was Ms. Flack.

I watched as she approached and forced a smile. It wasn't that I was unhappy to see her, but she was carrying what I suspected was a bundle of flyers for her campaign under one arm. I also suspected that offering to help her hand them out would be a nonverbal commitment to helping with her campaign. Ordinarily, I'd be happy to help. But I wasn't going to have much free time once I signed up for my class and didn't want to tie up what little bit I had left.

"Hey, girl, what brings you here?" she said with such a friendly smile that I felt bad. She looked cool in a sleeveless white blouse that showed off her golden tan, a pencil slim denim skirt, black leather wedge heeled sandals, and a silver ankle bracelet. Her hair was pulled back in a ponytail that hung down her back. She didn't look much older than the college students playing Frisbee and lounging around the college green on blankets.

"Guess who's about to be a student again?" I rolled my eyes melodramatically.

"Not little Miss I'm-never-going-back-to-school? Are you finally going to get that Master's degree I've been bugging you about?" She shifted the bundle of flyers to her other arm. I noticed two of her fingertips were bandaged.

"Not a chance. I was told today that if I didn't take a class I need to have my teaching certificate renewed by fall, I'd be out of a job."

"Well, I knew some kind of threat had to be involved." We both laughed.

"What happened to your fingers?" I asked, nodding towards her hand.

"Oh, it's nothing. My cat, Tamsin, knocked a big can of peas off the shelf onto my fingers and broke two of my nails off to the quick. I won't be able to see my manicurist until next week."

"You're lucky your fingers didn't get broken. What brings you to campus?"

"I just picked up some flyers I had copied at the student center," she said when she noticed me looking at the bundle. "I get a discount since I'm an alumni and I need all the help I can get. This campaign is going to cost a fortune and I'm broke. I had to have a new roof put on my house this summer, and I had to by a new car. I make good money but I don't know where it goes." She gave me a sulky look, confirming my suspicion that she was expecting me to volunteer to save her the cost of paying campaign workers. Instead of pointing out that maybe all her expensive clothes, shoes, and that new Mercedes might be the cause of her money problems, I changed the subject.

"Hey, what was up with everyone's weird reaction to Cherisse's suggestion for a tribute to Julian Spicer. I'd have thought they'd have been all over that, especially Audrey. I mean Julian was tight with all of them back in high school. Did they all have some kind of falling out?"

26

"You mean you don't know?" she asked, suddenly somber.

"Know what?"

"Cherisse used to be Julian's secretary. He fired her the morning of his death."

"Why?" I'd completely forgotten that Julian had started his own accounting business about a year before he died.

"Apparently, Cherisse either forgot or misplaced an important phone message for Julian from some big company looking for a new accounting firm to oversee their client accounts. By the time Julian found out, it was too late and he lost out on the job to another, larger firm."

"Ouch." I finally understood why everyone had acted so strangely at the meeting.

"Ouch, is right. All of Julian's friends think that if he hadn't been so upset over missing out on that account, he wouldn't have been distracted, lost his footing, and fallen off the roof."

I shook my head at the thought of Julian's life cut so short. But for some strange reason, I felt just as bad if not worse for Cherisse. Julian's fall could have been caused by his being distracted over the missed message, or it could have been caused by something as simple as losing his balance after swatting a fly. Either way, it was unfair of them to blame poor Cherisse for his death. But I wasn't really surprised Julian's round table buddies would act the way they did. Back in high school if one of them was mad at you, all of them were mad at you, and they didn't hesitate to retaliate against anyone who crossed them. I ought to know because I'd been on the receiving end of it once myself. Surely, Cherisse hadn't forgotten how they were, which made me wonder why in the world she'd volunteered to be on the reunion committee in the first place.

After a few more minutes of small talk with Ms. Flack, and registering for my class, I headed over to Estelle's, my uncle Alex's restaurant that I hostess at part-time. All the parking spots in front of the restaurant were taken. So I circled the block once more and finally found a spot about a block down the street. As I approached the restaurant, I spotted my sweetie, Carl Brumfield, standing in front of Estelle's looking good enough to eat in a dark brown suit and gold tie. Assuming he was waiting for me, I quickened my step but stopped short when I saw that he wasn't alone. He was with a woman, and not just any woman. Carl was talking and laughing with his ex-wife, Vanessa Brumfield-Carver. Not only was Vanessa Carl's ex-wife but she'd also graduated from Springmont High School with me and had been a member of the infamous round table gang. In fact, she was Audrey Grant's best friend. I did not need this.

As I approached I could see that Vanessa looked like she'd put on a little weight since the last time I'd seen her, which shouldn't have made me happy but did. She was laughing so hard at something Carl was saying that she was in danger of having a seizure. I rolled my eyes. I knew my man had a wicked sense of humor on occasion but he was hardly Eddie Murphy. I couldn't think of a single thing he'd ever said to me to elicit such a response. Phony cow. But, Carl, being a typical man and enjoying having his ego stroked, grinned goofily, making me put an extra pep in my step. Before I could even open my mouth to call out a greeting, they turned and headed off together down the street in the opposite direction. They hadn't even noticed me. They appeared to be in their own little world and were practically skipping down the street. Okay, I'm exaggerating about the skipping...a lot. But did I mention I didn't need this?

I ended up at my grandmother's for dinner that night. That hadn't been my plan but I was so annoyed about seeing Carl and Vanessa together I drove around trying to clear my head. It's not that I don't trust Carl; I do, mostly. And it's not as if I've been one hundred percent true blue myself. It was Vanessa that I didn't trust. Plus, I couldn't understand how Carl could be so chummy with a woman who'd left him high and dry after her father offered her money to end her marriage to Carl, whose skin color didn't agree with him. It didn't take a psychology degree to figure out she never loved him.

Even though Vanessa had recently remarried a bank manager named Drew Carver, who I'd had a disastrous blind date with last year, I fully believed that Vanessa was out for anything and anybody who could improve her standard of living. In other words, she was a gold digging ho. I went to Frisch's Big Boy for a Chocolate therapy session a.k.a hot fudge cake but realized I used the last little bit of cash I had to pay for my class. I ended up at Mama's, instead.

"Is something wrong with you or the meatloaf?" Mama nodded towards my barely touched dinner plate.

"Sorry, I'm just lost in space." I put a forkful of Mama's heavenly meatloaf in my mouth. I'm not being heavy-handed with the adjectives, either. Estelle's was named after Mama, and she gave my uncle Alex many of her recipes to use when he started his restaurant. Mama's Heavenly Meatloaf was one of the most popular items on the menu.

"Are you worried about the trial?" she asked softly. "You know that trial may never see the light of day, baby." She squeezed my hand.

The trial she was referring to was the upcoming

trial of Stephanie Preston, a woman who murdered a popular former actress, and in an attempt to cover her tracks, had kidnapped my best friend, Lynette, and me and tried to kill us both as well. The trial had been scheduled for fall. But Stephanie Preston had been badly burned during her attempted murder of Lynette and me and was in and out of the hospital due to her injuries. Last I'd heard she wasn't doing well at all. It had been a while since I'd even thought about the trial but I didn't want to talk about Carl to Mama. So, I nodded my head pitifully.

"Don't worry. It'll all be okay. I've got cheesecake for dessert," she said like food was the answer to all my problems. Ah, how well she knew me. Over dessert I told her about my upcoming class and how badly the reunion committee meeting had gone.

"Oh, it couldn't have been that bad."

"No, a root canal isn't that bad. That meeting was brutal."

"Oh, quit exaggerating," she said, chuckling.

"You weren't there. It was déjà vu. Nerdy Kendra up against the popular kids."

"But you're all grown folks now," she reasoned.

"Grown, yes. Mature, hardly."

"And since when is being a nerd a crime. You don't see Bill Gates whining about it do you?"

"Bad example. I wouldn't be whining, either, if I had his billions. And technically, he's a geek not a nerd." I noticed that even my own grandmother couldn't deny that I was a nerd.

"Oh, hush. You may not have run around with those popular kids but you had lots of friends and you were in all those clubs."

I nodded my head to show I was paying attention to her vigorous defense of my high school credentials, like being in the library and science clubs was proof of how cool I really was deep, deep down inside. But I'd drifted off into outer space again. Thinking about science club reminded me of how I'd been madly in love with Mr. Fields, my science teacher.

Mr. Fields had been in his early twenties and a serious geek but he was cute and funny and pretty cool as far as teachers went. He let me work for him during my study hall hour and I and ran copies and errands and helped him clean the science lab. We were friends and I could talk to him and about music and movies because we weren't that far apart in age and had similar tastes. I think he knew I had a crush on him and thought it was cute.

Then towards the end of that year, before finals and graduation, I made a huge mistake. Audrey Grant, or Fry as she'd been back then, cornered me in the bathroom one day and asked me to get her a copy of

Mr. Fields' science final. She dangled an invitation to her graduation party in front of my face. As much as I wanted to go that party, I just couldn't do that to Mr. Fields or the rest of the kids in the class, like me, who'd actually studied for the test. I lied and told Audrey I didn't have access to the test. She was not happy, and if she wasn't happy, neither was the rest of the round table gang.

Suddenly, I was a girl with a target on her back. Someone spray painted the word bitch on my locker in neon pink paint. A week after that, someone filled my backpack with dog shit. I found cigarette butts in my food at lunch and I couldn't walk the halls or sit in class without a member of the round table spitting hockers or flipping rubber bands at me or trying to trip me. There were prank calls to my house. And I won't even discuss the vicious rumor that circulated that I'd had a secret abortion over Spring Break and didn't know who the baby's father was. If it had just been Audrey, I could have ended the abuse by way of my fist to her face. But I didn't stand a chance against the whole gang. There were about a dozen of them. They were like the mafia, powerful, all knowing, and all seeing. The dweebs willing to do anything they asked to get into their good graces were legion. Me not cooperating wasn't something they were used to.

At age 29 I can think of ways I could have handled the situation differently, but at 17, I just wanted to curl up and die. Finally, after a few weeks of torture, I gave in and gave Audrey a copy of the test. The abuse ended immediately and so did my job with Mr. Fields. He never confronted me but he sent me back to study hall confirming to me that he knew or at least suspected what I'd done. I felt lower than crap. As for Audrey and her crew, they acted like nothing ever happened and that I no longer existed. I wasn't invited to her party, not that I'd have gone. I would bet money that even today if I asked any of them about it, they'd act like they didn't know what the hell I was talking about.

After eating two pieces of cheesecake, I headed home to my duplex on Dorset. Usually my elderly landlady, Mrs. Carson, would be sitting regally on her front porch with her Siamese cat, Mahalia. But Mrs. Carson had been dragged, kicking and screaming, on a Caribbean cruise for her birthday by her kids and would be gone for ten days. I had no idea who was watching Mahalia. And since the cat didn't like me, and had almost killed me once already, I didn't care. I pulled up the same time as Carl. He smiled his panty-melting smile when he spotted me and I had to suppress the urge to scowl at him. After all, I'd only seen Vanessa stroking his ego not the part of him that she'd given up rights to when they'd split up.

"Don't I even get a kiss?" he asked, interrupting my thoughts and following me to my front door. I turned and gave him a quick peck on the lips. Once inside, he pulled me close.

"Now, I know you can do better than that." He laid a real kiss on me that took my breath away. He hugged me close and I enjoyed his warm familiar scent of Obsession. I didn't realize how much I needed that hug and by the way he held me tight, he must have needed one, too.

"You okay?" I asked.

"Of course. Why, don't I look okay?" He tossed his suit jacket on my couch.

"I thought I saw your ex today," I said casually. "At least I thought it was her. Looks like she's put on some weight."

"Yeah, most pregnant women do," he replied dryly. I turned to look at him and caught the tail end of a frown.

"She's pregnant?" I followed him into my tiny kitchen. He opened my fridge and pulled out a bottle of Japanese plum wine. I handed him two wineglasses from the cabinet.

"I ran into her when I went over to Estelle's to see if you wanted to go out to dinner. She asked me to have a coffee with her. That's when she told me her good news. She's six weeks along."

He handed me a glass of wine and I sipped it as I watched him down his glass and pour himself another. I wondered how he was really feeling about his ex-wife's pregnancy. Carl and Vanessa were planning to start a family right before she abruptly left him. I knew on some level this news had to sting. I also couldn't shake the feeling that something between Carl and me had just changed.

Chapter Three

BEING SUPER BUSY ALLOWED me to put my worries about Carl out of my head over the next few days. We were short staffed at Estelle's. On top of working my regular shift as a hostess, I was working extra hours as a server until Alex hired more help. My pitiful bank account would appreciate the extra funds, but my feet were singing the blues, and my nerves were shot to hell. I hate waiting tables. Having to wait on a diner who sends their steak back fours times because it's not rare enough, or thinks it's funny when their toddler throws his catsup drenched chicken fingers at me, is enough to make anyone want to go live on a mountaintop.

I'd just left the literacy center and was on my way to the restaurant when my cell phone rang. I answered it with an irritable hello.

"Kendra?" said an uncertain female voice that sounded familiar.

"Speaking," I said, softening my tone.

"It's Ivy Flack. Is this a bad time?"

"Oh, hi. No. I'm just on my way to work. What's up?"

"Well, I'm sorry to bother you. But I'm calling an emergency meeting of the reunion committee tonight at eight at the high school. Can you come?"

Damn. My plans were to be in a hot bubble bath nursing a glass of wine or a cold beer at eight. I was tempted to say I'd still be at work. However, something in her tone changed my mind.

"What's wrong?" By the time I'd pulled into a spot in front of the restaurant, she still hadn't answered me. "Ms. Flack, are you still there?"

"Sorry. I'd rather not say until I get the whole committee together. Can you make it?"

"Yeah, I'll be there." I started to ask if there was anything I needed to bring but she'd already hung up.

Curiosity, or in my case, outright nosiness, had me wondering all afternoon what Ms. Flack wanted to see the committee about. I noticed her red Mercedes already in the parking lot when I arrived at the high school a little before eight that evening. Summer school was in session but the students and most of the staff were long gone by eight. I headed inside and thought I heard faint disembodied moaning coming from someplace. I stopped to listen but heard nothing and proceeded on.

The cafeteria was located just off the school's front entrance and down a flight of about a dozen steps. The same old smell of tomato soup, peanut butter, and bleach that accompanied every high school lunch I ever ate, greeted me as I approached the stairs. Back in my day the steps leading down to the cafeteria were carpeted in a sickly greenish yellow. Now, the carpet was gone, which made for a much cleaner look, not to mention being easier for the custodians to clean up dirt and the occasional vomit.

I rounded the corner and was at the top of the steps when I discovered the source of the moaning. It was Ms. Flack. She was at the bottom of the steps on the floor. I hurried down to her.

"Are you okay?" I helped her into a sitting position. She pulled down her black skirt, which had ridden up exposing her lacy silk slip. She only had one shoe on. The other kitten-heeled pump was a few feet away. I went to retrieve it.

"I feel like the biggest fool. I slipped and fell down the steps. The custodians must have mopped the floor and it hadn't dried yet."

"Are you hurt? Do I need to take you to the emergency room?" I handed her her shoe and then helped her to her feet after she put it back on. She winced and sat down on the bottom step.

"I think I'll be alright. I'm more embarrassed than anything. I just twisted my ankle a little. I'll live." She rubbed her ankle and then flexed it.

"Well, someone really needs to tell the custodian you fell. They should have put up a sign." I got up and looked around for the offending party. I started to head back up the steps to go look for the custodian when she stopped me.

"Kendra, don't worry about it. It's partly my fault. I usually tell them when I'm going to be here late. This time I forgot. There's no reason to put out a sign to warn people about a slippery floor when you don't know there are going to be people in the building."

She stood up slowly and I followed as she limped over to the infamous round table. She was quiet and subdued as I helped her set up the table with cans of soda and a platter of cookies. I started to ask her again what was wrong when I heard the sound of voices. The other committee members were arriving and they didn't sound happy.

"I can't stay long. I had to get my sister to watch the kids and she has to leave in half an hour," said Audrey Grant, looking annoyed. She wasn't wearing any makeup and had dried baby food smeared on her T-shirt. She'd arrived along with Gerald Tate.

"And I can't really stay at all. I'm having dinner with a client this evening. I just stopped by on my way to see what's up," he said, making a show of looking at his expensive black Movado watch and making me wonder if he was really concerned about the time or just showing off. In contrast to Audrey, he was dressed in a grey suit and black crew neck shirt and loafers.

Dennis Kirby was next to arrive followed closely by Cherisse Craig. Dennis was being his usual obnoxious self but didn't seem as bothered by the last minute meeting as Audrey and Gerald.

"Okay, where's the fire, Flack?" He plopped down at the table popped the top on a can of coke and helped himself to a cookie. His dark blue nylon warm-up suit crackled when he moved and made him look like a giant blueberry.

Cherisse, on the other hand, had opted not to sit at the round table and sat down at the table next to it. She looked around the room, not so much timid but expectant like she knew she was about to be attacked and had resigned herself to her fate. She was the only one so far who hadn't asked what the meeting was about.

"Since we're all here, I'll go ahead and get started," said Ms. Flack.

We all turned to stare at her.

"Earlier today I went to the bank to check on the funds for the reunion. It was my understanding that about thirty-five hundred dollars had been collected last year and since the reunion was cancelled, that money should still be there but—"

"That's right," said Audrey, interrupting her. "I

was on the committee last year. We had a fundraiser and the rest of the money came from alumni donations."

"Is there money missing from the account?" I asked. Everyone's gaze shifted back to Ms. Flack, everyone except Gerald that is. He stood staring at his black tasseled loafers.

"Try all of it," said Ms. Flack bluntly, a faint blush tinting her cheeks.

Everyone went silent. Even Dennis's chubby cookie-stuffed hand froze halfway to his mouth.

"The money's gone!" exclaimed Audrey angrily. "All of it?" she screeched.

Ms. Flack nodded solemnly.

"How the hell can it be gone if the reunion got cancelled?" asked Dennis with an angry snort, looking suspiciously at all of us. Gerald was now picking imaginary lint from his black shirt.

"Okay, hold up, everybody," I said to try and relieve the sudden tension in the room. "Now, who was in charge of making deposits to the account?"

"Yeah, who was on the committee last year?" piped in Cherisse speaking up for the first time.

"You can count me out on this one. I was still living in San Diego this time last year." Dennis shoved another cookie into his mouth. I made a mental note to grab one before he ate them all.

Audrey, in the throes of some kind of high school flashback, threw up her hand like she was in class, while Gerald finally looked up and reluctantly held up an index finger.

"Which one of you was in charge of making deposits to the account?" asked Ms. Flack.

Audrey and Gerald stared at each other.

"Julian was in charge of the reunion fund account," said Gerald softly. "Julian insisted all our names be on the account, to avoid this very thing. But we let him handle all the money because he was an accountant." He ran a hand over his balding head.

"He was the head of the committee. He was the one who opened the account and had all the paperwork and account number," added Audrey.

"Yeah, right. Blame the dead guy. I knew you guys were gonna try this shit. I can't believe you think my cousin fucked with that money. Either one of you could have done it." Dennis stood up abruptly. A flood of cookie crumbs cascaded down the front of his warm-up jacket.

"Oh, shut up, Dennis! No one accused Julian of stealing anything. They asked us who was in charge of the money, and we just answered the question. And how dare you accuse us of stealing." Audrey jumped forward to get in Dennis's face.

I looked over and saw that Cherisse appeared to

be having the time of her life witnessing the round table gang turn on each other. She sat watching the drama with a big ole' grin on her face. In fact, I don't ever remember seeing her look so happy. It suited her.

Dennis and Audrey were red-faced and staring each other down. Gerald was looking at his watch again.

"All right, everyone." Ms. Flack stepped between Audrey and Dennis. "We need to calm down and figure this out. Why don't we all sit down and have some refreshments."

"Sorry, but I really gotta bounce. My client is probably wondering where I am." Gerald backed up towards the steps. "Ms. Flack, I'll touch base with you tomorrow. I'll see you guys later," he said over his shoulder as he headed up the steps.

Audrey rolled her eyes at his retreating back then sat down and grabbed a can of diet Coke. Dennis reluctantly sat down, too, but was still glaring at Audrey.

We were all silent for a few minutes. But apparently a certain someone hadn't had enough drama.

"Then if neither you nor Gerald took the money, and you don't think Julian took the money, then what could have happened to it? One of you had to have taken it," Cherrise said in a not so subtle attempt to fan the flames further. Audrey didn't even acknowledge that she'd spoken and swung around to face Ms. Flack.

"What I'd really like to know is how *you* got access to the account?" Audrey took a long sip of soda and waited.

"That's simple. Julian thought that since I was the principal it would be a good idea to list me on the account in case of some kind of an emergency. All the reunion fund stuff has been in an envelope in my desk drawer for a year. Today is the first day I took a look at it," Ms. Flack replied completely, unfazed.

"How convenient," mumbled Dennis, his mouth filled with cookie. Ms. Flack just laughed.

"I make sixty thousand dollars a year being principal of this school. I have no need to steal a measly thirty-five hundred. I spend more than that a year on shoes alone."

"Well since you, Audrey, and Gerald were all listed on the account, shouldn't you all have been receiving bank statements showing deposits and withdrawals?" I asked.

"I never got any statements. As far as I know the bank sent Julian all that stuff and that was fine by me. I've got five kids and a husband to take care of and I don't have time to worry about stuff like this, which reminds me," Audrey said, jumping up abruptly. "I gotta scoot. My sister's going to kill me if I'm not home in ten minutes. She has a date tonight. I'll see you guys at the next meeting." She drained her soda can and hurried up the steps.

"I never got any bank statements, either. That's why I had to go to the bank to check the account. I didn't have any statements showing the account balance and I wanted to make sure of what was in there before we started writing checks off that account to pay a caterer or rent a banquet hall," said Ms. Flack to the rest of us in a weary sigh.

I didn't know what else to say and grabbed a cookie myself.

"Okay, so the money's missing. The bigger question is, what are we going to do about the reunion?" asked Cherisse.

"No money. No reunion," snorted Dennis in disgust.

"As head of the committee, I don't want to make any decisions about the reunion until we can all meet again. Maybe we can have a picnic down at Lake Mead. That's pretty cheap. Right now I'm too tired to think about this anymore tonight. I need to get home to feed my cat."

We all stood to go and as we headed up the steps I noticed the remains of a small slick spot near the top step. This must have been what Ms. Flack had slipped on. As the others headed out to the parking lot, I stopped to examine the spot. I noticed it was way too shiny to be water. I bent down to get a closer look and rubbed the spot with my fingers. I was right. It wasn't water. It was baby oil. Why would baby oil be on the floor at the top of the steps? Could someone have put it there on purpose so someone would fall? That didn't make any sense. I realized I was tired, too, and headed out to my car. Dennis and Ms. Flack were already pulling out of the parking lot, but Cherisse was still in the process of putting on her seat belt. A thought occurred to me. I tapped on her window, startling her. She rolled it down looking a little impatient.

"Sorry. I just had a question for you."

"That's all right. What did you want?"

"Well, I was just wondering since you used to be Julian's secretary if you had any idea what could have happened to the money? Did he ever mention it at all?"

I thought it was an innocent, straightforward enough question. Apparently, I was wrong. Cherisse's face tensed up angrily and her head jutted out of the driver's side window like an angry chicken ready to peck my eyes out. I took half a step back from the car.

"Don't you think if I knew anything about that damned money I'd have said so in the meeting? Why are you asking me this?" she said with more aggression then I'd have thought her capable of.

"Hey, there's no need to snap at me. I'm just trying to figure out what could have happened to the money."

Her shoulders slumped and she let out a long breath then gave me a contrite look.

"I'm sorry." She grinned sheepishly. "Anytime anyone asks me anything about Julian, it's usually to imply that I'm to blame for him falling off his roof."

"To be honest, I'm really surprised you even volunteered to be on the committee. A lot of people made your life hell in high school. Why would you want see any of these assholes again, especially since you know they think you're to blame for Julian's death?"

She seemed to think for a minute before responding.

"I spent the majority of my high school days living in terror of Audrey and her crew. Even after high school when I'd see one of them at the grocery store or the mall, I'd turn and walk in the opposite direction. But I'm almost thirty. I need to get past what happened to me in high school. I thought serving on the reunion committee would help me do that. I thought things would be different since we're all adults now. The only difference now is they hate me because of what happened to Julian and Julian's death wasn't even *my* fault," she said bitterly.

My ears perked up at that last part.

"Whose fault was it?" I watched her closely. For a minute I thought she was going to say something. I could see the indecision in her eyes. Then, as if a curtain had fallen, her face went blank.

"I gotta go. It's getting late and I have to be up early tomorrow. Bye," she said, avoiding my gaze.

I watched as she pressed the button to raise her car window and stepped back as she pulled out of the parking space and drove away. I wondered. Could Julian's death have been anything other than a freak accident and did it have anything to do with the missing money? And why didn't Gerald seem at all surprised the money was gone?

It was after nine by the time I left the high school, and I'd yet to eat. I called Carl to see if he wanted to meet me for a late dinner. He answered the phone on the first ring.

"Hey, sweetie. Have you eaten yet?"

"Um. Sort of," he said slowly.

"What do you mean sort of? Either you've eaten

or you haven't." I laughed because I thought he was being silly.

"Yeah, I just ate. I'm uh…I'm kinda busy right now. Can I call you back?" he replied with an annoyed little sigh.

"What's wrong?" I was confused by his tone.

"Nothing. I'll call you back, okay?" More sighing.

That's when it hit me. He hadn't even referred to me by name and he was trying to rush me off the phone. He wasn't being silly. He was being shady.

"Where are you and who are you with?" I demanded, anger making my voice rise a whole two octaves.

"I'll give you a call tomorrow," he replied quickly and then hung up.

I was sitting at the light at an intersection staring at my cell phone with my mouth hanging open. No he didn't just hang up on me. I hit redial twice and got his voice mail both times. I started to leave a scathing message when a loud car horn blasted from behind me and made me jump. The light was green and I sped through it, rounded the next corner, and coming to screeching halt in front of Frisch's Big Boy. Hot fudge cake here I come.

I was waiting to be seated in the near empty restaurant when I noticed a bald, brown-skinned, handsome older black man sitting at a booth in back. It was Reverend Morris Rollins. My stomach did a flip-flop. Morris Rollins was a local minister just as well-known for his way with women as for his fiery sermons. I'd met him a year ago, under tragic circumstances, and he'd been trying to get into my pants ever since. Not that the thought of letting him wasn't extremely appealing; but he was old enough to be my father and I wasn't sure how much I trusted him. I'd already locked lips with him on more than one occasion, which deep down inside made me think I probably deserved whatever Carl was doing behind my back.

Rollins looked up suddenly like he'd sensed my presence, and his smile lifted me out of my murderous mood. He got up and came over to where I was standing.

"She'll be joining me," he told the hostess, who went to put another place setting at his table. Then he grabbed my hand and grinned.

"Kendra," he said pulling me into an embrace.

"I know. It's been a while, hasn't it?" I pulled back to look up at him. He was over six feet tall.

"I haven't seen you all summer long? You never returned any of my phone calls." He led me back to his table.

"I'm sorry. I've been busy with —" He held up his hand to stop the lie that was about to spring forth from my lips.

"No problem. You don't have to explain to me. I just moved on to plan B." He was laughing at me like he always did when he knew I'd been avoiding him.

"Plan B? What are you talking about?"

"I know you come here a lot. Do you know how many nights I've eaten here trying to run into you?" he asked, suddenly serious. I was stunned.

"You're telling a tale and you know it," I said, laughing nervously.

"No, I'm not and *you* know it." His eyes held mine and I looked away first.

"Now, I don't care what you say. I'm buying you dinner. What do you want to eat?" he asked in a low seductive voice.

Talk about a loaded question.

Chapter Four

I WAS EXPECTING A call from Carl the next morning. By 10 o'clock it still hadn't come. I started to call him. Then the pleasant memory of my evening of food and flirting with Rollins stopped my fingers before they could punch the numbers. Spending my evening with another man, and dread over wondering what was up with my own man, made me suddenly not quite so eager to know what was going on. I was sure I'd be finding out soon enough. Instead, I put on a pot of coffee and settled down at my kitchen table with a cranberry muffin and the newspaper. I was scanning the local news section, glancing over the emergency squad runs from the night before, when a name jumped out at me: Audrey Grant. I quickly read the brief blurb.

Audrey Grant, 29, of 1291 Pensacola Pike, taken by squad to the emergency room of Willow Memorial Hospital due to illness. Admitted for treatment.

Audrey was in the hospital? I wondered what could be wrong with her. She seemed healthy enough at the meeting last night, maybe a little tired from chasing around five kids, but otherwise healthy. I wondered if she was still in the hospital. There was only one way to find out. I made a call to Willow Memorial and asked to be connected to Audrey Grant's room.

"One moment, please," replied the mellow-voiced operator. Seconds later the sound of a busy signal filled my ear.

"Ma'am, that line is busy. Would you like me to put you on hold or will you call back later?"

"I'll call back. Thanks."

So, Audrey was still in the hospital and judging by the busy signal she wasn't ill enough to not be on the phone, which made me even more curious about what was wrong with her. I hung up and headed for my bathroom. It was Saturday. I had nothing else to do that day and decided that visiting Audrey would be better than sitting around waiting for Carl to call.

An hour later, and armed with a cactus plant from the gift shop, I was standing awkwardly in the doorway of Audrey Grant's hospital room. She was propped up in bed dressed in the requisite blue gown with the same plaid headband she'd had on in the meeting last night, only now it was crooked and pieces of hair had escaped and were falling in her face. She was also as pasty as the white sheet that was bunched up under her large breasts. Dark smudges under her eyes looked like bruises on her pale skin. An IV of clear fluid was hanging from a pole on the right side of the bed with the line inserted into the back of her right hand and held in place by clear tape. Audrey was staring off into space in a daze. I knocked softly on the open door and she snapped out of her trance and looked over at me.

"Kendra?" she said in a surprisingly strong voice for someone who looked so ill.

"I hope you don't mind," I said, coming into the room and standing by the side of the bed. "I read in the squad runs this morning that you'd been admitted to the hospital. Are you okay?" I set the cactus down on the table by the bed.

She glanced at it then back at me without speaking. She continued to stare at me without speaking and looking quite confused, I might add, for a full minute and it took everything in me not to squirm.

"Okay. Well, I should probably go so you can get your rest. Sorry to have bother you." I turned to go.

"Wait," she called out, stopping me before I could get out the door. "I'm sorry. That was rude. I'm just a little out of it." She shook her head as if to clear it and gestured for me to sit in the chair by the bed. I sat.

"What happened? You seemed fine last night."

"That's a good question," she said with a laugh.

"What do you mean?" I leaned forward in the

chair.

"They told me that I had a bad reaction from mixing my antidepressants with alcohol. My husband found me unconscious on our bedroom floor when he got home from work last night."

"Then why do you say you don't you know what happened?"

"Because I don't drink. I haven't had a drink in years. This has to be some kind of big mistake. We don't even keep any alcohol in the house." She pulled her headband off and tossed it on the bed in frustration.

I felt for her but couldn't help but remember the hard partying Audrey of old. The same Audrey who I sat behind in science class senior year and who reeked of stale beer and weed on more than one occasion. Sitting behind her all those years ago, and bearing witness to a level of popularity only rivaled by a pop star, I never pictured her becoming the dumpy, plaid wearing, stay-at-home mom I was currently looking at.

If I recalled correctly, I remembered overhearing her telling her fellow round table cronies more than once that she planned to model after high school. It's no mystery why that plan didn't work out since the modeling world isn't real big on 5' 3" models, at least not any that wear clothes. Of course I could have told her that back then but she didn't ask me. I wondered if that's why she was being treated for depression. Was there such a thing as Failed Model Syndrome?

"Could you have accidentally had some alcohol?" I asked for lack of anything better to say.

She thought hard for a minute and then buried her head in her hands and groaned. "No! It's just not possible. I know not to mix alcohol with my prescriptions. I would never make that mistake. I know my husband probably thinks I'm lying but I swear I didn't have a drink." She started to cry and I handed her the box of tissues on the bedside table.

"How long are they going to keep you in here?" I asked softly.

She shrugged miserably and leaned back against the pillows, causing her tears to run down the side of her face.

"Well, I'm going to leave now so you can get your rest. Is there anything you need before I go?" I figured my curiosity had been satisfied sufficiently.

"Oh, I need my cell phone. Can you hand me my purse. It's in the closet," she said through her tears.

I grabbed a large tan leather purse from the floor of the narrow closet and walked over to hand it to her. But in her weakened condition, she didn't get a good enough grasp on her heavy purse and dropped it. It fell on the floor spilling some of its contents. She mumbled an expletive as I bent down to pick up everything. Amongst the wallet, brush, can of hair spray, box of wet wipes, and set of keys on a unicorn key chain, I spied something surprising. It was a half empty bottle of baby oil. Hadn't baby oil been what Ms. Flack had slipped on last night? I looked at Audrey as I stuffed everything back into her purse. Her eyes were closed. Was she the one who put baby oil at the top of the cafeteria steps? It didn't make any sense. Then I remembered that Audrey had arrived *after* Ms. Flack and me and couldn't have put the baby oil on the steps. I realized how paranoid I was being. Because why in the world would Audrey want Ms. Flack, or anyone else, to fall down the steps?

I handed Audrey her purse and headed out of her room, almost colliding with a nurse in green scrubs and a white lab coat. It was Audrey's best friend and Carl's ex-wife, Vanessa Brumfield. Vanessa was a nurse at Willow Memorial, though to be honest I was surprised she was still working. She'd inherited a large sum of money from her father when he died, money she only got because she ended her marriage to Carl. Her greedy behind must have spent it all. I stepped aside and held the door open for her. She gave me a dismissive look before walking past me into the room.

"You're welcome," I said when it was obvious she wasn't going to thank me. She rolled her eyes and flipped a piece of her long dark curly hair over her shoulder before closing the door in my face.

I couldn't tell if she was just being bitchy or if there was something she was going to be talking about that she didn't want me to hear? And if so, was it about Carl? Had she left the door open I'd have gladly left. But to someone as nosy as me a closed door only meant one thing: an invitation to eavesdrop. I looked up and down the hall to make sure no one was coming, then pressed my ear to the door. I could only hear muffled snatches of what they were saying. So, I pushed the door open just a sliver.

"What am I supposed to be listening to?" I heard Vanessa ask Audrey with barely concealed annoyance.

"Just listen. It's the third message," Audrey responded tensely.

I pushed the door open a little further and peeked in. Vanessa was sitting on the hospital bed with her back to the door with a cell phone pressed to her ear. Thankfully she was also blocking Audrey's view of the door and neither woman had noticed me spying on them. Vanessa must have been listening to Audrey's voice mail messages.

"What have you done now?" Vanessa asked when she was done. She was waving the cell phone in Audrey's face.

"What do you mean what have I done? I have no idea who that message is from let alone what they're talking about," wailed Audrey.

"The message said, *you will pay for what you did.* All I'm asking is what is it you did to piss someone off?"

"Nothing! I've done nothing," insisted Audrey. I could see Vanessa crossing her arms and turning to stare out the window.

"Just forget it! Go on back to work. I just thought since you were my best friend you might care that someone threatened me. My mistake." Audrey's voice rose angrily with each word.

"Oh, calm down," Vanessa said in disgust.

"Calm down. Someone left a threatening message on my voice mail and all you can say is calm down. *You* fucking calm down."

"I'm sorry. But are you *sure* you don't know who left that message?" Vanessa stood up abruptly. I quickly closed the door a smidge.

"You obviously have something on your mind. Just say it." Audrey's voice was hard and cold as ice.

"All right. Are you sure one of your little friends didn't leave that message?"

I didn't hear a response. I peeked in again and saw Audrey glaring at Vanessa. She looked so mad her pale cheeks had turned bright pink.

"No one I know would have any reason to leave me a message like that," Audrey said, through gritted teeth.

"I certainly hope not. Because if you don't cut it out, you're going to lose everything you have."

Vanessa stood up to leave and I hot-footed it across the hall and into another hospital room. I peeked through the door and watched as she stalked off down the hall. I started to leave when I heard a familiar voice coming from behind me.

"Well, ain't this a surprise! Hey, baby doll, you just in time to help me wit my sponge bath. Come on in here, girl, and let me look atcha."

I whirled around and found myself face to face with Lewis Watts, of all people. Just great. I'd made Lewis's acquaintance last spring at a local hole-in-the-wall called the Spotlight Bar & Grill. Lewis was height challenged, thought he was a Don Juan, and dressed like he shopped at Pimps R Us. The seventies had been Lewis's glory days, and he wasn't about to let that decade go without a fight. The last time I'd seen Lewis was when he'd caught me hiding in a house I'd snuck into while he was delivering furniture. He'd tried to feel me up in exchange for not busting me and only kept his mouth shut after I'd threatened to report him for disability fraud. In other words, we're not friends.

He was sitting upright in the hospital bed nude from the waist up exposing his thick muscular arms and a barrel chest lightly sprinkled with grey chest hairs that were in great contrast to the jet black processed hair on his fat head. A plastic tub of soapy water was sitting on a tray positioned in front of him. He leered at me and tried to hand me the sponge in his hand.

"I don't think so." I backed up towards the door.

"Hey, wait a minute, Kelly. I'm just kiddin'," he said with a devilish laugh. He tossed the sponge into the tub and pushed the tray aside. "You mean you really didn't come to see ole' Lewis?" He looked genuinely hurt.

"It's Kendra and, no, I didn't come to see you. Bye."

My hand was on the door handle but before I could pull it open, it was pushed opened from the other side and in walked a nerdy looking doctor staring at the chart in his hand and not where he was going. I was pushed backward, slipped on Lewis's hospital gown, which was on the floor, and practically landed in his lap. When the doctor finally looked up, Lewis had his arms wrapped around me and was nuzzling my neck while I tried in vain to break free.

"Ah, I see you're feeling much better, Mr. Watts," said the doctor who's name tag identified him as Dr. Samuel Kincaid.

"Yeah, Doc, my lady here has a way of making

me feel a whole lot better if you get my meanin'."
Lewis winked at the doctor. Both men laughed. My
face was burning.

"I'm not his —," I began but didn't get far.

"Are you ready to be discharged?" Dr. Kincaid cut
me off. I was finally able to break free and stood up
glaring at both of them.

"Don't worry, Miss. We'll be releasing your *Boo*
within the hour," he said in an attempt at sounding
black and only succeeding in making me want to slap
him. "But only if you promise to drive him straight
home. Understand?"

"I got it, Doc. Kelly here's gonna take me right
home, ain't you, girl?" His eyes were pleading with
me and I realized he probably had no other way home.
Great. I nodded my head in agreement.

The doctor left and I rounded on Lewis. "Call a
cab," I spat out at him and turned to go.

"Hey, wait. I ain't got no money and I only live
'bout five minutes from here over in the Pullman
Apartments. Come on, Kelly. Help a brotha out."

"You mean to tell me you don't have a girlfriend
who can come and get you?"

"Naw, I'm between ladies at the moment. See, my
lady left me when my disability got cut off back in
May. Once I didn't have no check to spend on her, she
bounced," he said matter-of-factly.

"Finally caught up with you didn't, they. What happened? Did Social Security find out you were delivering furniture when your back was supposed to be bad?"

"Yeah, my ex-lady called and told on me when I cheated on her with my last lady," he said smugly, like he was proud that the loss of his love pushed women to drastic measures.

"So now you have to work like the rest of us," I said, laughing. But Lewis didn't laugh.

"Yeah, you lookin' at the custodian at Springmont High School." He shook his head sadly.

After dropping Lewis at his apartment, and grilling him about how often the floors got mopped at Springmont High, I headed over to the Kingford College bookstore to buy the book for my class. According to Lewis, he mopped the floors at least three times a week. But he'd been in the hospital since Friday morning with chest pains and hadn't mopped the floors since Thursday, and he doubted the custodian who subbed for him Friday would have mopped. So, anybody could have spilled the baby oil on the floor in front of the cafeteria steps anytime on Friday. Most likely it was one of the summer school students. I felt stupid for thinking it could have been Audrey.

The Kingford College bookstore was in the student union. Since it was the summer session, which is always a slow time for the college, I was the only other person in the bookstore besides the staff. I quickly located the book I needed for my class. After getting over the shock of having to fork over sixty bucks for a used copy, I headed to the checkout counter and was surprised to see a fellow member of the reunion committee running the register. It was Dennis Kirby. He looked just as surprised to see me as well. He had a bruise on his forehead and his left wrist was wrapped in an Ace bandage. The nametag he was wearing pinned to his yellow button-down shirt identified him as the manager.

"Dennis, I didn't realize you were working here." I handed him my book.

"I just started last week. It's only temporary, though, until something in my field opens up," he said nonchalantly. I could tell he was embarrassed for me to see him working a job he clearly considered beneath him.

I knew Dennis's field was sports medicine and that he'd worked for a college baseball team in California before moving home to help his parents after his father's triple bypass. Willow wasn't exactly a booming area for the sports medicine field. Dennis was in for a long wait.

"Did you have an accident?" I asked, gesturing to his wrist and forehead.

"Oh, this?" He rubbed the bruise on his forehead. "I didn't exactly have a great evening starting with that bullshit meeting. When I got home I found out someone had broken into my parent's garage and trashed it. Red spray paint all over the fucking walls. I slipped on some spilled lawn fertilizer and slid into the wall. I bumped my head and sprained my wrist and knocked down a shelf. Then when I got out the Dustbuster to vacuum up the fertilizer, I plugged it in and almost got electrocuted." He chuckled.

"What masterpiece did they paint on your walls?" I asked, trying hard to shake the image of big Dennis sliding into the wall.

"Huh?" He was looking like I'd spoken to him in a foreign language.

"You said there was red spray paint all over the walls. Did they spray paint something crude?"

"It wasn't pictures. It was words and misspelled ones too. It's great to see our education system at work." He laughed loudly, a little too loudly.

I asked him if he'd heard about Audrey being in the hospital.

"No, what happened to her?" I could tell he

wasn't all that interested. He was shifting from foot to foot and I got the distinct feeling he wanted me to leave. Instead, I filled him in on what happened to Audrey. He whistled and shook his head.

"You know, I wouldn't be surprised if those rug rats of hers have driven her to drink. And I wouldn't put it past her to lie about it, either. Honesty's never been real important to Audrey."

"Really," I said, my curiosity flaring up.

"I wouldn't expect you to know this, but Audrey's been on antidepressants since our senior year in high school. She started taking them after she got depressed and overdosed on sleeping pills." He smirked nastily, which surprised me.

Dennis and Audrey, being fellow members of the round table crew, had been tight. I knew eleven years was a long time for some people to maintain a high school friendship. But I could tell that Dennis was getting a big kick out of Audrey's troubles and wondered what had happened to change things.

"She tried to kill herself?"

"She claimed it was an accident. Personally, I think she was just looking for some attention."

"Any idea why she's so depressed?" I asked, handing him my credit card.

67

"I guess she never got over her one true love," he said, staring off into space. Audrey's one true love had been Dennis's cousin Julian Spicer. They'd dated all throughout high school until she mysteriously dumped him halfway through our senior year.

"But she dumped him. Why would she try to kill herself over a relationship she ended?"

"I think she tried to get back with Julian but my cousin had moved on to greener pastures."

People would do a double take when Dennis told them Julian was his cousin. Julian had been biracial but looked more like his black father than his mother, who was Dennis's aunt. Dennis and Julian's mothers had been born into the wealthy Aldridge family. Mama used to be their maid back in the days before she married my grandfather and stayed on good terms with the family after she quit. Dennis's mother, Emma, was the beauty of the family and married into the equally wealthy Kirby family.

Emma's older sister, Helen, was quiet, shy and plain, destined to become the family spinster, until she fell in love with and ran off and married Jimmy Spicer, the family's black handyman. Both sisters gave birth to sons within months of each other. Dennis and Julian had very different childhoods. Helen had been cut off financially by her parents and she and Jimmy struggled to live off of Jimmy's salary as a bus driver, while Dennis lived a life of privilege. Tragically, Helen and Jimmy were killed in the Highland Hills Supper Club fire of 1977, while celebrating their anniversary, an occasion Jimmy had spent months saving up for, and nine year-old Julian went to live with Dennis and his parents. Dennis and Julian became as close as brothers. They were inseparable.

"I was real sorry about what happened to Julian, Dennis," I said, finally after an awkward silence.

"Yeah, life sucks, doesn't it?" he replied shrugging his thick shoulders and handing me the plastic bag with my book in it. I didn't notice until I looked at my receipt later that he'd given me his employee discount.

Chapter Five

MONDAY EVENING I HEADED to Beekman Hall on the Kingford College campus armed with my book and ready to be bored out of my mind. A class on education theory couldn't be anything other than a chance to catch up on some z's. The class was held in a large lecture hall. I was one of about sixty students, a handful of who looked like other teachers in the same boat as me.

My professor, a thin, intense-looking woman named Dr. Petra Garvey had a loud, harsh voice that cut through me like a knife. Her tight dark green knit dress clung to her like a second skin emphasizing her angular figure and making her sharp collarbone, pointy elbows, and jutting hipbones hard to look at without wanting to force feed her. Dr. Garvey was also big on class participation and liked to call on those who didn't look like they were paying enough attention to the profound wisdom she was dropping on us, which meant sleeping was out. I tried hard to look bright-eyed, bushy-tailed, and interested so she wouldn't call on me. But by hour two of listening to her drone on and on without a break, I was wilting like warm lettuce and ready to slide out of my chair.

"You in the back in the purple top. What can you tell me about the Montessori Method?" she screeched making me jump and bump my knee on the underside of my desk. It took me a few seconds to realize she was talking to me. I heard the distinct sounds of muffled laughter and felt my face get hot.

"Well?" she asked, waiting for my reply with her hands planted on her bony hips.

Everyone was staring at me and I had to dig deep into my subconscious, all the way back to my college days at Ohio State as an education major, for an answer that danced on the edge of my memory before disappearing altogether. I started to open my mouth to apologize before I remembered that I was there to learn from *her*.

"Excuse me, Dr. Garvey. But, I thought the purpose of this class was to learn about education theory. Shouldn't *you* tell *us* what the Montessori Method is?" My words were met by more muffled laughter.

Dr. Garvey's nostrils and lips were pinched together in anger and I wondered how air was getting to her brain. She shook her head and walked quickly back to her desk.

"Okay, class, we'll go ahead and end now. For class on Wednesday I'd like you all to read chapters one through three in your textbooks, and I want a five page paper on the Montessori Method of teaching," she said, smiling triumphantly.

Just great. Amid the groaning and heavy sighing, everyone was glaring at me like it was my fault. I gathered up my stuff and got the hell out of there. In my rush to get to my car before I was pummeled with spiral notebooks, I ran right smack into a young woman, knocking her book bag off her shoulder. It turned out to be Cherisse Craig.

"Whoa, what's the rush?" she asked as she picked up the book bag and flung it over her shoulder. She was dressed down in jeans, a blue cotton tunic, and espadrilles. Her long blonde dreads were pulled back with an elastic scrunchy.

"Sorry. I've just been to my first class since college and I was just reminded of why I didn't further my education." She laughed and it lit her whole face up.

"Are you taking classes, too?" I asked, following her to the parking lot.

"Uh huh, for about a year now. Just a couple of classes a quarter. It's all I can manage working full-time. After I lost my job with Julian last year, I decided to go back to school and get a degree. I'm just taking electives right now. I haven't declared a major yet."

"That's great," I told her. Once we'd reached my car, my stomach rumbled loudly reminding me that it hadn't been fed.

"You want to go have dinner?" Cherisse asked timidly.

Her shyness made me wonder if she'd made many friends in the eleven years since high school. Back then her only friend was her twin sister, Serena. I had no other plans since my so-called man was avoiding me like I was plague stricken, claiming he was swamped at work.

"Sounds like a plan." I agreed.

We met ten minutes later at the Red Dragon Chinese Restaurant. The usually jam-packed restaurant was half empty on a Monday night and we were seated right away. I ordered my usual cashew chicken and fried rice while Cherisse ordered shrimp lo mein. We both had mai tais and egg rolls.

"You know, I always wondered what happened to you after high school. You were one of the few people who didn't torture me," Cherisse said after we'd placed our orders.

"I wasn't exactly Miss Popularity, either. Picking on you would have been dweeb on dweeb violence."

She laughed so hard I thought mai tai might squirt out of her nose.

"Can you believe how fat Audrey and Dennis got?

I can understand gaining weight when you've had five kids but what's Dennis's excuse?" she asked.

I wasn't going to touch that one since my scale regularly swung back and forth between fat and fabulous.

"Remember how Audrey and her crew all acted like they were going on to big things after graduation? Audrey was going to model. Dennis was going to play pro baseball. Julian was going to be a brain surgeon. Remember how they bragged about all their big plans?" I asked, chuckling. Cherisse laughed too.

The waitress brought us our egg rolls and I took a bite without waiting for it to cool and almost burned my tongue.

"Gerald seems to be the only one doing well professionally but then again he has three ex-wives and four kids. He must be spending a fortune on child support and alimony, " she said.

I nodded in agreement and suddenly remembered the missing reunion fund money and Gerald's reaction at the meeting. Thirty-five hundred dollars might not be a fortune but to someone like Gerald with ex-wives and children to support, it wasn't exactly small change.

"Gerald used to visit Julian at his office a lot. Do you know he had the nerve to act like he didn't remember me?" She curled her lips in distain.

"Well, you do look a lot different now, more stylish," I said giving her a smile.

"Thanks." I could tell she was flattered.

"Can I ask you a question?" I was unable to contain my curiosity about the Julian situation any longer. I wanted to know if her version matched what Ms. Flack had already told me. She laughed and took a big gulp of her drink.

"Go ahead and ask. It's what everyone wants to know," she said dryly.

"What happened? Why'd he fire you?"

"It's simple. I forgot to give him an important message from a potential client. He lost out on the account and I got fired as a result. But to be honest, I don't think Julian firing me was completely my fault."

"Why?"

"Julian had just broken up with his girlfriend and was acting like a crazy person. He was so upset and then I messed up by not giving him that damned message and I think he just took everything out on me," she said shrugging.

"Wow. Who was the girlfriend?" I asked before taking another bite of egg roll. But she just shook her head.

"I'd rather not say. She did me a big favor by helping me get that job with Julian in the first place. I don't want to talk about her behind her back."

I could respect that so I moved on.

"So you never left Willow after high school, huh? I just figured you probably joined Serena wherever she went." The minute it was out of my mouth I regretted it. Her face almost fell into her drink.

"Serena's dead, Kendra," she said softly, her eyes filling with tears.

"Oh my God, Cherisse. I'm so sorry. When did she die?" I reached across the table and squeezed her hand. She didn't pull away, but her hand was as limp and cold as a dead fish.

"I don't know." She shrugged and stared at me.

"But I thought you said —"

"Serena never came back home. She never wrote or called. I'm her twin. Why wouldn't she have called or written to let me know she was okay? She has to be dead. That's the only explanation."

Serena Craig was the polar opposite of her sister, Cherisse. She was a wild child, a bad ass. She smoked and drank, had a vocabulary that would make a felon blush, talked back to teachers, and regularly cut class. She also had her own very distinct style of dress that included mini skirts or baggy shorts, tight T-shirts, fishnet stocking, and combat boots worn with long coats and blazers. She wore her hair in a big curly Afro when most other black kids back then were sporting Jheri Curls or asymmetrical cuts. She was beautiful and untamed, like some kind of wild exotic animal, the kind that don't thrive in captivity. Strangely enough, the round table crew left her alone. I think even they were in awe of her. But their deference to Serena didn't stop them from going after Cherisse. I sometimes wondered if they gave Cherisse a double dose of bullying to make up for what they didn't have the nerve to do to Serena. She protected her twin as best she could when she actually came to school, but it wasn't enough.

Our food arrived and we started eating.

"Did your parents file a missing person's report?" I asked between bites.

"My parents were really hurt when Serena left home. They thought she did it to get back at them and that she'd turn up eventually. When she never came home, they just acted like little kids in a staring contest trying to see who would blink first, them or Serena. I think they were trying to practice tough love. You know, trying to show her they couldn't be manipulated by her actions anymore."

"Get back at them for what?"

Cherisse pushed noodles around her plate for a few seconds before answering.

"Serena was a lesbian."

I stopped eating and stared at her until she continued.

"I'd known since junior high. I didn't care. She was my sister. I worshipped her. But she came out to our parents about a month before she left. They kicked her out of the house. She didn't have any money, and she was sleeping on the streets. I begged them to let her come back home. They only agreed to let her come back if she promised to attend one of those reversion programs. You know the kind that are supposed to turn homosexuals straight?"

"I've heard of those programs. Don't they use some kind of aversion therapy to repeal homosexual urges?"

"Yeah. She agreed to go. And my parents enrolled her into a program run by this Christian organization. She was gone for two weeks and when she came home for a weekend visit she was like a different person. She was so quiet and subdued. My parents were happy. They thought the program was working. But I knew she was faking. She told me she was leaving to go live with our aunt in California. Then before she had to go back to the program, she was gone and we never heard from her again."

"Didn't anyone contact your aunt to see if she was there?"

"My mom and my aunt Carmen hadn't spoken in years. She's a lesbian, too. My mom didn't approve of her lifestyle. I never told my parents where Serena was going. She was under-age and I didn't want them dragging her back here. I wanted her to be happy. After graduation, I called my aunt to talk to Serena and she had no idea what I was talking about. Serena wasn't there and she hadn't seen or heard from her, and since I never heard from her again, I figured something bad must have happened to her on her way to California."

"Where did she even get the money to go to California?" I asked.

"I had jars of pennies that I'd been saving since I was twelve. I cashed them in at the bank and gave it to her. It was only about three hundred dollars, but enough to get her a bus ticket."

"It's been eleven years. Don't your parents wonder where she is?"

"My father died of a heart attack five years ago and mom died of cancer six months ago. Until the day they both died, they still thought she was just staying away out of spite just to hurt them. They refused to look for her."

"Maybe it's time you found out what happened to her," I said.

"You know, I don't know what would upset me more, if I found out she was alive and just didn't want to see me, or if I found out she was dead. I'm almost too afraid to find out for sure."

"If she was my sister, I'd want to know what happened to her."

"I really do think she's dead." Cherisse pushed her half-eaten plate away. "I know you wouldn't understand. It's a twin thing. It's like I can't feel her energy anymore. It's like half of me is gone forever."

"All the more reason to find her," I insisted.

Forty-five minutes later, we were standing at the curb in front of the restaurant saying our good-byes. Cherisse gave me a hug.

"Thanks for having dinner with me. It really felt good to talk to someone about Serena."

"No problem, girlfriend. Anytime you want to talk, you just give me a call." I handed her a slip of paper with my number on it.

I watched as she stepped off the curb to cross the street to her car. When she got to the middle of the street, I heard tires squealing and saw a dark colored car pull out from down the street and barrel straight for her. Cherisse was frozen to the spot.

"Cherisse! Look out!" I screamed and ran out grabbing Cherisse and pushing her out of the way just in time. The car never stopped.

"Are you okay?" I asked. We were on the other side of the street by her gold Ford Escort. She was clinging to my arm and staring after the car.

"Did you see that? They didn't even stop!" she said breathlessly.

But I was too busy staring at the side of her car to answer her. She noticed me looking and looked down, too.

"Oh no!" she said, covering her mouth with her hands.

Someone had keyed the words, "You Will Pay For What You Did" on the driver's side door.

I tried to get Cherisse to report the vandalism of her car—and almost being run down—to the police. She refused. She was too rattled and upset and just wanted to go home. Understandably, Cherisse thought the message on her car was from yet another person who held her responsible for Julian Spicer's death. Thinking back on the conversation I'd overheard between Vanessa and Audrey about the strange voice mail message left on Audrey's cell phone, I wasn't so sure. Then there was what Dennis Kirby had told me about coming home to find his garage vandalized. The vandal had painted some kind of message on his garage wall. Was his message the same as Audrey's and Cherisse's? If so, could all three messages be from the same person? Was this person also the one who almost ran Cherisse down and was behind Audrey's drug and alcohol interaction and Dennis almost being electrocuted? And what about the baby oil I found at the top of the cafeteria steps Ms. Flack fell down. Had she gotten a message too? She certainly hadn't mentioned receiving one. More importantly, what were the messages about? What were they going to be made to pay for?

I followed Cherisse to make sure she got home okay before heading home to read about the Montessori Method.

Chapter Six

I WAS STILL THINKING about the message on Cherisse's car the next day at work. If I was right, and Audrey, Dennis, Cherisse, and possibly Ms. Flack had all gotten the same message, after suffering near fatal accidents, then Gerald and I should be next. That is, if Gerald hadn't already received a message. I had to find out. During my two-hour break between the morning and afternoon class session, I headed over to Wheatley Financial, where Gerald worked, to pay him a little visit.

Wheatley Financial was in downtown Willow on the second and third floors of a beautifully renovated three-story brownstone. The first floor had been occupied by a real estate company that had recently moved to larger office space, at least that's what the sign on their closed office door said. I headed upstairs and found myself in an open landing that had been turned into a warm and inviting waiting room. The walls were robin's egg blue and abstract art in muted watercolors hung on the walls, thick plush brown carpeting cushioned my footsteps. A young black woman with braids, dressed in a white suit and seated behind a glass topped desk, looked up and smiled as I approached.

"May I help you?" she asked in a well-modulated, slightly accented voice. The brass nameplate on her desk informed me she was Sunny Abou, receptionist.

"I hope so. I'm here to see Gerald Tate. I'm an acquaintance of his. I don't have an appointment. I just wanted to see if he could spare me a few minutes."

"Really," she said, staring at me quizzically for a moment. "Let me check to see if he's free." Sunny, the smile never leaving her face, consulted a leather bound planner on her desk before picking up her phone and punching in a number.

"Mr. Tate a—" She looked up at me expectantly.

"Kendra Clayton," I supplied when I realized I never told her my name.

"Kendra Clayton is here to see you." I watched as she listened to his reply nodding her head in agreement to whatever he'd told her.

"You can go on back. It's down the hall, the third door on your left," she said half standing and gesturing down a long narrow hallway.

I thanked her and headed back. Before I got halfway down the hall, Gerald appeared in the doorway of his office.

"Kendra? What brings you by?" He had a slightly confused expression like he couldn't decide if he was happy to see me or not. He shot a quick, nervous glance over my shoulder and I turned to see Sunny staring at us with a tight smile. Gerald's tie was loosened and his shirtsleeves were rolled up. He wasn't sporting any bandages or bruises indicating a recent accident, which meant I was going to have to do some digging.

"I hope I'm not bothering you. I just needed some financial advice and I thought who better to consult me than Gerald, right?" I didn't wait for his reply and walked past him into his office and took a seat in one of the two chairs in front of his desk, which was a larger version of Sunny the receptionist's. His office was small and much plainer than the waiting room with stark white picture-free walls and cold chrome furniture. But it was free of clutter, if a little impersonal, and he'd maximized what little space he had.

"So, what kind of advice are you looking for?" He sat behind his desk and closed his laptop computer so he could give me his full attention. Gerald was a handsome guy and someone I could have been attracted to if I didn't know what an asshole he could be. Plus, with three ex-wives and four kids, he had way too much baggage.

"That's a good question," I said, laughing. "I recently came into a sum of money and I have no idea what to do with it. That's why I'm here. I can't decide if I should invest it or just stick it into my retirement fund or what." I knew that there was probably no reason for me to lie about why I was really there but I still wasn't sure there was any connection between what had happened to Dennis, Audrey, and Cherisse and didn't want to come across as crazy or paranoid.

"How much money are we talking about?" he asked. I couldn't help but notice he had perked up considerably at the mention of money and was again reminded of the missing reunion fund cash.

"About five thousand dollars," I said, wishing I was talking about real money.

"Are you enrolled in a four hundred one k plan through your job?"

"Actually, I'm only part-time and not eligible for the four hundred one k plan my job offers. But I am enrolled in the school system's retirement fund," I told him truthfully. At 29 I wasn't thinking as much about my financial future as I should be and hoped I wasn't going to be dining on cat food cuisine in my old age.

"Then I'd recommend opening an IRA." He pulled open a desk drawer and pulled out some brochures on the types of IRA accounts Wheatley Financial offered and the pros and cons of each. He really seemed to know his stuff.

"I think I'd like to take these home and give it

some more thought," I told him when he'd finished. "I just hope I live long enough to retire. It was so sad about what happened to Julian, which just goes to show that you never know when your time is up." I was hoping to get the ball rolling. Gerald stared at the top of his desk and shook his head slowly.

"I know that's right. Hell, I almost joined Julian." He leaned back in his chair and gave me a grim smile.

"Really? What happened?"

"I fell asleep on my couch and woke up and the house was filled with smoke. I'd left a cigarette burning in an ashtray in my kitchen next to an open kitchen window. A breeze must have blown the curtains against the cigarette and caught them on fire. I woke up just in time to put out the fire before my whole kitchen went up in flames."

"*Damn*! You were lucky you weren't killed," I said with genuine feeling.

"And do you want to know what the craziest part is?" He was tapping a pencil nervously against his desk. I shook my head and he continued.

"I only remembered smoking half of that cigarette before putting it out when I left the kitchen. But after I took care of the burning curtains, I noticed a whole smoldering cigarette in the ashtray. Isn't that crazy?"

"That does sound weird." I also didn't remember it being breezy last night, either, but decided not to mention that. Instead, I filled him in on what had happened to Audrey, Dennis, and Cherisse.

"Maybe it's some kind of reunion curse," I told him jokingly after I'd finished. Gerald laughed. Clearly he didn't see any connection between his and the other accidents.

"Naw. I can't speak for the others, but I really need a vacation. I didn't realize how much until last night. I must have been really tired to have forgotten to put out that cigarette."

"Maybe you should just quit smoking," I suggested. He cocked his head and looked at me like I was clueless.

"Maybe," he said with a bored shrug.

"Speaking of the reunion, what do you think about that missing money?" The smile vanished from his face making me smile in turn.

"Hard to say what could have happened to it." He laughed nervously. He made a point of looking at his watch and then stood up. I knew he wanted me to leave but I wasn't finished yet.

"You haven't received any strange anonymous messages have you?" I asked. He blinked nervously a couple of times and shook his head slowly but never looked me in the eye.

"I have no idea what you're talking about. Look, I'm glad I could help you out, Kendra. But I've got another client coming pretty soon. Go on home and think about which IRA you'd like then we can schedule another consultation and we'll have more time to talk." He walked over to his office door and held it open for me.

He wasn't the worst liar I'd ever seen but he sure was close. Just for fun I sat and stared at him for a minute without speaking and watched him twist in the wind. He rocked back on his heels, looked at his watch again, pulled on his earlobe, looked up and down the hall. Finally, he looked away from me and down at his highly polished shoes.

"Thanks for the advice. I appreciate you taking the time to see me." I got up and walked out the door.

I sat in my car across the street from Wheatley Financial to think. Something was very wrong. Gerald's kitchen curtains had caught fire last night. He admitted the kitchen window had been open and assumed a breeze had blown the curtains against the cigarette in the ashtray. It hadn't been breezy last night. In fact, it was muggy and humid. The heat had hung thick, stagnant, and unmoving in the air. I ought to know. The air conditioner in my apartment was broken and I was miserable.

With Gerald's window being open, it would have been easy for someone to reach through the window, put a burning cigarette in the ashtray, and hold the curtains against the cigarette to catch them on fire. Just as it would have been easy to put baby oil on the cafeteria steps Ms. Flack fell down, spike something Audrey drank with alcohol, tamper with Dennis's vacuum, and try and run Cherisse down in the street. I knew Audrey and Cherisse had gotten strange threatening messages. Even though Dennis had never told me what had been painted on his garage wall, I would bet anything it had been the same message saying: "You Will Pay For What You Did". Now I just had to find out if Gerald had gotten a message, too.

I knew the black BMW convertible parked in the small lot next to Wheatley Financial was Gerald's. I got out and went over to inspect it. There wasn't anything keyed in the paint like on Cherisse's car. I heard the sound of an approaching voice and ran over and hid beside a large dumpster next to the building. I stood on tiptoe, peaked over the top of the dumpster, and watched as Gerald came around the corner talking and laughing on his cell phone. The playfulness in his voice, and his soft seductive laughter, told me he was talking to a woman and it wasn't about IRAs. He must be working on wife number 4. I watched him hop in his car and drive away and decided to have a go at his office.

Sunny Abou, receptionist, was on the phone when I went back inside. She covered the receiver with her hand and gave me a quizzical half-smile.

"Sorry, but I left me keys in Gerald's office. I can see you're busy so I'll just pop in and get them." I started down the hall. Sunny looked uncertain and stood up to stop me before whoever she was talking to on the phone commanded her attention and she absently waved me on.

Gerald's office door was closed but unlocked. I walked in and pulled it shut behind me. I put my ear to the door and could hear Sunny still talking on the phone. I quickly went over to his desk and looked through a thin stack of papers in a steel wire tray. No message. I looked in the metal wastebasket by his desk but found nothing except receipts for gas and coffee, an apple core, a newspaper, an empty Pepsi can, and four pink telephone message slips all from someone named Clair Easton wanting him to call her about her account. On a whim, I grabbed one of the pink slips and stuffed it in my pocket. Next, I turned my attention to his laptop. The top was open and I could see he was still logged into his e-mail. I skimmed through his inbox but didn't see anything unusual until I got to an e-mail marked urgent with the name Clair Easton in the subject line. I opened it. The message was from one of Gerald's coworkers questioning him about some inaccuracies with Clair Easton's account.

I skimmed through the rest of the messages and

found nothing else of interest unless you counted the numerous e-mails he was getting from someone with the address wetnready@letsplay.com. I resisted the urge to open one and tried his trash folder instead. Bingo. Five messages down from the top I found one with "You Will Pay For What You Did" in the subject line. I opened it and saw that it was the same message repeated over and over all the way down the page. The e-mail address the message had come from was vengence1986@youmail.com. I grabbed a pen and wrote down the e-mail address just as I heard the sound of footsteps coming down the hall. I pulled out my keys and was at the door as Sunny, the receptionist, opened it. I shook the keys in front of her face.

"Found them. They were hiding under Gerald's desk and I had a hell of a time spotting them." I brushed past her on my way down the hall. I looked back and saw Sunny looking into Gerald's office with a frown on her face. I ran down the steps and back to my car.

I still had more than an hour to kill before I had to be back at work and had yet to eat lunch. I was sitting at a red light, trying to decide what my taste buds were in the mood for, when I happened to look to my right and spied a man through the window of a shop called the Coffee Break Café. It looked like Carl. But it couldn't be Carl because it was the middle of the day on a Tuesday and Carl should be half an hour away at work in Columbus. I parked and went in to get a better look to see if it was indeed Carl, the man who'd been blowing me off for the past several days claiming to be busy at work.

The coffee shop was cute and cozy and about as big as my apartment. There were only four other people in the café besides the person behind the counter. Two of them were women sitting separately as they drank their coffees and read. The other two people, a black man and a white woman, were sitting together, laughing and talking more like two old friends instead of ex-spouses. It was Carl and Vanessa.

Carl looked up as I approached the table and gave me a deer caught in the headlights look, while Vanessa, who turned to see what he was looking at, sighed heavily and rolled her eyes like a pissy teenaged girl.

"Well, this is a surprise," I told them as I sat down at the small table next to Vanessa. The table was really only meant for two people, so Vanessa was squeezed up against the window when I sat down, giving her a real reason to be pissy.

"I hear congratulations are in order. When are you due?" I looked at her stomach, then at Carl who was silently sipping his coffee and staring straight ahead.

"February," she said simply and started gathering her stuff together.

"How's Audrey doing? Is she still in the hospital?" I continued undeterred by the awkwardness of the situation.

I could tell my friendliness was more irritating to Vanessa than if I'd come charging into the café, making a scene, and calling her names. As for Carl, he just looked grim, like he'd resigned himself to his fate. Vanessa stood up and squeezed past me.

"She's fine and back at home." She turned to Carl. "Thanks for the coffee, babe. I'll give you a call later." She tossed me a shit-eating grin and headed out of the café.

"You don't have time for me, but you have time to come here in the middle of your workday to have coffee with the woman who walked out on your marriage when her daddy dangled money in her face?"

"It's not like that," he said softly, turning to stare moodily out the window.

"Well, I wouldn't know what it's like cause I haven't heard from your ass since Friday. So, explain it to me." I glared at him.

"Vanessa just needs a friend right now. She's going through a hard time."

"Is she the one you were with when you hung up on me Friday?" He just stared down into his coffee cup and I had my answer.

I sucked my teeth in disgust, which must have pissed him off because he slammed his cup down on the table and leaned forward angrily.

"She called me Friday. She was really upset and asked if I could meet her to talk. All we did was talk. She just needed a shoulder to cry on," he said loudly causing one of the other women in the café to turn and stare at us.

"Hmm, a shoulder to cry on. Well that sounds to me like a job for her *current* husband, not her *ex*-husband. You're not married to her anymore, remember?"

He sighed heavily. "Her husband is the problem. He doesn't want this baby and it's tearing her apart. She just needs someone to talk to."

She sure as hell didn't look too broken up the last couple of times I'd seen her. And why in the world couldn't she talk to her best bud, Audrey Grant, if she was in so much distress?

"No. She and her husband need to be talking or going to counseling or something. You're a lawyer not a therapist. And if you ask me, it's poetic justice," I said, not so subtly referring to the fact that Vanessa had had an abortion not long after she split with Carl, a baby that could have been his, even though she'd been sleeping with two other men at the time. A child Carl would have welcomed. How ironic it was that she was now pregnant, again, by a man who didn't want a baby.

"Well, I didn't ask you and I'm seeing a side of you that I'm not liking much," he said in disgust. "You shouldn't take so much pleasure in Vanessa's problems. I didn't know you were like this," he spat out at me before I had a chance to respond. I stared at him in shocked silence, willing the tears not to come. How dare he say that to me?

"And I didn't know what a big fool you were." I was so angry I could barely get the words out. "Vanessa must have spent all that money her daddy left her and is just lining up another sucker to take care of her and her baby in case her husband bounces. I cannot believe you're stupid enough to fall for her shit. And if you don't like this side of me." I stood up and turned around, "then you can *kiss* this side of me." I smacked my ass and stormed out of the café.

I was still furious with Carl when I arrived back at class an hour later. Even a lunch consisting of a double portion of hot fudge cake hadn't lifted my foul mood. I was on the first floor, getting ready to head up the steps to my classroom, when I spotted Audrey Grant about to head into the room where the summer day camp program was held. She must be there to pick up her kids. I called out to her and she turned and gave me a tight smile when she saw it was me. She still looked a little tired and her black sundress emphasized her paleness but she still looked better than she had in the hospital.

"Are you feeling better?" I asked, walking over to her.

"A lot better, thanks," she acknowledged with a genuine smile this time.

"I didn't realize you had kids old enough to attend summer day camp."

"My oldest daughter, Cassidy, turned five this summer. She starts kindergarten this fall and I thought it would be a good idea to get her used to being around other kids besides her brothers and sisters. Plus, I really needed the break."

"It's a great program. She'll have lots of fun."

Just then a slightly chubby little girl with long curly blonde hair and big blue eyes dressed in denim shorts and a pink Barney tank top ran up and grabbed Audrey's hand tugging her towards the day camp room.

"Come see my picture, Mommy," she said lisping excitedly. Her two front teeth were missing and she

97

sounded precious, though I wondered how cute I'd think it was if I had to listen to her all day long.

"You're being rude, Cassidy. Say hi to Kendra." Audrey tousled her daughter's curls affectionately. Cassidy stared up at me shyly and started sucking her finger. I knew all of Audrey's kid's names started with C. She'd shown us all pictures of them at the first reunion meeting.

"Hi, Cassidy. That's a pretty name." The little girl just ignored me and started pulling on her mother's hand again.

"Mommy is talking right now, sweetie. Go on back into the classroom and I'll be there in a minute, okay." Audrey gave her daughter a gentle nudge in the right direction. Cassidy poked her bottom lip out and then ran back the way she came.

"She's adorable," I commented and could tell Audrey was pleased.

"I'm not supposed to pick her up for two more hours. She was really scared when I was in the hospital all weekend," she said, expressing the kind of guilt that only a mother can feel. "I thought I'd come get her early so we can get some ice cream, just the two of us."

"So did you ever figure out about the alcohol?" I asked.

"It's still a mystery to me. All I drink is Diet

Coke. But if you ask my husband, I'm just a big liar," she said bitterly. "I don't know. I'm honestly beginning to wonder if maybe I did have a drink and just don't remember." She shrugged

"I wouldn't be so hard on yourself." I quickly filled her in on what had happened to Dennis, Gerald, Cherisse, and Ms. Flack.

Just like with Gerald, I didn't quite get the reaction I'd been hoping for. Audrey just gave me a blank stare.

"Don't you think all these accidents are strange?" I asked in exasperation.

"Maybe a little," she admitted slowly, looking at me like I didn't have good sense.

"I think someone is behind them. I think someone spiked something you drank with alcohol, tampered with Dennis's vacuum, set Gerald's kitchen curtains on fire, tried to run down Charisse, and put baby oil at the top of the cafeteria steps so Ms. Flack would fall."

Audrey looked alarmed then asked me anxiously, "Have you had an accident?"

"Well, no. Not yet," I admitted, which made her relax and let out a relieved laugh.

"I think you're being a little paranoid. Why would anyone want to hurt us?"

I hesitated then asked, "Have you gotten any weird messages lately?" That got her attention.

"You know, there was a weird message on my cell phone's voice mail when I checked it on Saturday. I just thought it was a prank call or a wrong number. Are you telling me everyone else got the same message?"

"Can I hear it?" I asked, ignoring her question. I wasn't exactly ready to admit how I knew about the other messages. But she shook her head.

"Sorry, I erased it. I didn't take it seriously." The sound of children's laughter caused her to turn and look over at the door to the day camp classroom, and I knew I was losing her interest.

"What do you think about the missing money?" I asked and she swung back round to face me.

"Oh, that's easy. I didn't want to say anything at the meeting in front of everyone, but I'd bet anything that Julian used that money to help out some friend in need. Julian was like that. He probably borrowed the money and then died before he had a chance to replace it."

"Any idea who the friend could have been?"

"Only one I know who's needed money in the last year is Gerald. He got into some trouble on his last job over some missing money and I heard he was told to either resign and make restitution or be prosecuted for theft. Julian may have given the money to Gerald to help him out. But Gerald would never admit it."

I guess I wasn't surprised that Julian would help out a friend financially, even when the money wasn't his to give. However, though Julian wasn't quite as bad as the rest of his friends in high school, I certainly wouldn't have thought he was so generous. He must have changed in the decade before his death.

"Kendra," Audrey said tentatively making me look up. "I really want to apologize to you for the way I treated you senior year. I was desperate to get my hands on that test because if I failed science, I wouldn't have graduated. I thought I had a job lined up. But it didn't work out. I'm so sorry for what happened. I'm a different person now than I was back then."

I was too stunned to speak and just nodded my head. Cassidy ran back out of the classroom and grabbed her mother's hand.

"Come *on*, Mommy," she whined, pulling Audrey towards the classroom. This time Audrey allowed herself to be pulled and waved good-bye to me over her shoulder.

Later that evening, I was at Kingford College in the computer lab at Floyd Library typing up my paper on the Montessori Method. After I printed my paper, which was a five-page monument to my ability to bullshit, I pulled up an Internet browser and logged into my e-mail account. For the hell of it I typed, "I know who you are," and sent it to the vengence1986 e-mail address. I was bluffing and wanted to see if I'd get a response. I'd been thinking about the e-mail address ever since I saw the message in Gerald's trash folder. Nineteen Eighty-Six was the year we'd all graduated but it was the reference to vengeance that really had me worried. Was someone seeking revenge for something that happened in 1986? Was it something that someone on the 1986 reunion committee had done? The round table gang had been the cause of many bad high school memories. But what in the world had Ms. Flack or Cherisse done?

Before I gathered up my stuff to head home, I checked my e-mail to see if I had a response from vengence1986. No such luck. My e-mail had been returned as undeliverable. The vengence1986 e-mail account had been cancelled. Disappointed, I headed out of the library. I was at the bottom of the library's wide front steps, rifling through my tote bag for my car keys, when I heard a loud voice yell, "Look out!" I looked up to see a large stone planter hurtling down towards my head. I dove out of the way as the planter landed mere inches away from me, showering me with dirt and debris. Several people ran over to see if I was okay. One knee was scraped and I had a tiny cut on my cheek from the flying debris, but I was okay. I had to fill out an accident report with the campus police before they'd let me go home.

I was still shaking when I walked into my apartment. I was so rattled over almost being killed that I didn't notice that my living room window was broken until I turned on the lights and saw the broken glass. Lying amongst the glass on my living room floor was a large rock. I carefully picked it up. There was writing on it. Of course, I already knew what it said. The message was written in bright red magic marker and screamed, "You Will Pay For What You Did."

Chapter Seven

DETECTIVE TRISH HARMON WAS in a meeting when I arrived at the Willow Police Department the next morning. I had to wait almost an hour on a hard wooden bench in the hallway before she could see me. When I was finally able to go back to her cubicle, I could tell by her cynical expression that she was waiting for me to waste her time yet again with my overactive imagination. Trish Harmon doesn't like me. I can think of a few reasons for her dislike, namely me getting myself involved in some of her murder investigations, but mostly I think it's because she thinks in a straight line and has little or no use for the detours I try to put in her path. She only sees situations in black and white, while I can distinguish the shades of gray. Whatever the reason, her dislike of me was very much reciprocated.

I placed the rock on her desk and told her all about the strange near fatal accidents that me and the other reunion committee members had had. She tucked a loose strand of graying hair behind her ear before picking the rock up and reading it. She'd been letting her short hair grow out since the last time I'd seen her and it was now past her ears and made her look a little younger. To her credit, she actually listened intently to what I had to say, and I had hope that for once she wouldn't dismiss my concerns. When she finally spoke, I was surprised that she agreed with me, sort of.

"I have to admit that if all of these incidents are connected, then this does sound pretty strange," she said making me sit up excitedly in my chair. "Although, I have to wonder why you seem to be the only one who has reported these so-called accidents and threatening messages," she concluded with a slight shrug of her shoulders.

I sighed and sat back in my chair. If we ever actually saw eye-to-eye it would most likely be because our foreheads were superglued together. But at least she agreed that something weird was going on and for her that was saying something.

"I can't speak for the others. I don't know why they haven't reported what happened to them. All I want is for you to look into this before someone gets hurt or killed."

"And why do you think this is about something that happened back in nineteen eighty-six?"

I wasn't going to tell her about vengence1986

because then I'd have to admit to snooping through Gerald Tate's e-mail. I felt a little tongue-tied. "Uh, well, since members of the reunion committee are involved, I thought maybe someone is holding the class of eighty-six responsible for something—" My voice trailed off as I realized I had no idea why anyone would be targeting us.

Eleven years was a long time to hold a grudge for something that happened back in high school. I'd gotten my fair share of grief from Audrey and her crew back in the day and, yes, I'd wanted to cause them bodily harm back then. Now, I could at least look back on my high school days without cringing and like Audrey said, she was a different person back then. Weren't we all?

Skepticism clouded Harmon's face before it went blank with disinterest. I watched her put the rock into a plastic bag from her desk drawer. "I've already gotten your statement. The other committee members will need to come to me personally and report what happened to them. However, my guess is that no one else but you sees this as anything more than series of a coincidences."

She was back to talking like the Harmon I knew and loathed. I wasn't going to waste more time trying to convince her. I'd reported what had had happened to me and for now that was the best I could do.

I called into work to let them know I'd be a little late and headed over to Springmont High to talk to the one person I'd yet to discuss all this madness with, Ms. Flack. She'd suffered an accident too. In the times that I'd seen her afterwards, she hadn't mentioned receiving a threatening note. But why would she?

The parking lot was only partially full when I arrived. Summer school was in session and I could see a few students socializing at the tables near the gym's outside entrance. I went inside and headed to the office. Ms. Flack's secretary, Mavis Green, who'd been the school's secretary back when I was in high school, was filing papers in one of the office's large filing cabinets and turned to greet me as I walked in. Mavis hadn't changed much in the eleven years since I'd attended Springmont High. She still exuded the same nervous energy that had always unnerved me back then. With her prissy looking ruffled blouses, perfectly styled fluffy white hair, and manicured nails, she'd always reminded me of a high strung show poodle.

"Can I help you?" She eagerly rushed over to the counter. It suddenly hit me that I didn't think I ever remembered seeing Mavis sitting down. She was always up doing something.

"Is Ms. Flack in?" I looked past her at the

107

principal's closed office door.

"Is she expecting you?" Mavis leaned forward and whispered, "She's been in her office all morning and asked me not to disturb her. I don't want to bother her unless I have to."

I started to ask if I could leave her a message when the door of Ms. Flack's office opened and she stuck out her head.

"Mavis," she began, then stopped when she saw me. I could see that her eyes were red-rimmed. It could have been from allergies, but she looked like she'd been crying. It also looked like she wasn't up for company. "Kendra?" She opened her door all the way.

"I'm sorry to bother you. I know you're probably busy. I just needed to talk to you about something." I walked around the counter assuming she was going to invite me into her office. She didn't.

"This is kind of a bad time right now. Is it very important?"

I looked past her into her office and saw that her desk was piled with books and magazines. She noticed me looking and stepped outside her office and pulled the door partially shut behind her. Is that what she'd been doing all morning, reading? Hell, even I could do that for sixty grand a year.

"Actually, it is important," I replied. We stared at each other until she finally sighed and looked away.

"I'm in the middle of something. How about we meet later for lunch?"

I could tell it was an effort for her to be pleasant and decided not to push my luck. I agreed and she told me she'd meet me at Frisch's at noon.

On the way back to my car, my cell phone rang. It was Carl. I didn't answer. I was still upset over our argument and wasn't ready to talk to him. By the time I got into my car, my cell phone beeped indicating that he'd left me a voice mail message. I got in my car and listened to his message.

"Kendra, I'm really sorry about what I said yesterday. Please let me make it up to you. I hate it when we fight. This isn't like us at all. Please give me a call, okay."

I listened to the message two more times before erasing it. But I didn't call him back because while I was sitting in my car, Ms. Flack came rushing out of the building and hurried across the parking lot. She was in such a rush she didn't even notice me sitting in my car a few spaces down from where she was parked. I sat and watched her as she fumbled around in her purse. I figured she was hunting for her car keys. Instead, she pulled out a crumbled sheet of paper. She sagged against the driver's side door of her car, unfolded it, and read it. Then she angrily ripped the paper in half, stuffed it in her purse, hopped in her car, and drove away.

What in the world had that been all about? Had she gotten one of the threatening messages claiming "You Will Pay For What You Did"? I looked over at the empty space where Ms. Flack's car had been parked and saw something white on the ground. It looked like part of the paper she'd ripped in half. I quickly got out to go pick it up but someone else beat me to it. It was the custodian, Lewis Watts. I almost didn't recognize him without his usual attire, which consisted of a three-piece suit in some bright rainbow color with shoes and a hat dyed to match. When he saw me he grinned like a Cheshire cat.

"Damn, I know I got a powerful affect on the ladies, Kelly. But, if I didn't know betta I'd swear you was stalkin' me, girl."

"That's mine," I said, ignoring his ridiculous comment and reaching for the piece of paper. He held it out of my reach.

"Now, hold up. I just saw that fine ass Ms. Flack drop this. Why you so hot to get yo hands on it?"

He was shorter than me, and I should have been able to grab the paper from him. But he was holding it behind his back and kept jumping back every time I reached for it.

"Come on, Lewis. I don't have time for this. I need that paper. It's important," I pleaded.

"Yeah, I know. It's always important. You always want ole' Lewis to help you out but there ain't never nothin' in it for me," he pouted. It wasn't a pretty sight.

"Okay, I get it. You want money, right?" I reached into my purse and pulled out a five-dollar bill. Lewis turned his nose up in disgust.

"I ain't never taken a dime from no woman 'cept my mama in all my life," he said indignantly with his head held high. "But there's something else you could give me that would make me real happy." He was leering at my breasts.

I hit him over the head with my purse. He dropped the paper on the ground behind him. We both lunged for it. Lewis shoved me out of the way and got to it first…again. He started dancing around the parking lot waving it in the air while I chased him. The little booger was quick and as slippery as a greased pig. Finally, I resorted to the one thing that seemed to work on men every time. I started to cry. I leaned against my car, covered my face, and sobbed.

"Oh come on now, Kelly. I was just playin' wit you, girl." He was still panting from his romp around the lot.

"Then give me that paper and my name is Kendra!" I wailed.

"Look, girl, I need this job. If Ms. Flack finds out I done gave somethin' a hers to somebody else, she'll fire ole' Lewis. You gonna support my ass when she boots me outta here?"

"She doesn't even realize she dropped it, so how's she going to know you gave it to me?"

He thought for a moment and then grinned at me slyly. "Okay, I'll give it to ya. But you got to do somethin' for me in return, baby doll."

I raised my purse again and he flinched. "Naw, it ain't nothin' like that. See, you got a filthy mind, Kelly."

"What is it you want?" I said through gritted teeth.

"There's an annual ball in Dayton next weekend. I go every year. I was gonna take my lady, till she left me. I wanna go but I cain't show up alone. Not ole' Lewis, Mr. Playa Playa himself. How bout I give you this paper, and you be my date to the ball."

I stared at him with my mouth hanging open. This was not happening. I really needed to see what had upset Ms. Flack so much. I sure wasn't planning on having to make a deal with the devil to do it. *Damn!* Lewis started to walk away with the paper and I panicked.

"All right, whatever! Just give me that paper." I followed him. He turned and grinned at me before shoving the paper in my hand.

"It's a deal then. And don't try and hide from me, girl. I know where ya live. I'll be pickin' you up a week from this Saturday at seven thirty sharp." I turned my back on him and headed for my car.

"Oh, and Kelly," he called out before I could get to my car.

"What!" I screamed in frustration.

"You ain't exactly lookin' real fly right now. I hope you can get it togetha by next weekend. Ole' Lewis has standards, ya know." He looked me up and down. I did a slow burn as I watched him walk into the building whistling without a care in the world. I didn't know what I was more freaked out about, the fact that I had a date with Lewis Watts, or that he knew where I lived. Eew!

I got in my car and smoothed out the paper. It was torn right down the middle. I had the right half of the letter. It turned out to be from a Department of Corrections. The picture of the state of Ohio on the seal on the half I had told me it must be the Ohio Department of Corrections. From what I could make out, the letter was informing someone that somebody by the last name of Vermillion was going to be released from prison. The date of the release, the inmate's first name, and the name of the person the letter was addressed to must be on the other half of the letter that Ms. Flack had. I wondered who this Vermillion person was and couldn't wait until I met Ms. Flack for lunch so I could try and pry it out of her.

Later that afternoon, before I headed to lunch with Ms. Flack, I went to the drugstore to pick up a prescription for Mama. It was so crowded I had to wait for almost half an hour. I was in the magazine aisle flipping through the latest issue of People, when I spotted a familiar figure brush past me on their way to the greeting cards. It was Vanessa. I watched her as she perused the birthday cards for men. She was so engrossed she didn't even notice me. I had a sick feeling I knew who the heifer was picking out a card for. Carl's birthday was on Sunday. At least it would be if I let him live that long.

"Shouldn't you be shopping for baby clothes?" I approached her and she jumped.

"It's not nice to sneak up on a pregnant woman," she said and turned back to the cards.

"Just like it's not nice to dump your marital problems with your new husband on the ex-husband you left high and dry," I remarked casually.

"Last time I looked, Carl was old enough to make his own decisions and if he didn't want to be bothered with me, he would have told me, which he hasn't." She glared at me.

"Carl's too nice for his own good, which makes it easy for people like you to take advantage of him and—"

"Oh, shut up!" she yelled, cutting me off and causing people to turn and stare at us. "I've known Carl for a hell of a lot longer than you have and we'll always have a special bond whether we're married or not. He *wants* to be there for me. So, you better get used to it."

"If you were tending to your *own* man, you wouldn't have problems to bother *my* man about? And by the way, do you even know who the father of your baby is this time?" I spat out at her, getting loud myself. Vanessa started shaking and her face turned tomato red.

"Bitch!" She took a step closer.

"Skank!" I stepped up to meet her. I knew I couldn't punch a pregnant woman, but I wasn't going to run from one, either.

"Ladies!" said a voice behind us. We turned and saw the pharmacist, a short, elderly bull- dog of a man come charging down the aisle. "If you can't behave any better than this, I'll have to insist you leave at once."

"Gladly." Vanessa tossed the card in her hand on the floor and walked out of the drugstore.

I slunk off and hid in the candy aisle until Mama's prescription was ready.

Ms. Flack was almost fifteen minutes late for lunch. When she finally arrived, she didn't look any happier than she had earlier that morning, and looked uncharacteristically dishelved.

"You okay?" I asked as she slid into the booth. I was disappointed to see that she'd brought a different purse with her than the one she had earlier, which meant I wouldn't get a chance to snoop through it and find the other half of the letter.

"Fine," she assured me, picking up the menu and glancing at it before tossing it back down on the table when our server approached to take our orders. We both ordered tuna melts and fries.

"What's up? You said it was important," she asked when our server walked away.

"It's about last week when you fell down the cafeteria steps."

She looked confused and asked, "What about it?"

I told her about the other accidents I, Cherisse,

Gerald, and Audrey had had. I also told her about the message wrapped rock that had been thrown through my window and the message left on Audrey's voice mail. As I talked, I could see the color drain from her face. When I finished, she looked at me and burst into tears.

I instinctively grabbed her hand. "What's wrong?"

She reached inside her purse, pulled out a piece of paper, and slid it across the table at me. I got excited because I assumed it was the other half of the letter from the Department of Corrections. It wasn't. On the paper was a message made up of large irregular letters cut from a magazine. It said, "You Will Pay For What You Did."

Chapter Eight

"WHERE DID YOU GET this?" I asked, trying to keep my voice down. She wiped her eyes with the back of her hand. I handed her my napkin and she blew her nose before replying.

"I found it taped to the round table in the cafeteria before the emergency meeting last week right before we set up the table."

"I didn't see this on the table. Where was I when you found it?"

"Your back was turned. I saw it and stuffed it in my pocket."

"Why didn't you say anything about it?"

"Because I've been having problems with a group of tenth grade girls. Everyday I've had one of these kids in my office because of fighting. I just thought it was one of my summer school warrior princesses who'd left it to harass someone they'd been in a fight with. I just gave them all a warning and never gave it a second thought."

"Someone is targeting the reunion committee for some reason. I've already reported what happened to me to the police this morning. You all need to talk to

118

them, too. It's the only way they'll take it seriously enough to look into it."

"I can call another emergency meeting and have someone from the police department there to talk to us all," she suggested. I agreed and she said she'd schedule a meeting for the next night.

Our food arrived and we ate silently. She didn't seem to be nearly as upset as she had earlier but there were things that were still bothering me. Why did she hold onto the note when she thought it was no big deal and who did she know who was getting out of prison soon?

After two excruciating hours of looking at Dr. Petra Garvey's pointy shoulder blades every time she turned to write on the board, I went to the store and got a roasted chicken, garlic mashed potatoes from the deli, and some fresh asparagus from the produce section. I called Carl on the way home to invite him over for dinner and makeup sex. He didn't answer his phone. I left a message and went home, got everything ready, and even put on a little black dress and heels.

Carl didn't call back. So, I called him again. There was still no answer. Only this time, the phone went straight to voice mail, indicating that he was either talking to someone else and not bothering to answer my calls or the phone was turned off. Of course I was imagining all kinds of scenarios, all of them involving Vanessa Brumfield-Carver, and none of them platonic. An hour later, with still no call from Carl, I decided two could play this game. I tossed the now dried out chicken in the trash, called Morris Rollins and asked if he wanted to meet at Estelle's for a late dinner, touched up my perfume, and headed out.

"So, what'd he do?" Rollins asked halfway through dinner. Up until that point we'd been having a great time laughing, talking, and flirting. It certainly never occurred to me that he'd think my calling him out of the blue to have dinner was anything out of the ordinary. My ego told me he'd jump at the chance to spend time with me. No questions asked. As usual, my ego was wrong.

"Hmm? What do mean," I asked after swallowing a mouthful of Fettuccini Alfredo. He laughed his full-bodied laugh while I continued to stare at him in faux confusion.

"You know exactly what I mean. You and Carl must have had an argument or he stood you up for a date. Whatever's going on with the two of you, I'm under no illusions that you got all decked out in that sexy little dress just for me," he concluded dryly.

I didn't know what to say. I was embarrassed. Instead of trying to convince him otherwise, I filled him in on what had been going on with Carl and

Vanessa. He listened intently before commenting.

"I won't lie and tell you not to worry. He pulled slowly on his goatee. I could tell he was trying to find just the right words to tell me something I didn't want to hear. "Pregnancy affects men in strange ways. Marriages come and go, but a child is forever and a big commitment between two people. Carl might be realizing that—" His voice trailed off before he could finish but I had sick feeling I knew what he was getting at.

"You mean Vanessa re-marrying probably wasn't any big deal to Carl because as you've just said, marriages come and go, but her having a child with someone else means she's truly moved on?"

Rollins shook his head yes.

My God. Was that what Carl's problem was? Had he been secretly hoping he and Vanessa would get back together one day? I'd started dating Carl the week before his divorce from Vanessa had become final. Had he been simply killing time with me until he could find his way back into her life and her getting pregnant ruined his game plan? No. I just refused to believe that was true.

"Sorry, Reverend, I don't buy it." I shook my head angrily and tossed my napkin on the table.

"Well then what do you think is going on?" He was looking at me like he felt sorry for me and I wanted to scream.

"Carl isn't the kind of man who's going to turn his back on someone in need even if it is his ex-wife. I think Vanessa is using her marital problems to worm her way back into Carl's life *not* the other way around. I just wish he wasn't so naive when it came to her," I concluded huffily. I looked at him and saw that his lips were twitching. What was so damned funny?

"So you are capable of seeing a situation for what it truly is. Logic does somehow manage to prevail in that pretty head of yours." He laughed a little too condescendingly for my taste. He'd used reverse psychology on me and I'd fallen for it without even realizing what he'd been up to. I felt my face start to burn and my lips went tight with anger. I didn't speak and instead turned my attention back to my meal.

An awkward silence ensued as we continued eating and I felt bad. I'd lured him to dinner under false pretenses then unloaded my problems on him and he'd just tried to help me. I wasn't being a very good sport. We looked up from our plates at the same time.

"I'm sorry," we said in unison then laughed.

After dinner, we ordered the Wednesday dessert special of strawberry shortcake. While we savored the fluffy biscuits dripping in luscious strawberries, covered in clouds of whipped cream, I couldn't help but notice two women sitting on the opposite side of

the restaurant three booths down from us. They were
leaning close together whispering. One woman was
black, looked to be in her late thirties, and was dressed
in jeans and a blue silk blouse and a matching denim
blazer. Her hair was curly and held back from her face
with a multicolored silk scarf. She looked upset. The
other woman's back was to me. But I could see she
was a full-figured blonde white woman in her late
twenties, was dressed in the same black sundress she'd
worn when I'd seen last seen her except this time
she'd tried to dress it up with a red fringed shawl. It
was Audrey Grant. Whatever they were talking about,
it looked pretty intense and I couldn't help but stare.

"You know them?" Rollins asked, glancing over
to see who I was looking at.

"I went to high school with the blonde." I
continued to watch.

Audrey's companion abruptly stood up, causing
Audrey to grab both her hands and try to pull her back
down into the booth. They were still whispering
angrily and I couldn't hear what they were saying but
could tell by the tone of Audrey's voice that she was
pleading with the woman about something. The
woman pulled out of Audrey's grasp and rushed out of
the restaurant.

I excused myself and went over to say hello and
to ask if Ms. Flack had contacted her about the

emergency reunion committee meeting. It took two hellos and me finally waving my hand in Audrey's face to get her to acknowledge my presence. She stared up at me with tear-filled eyes.

"Audrey, are you okay? Who was that woman?" I sat down across from her. At the mention of her companion, Audrey looked so startled I thought she might faint.

"I've got to get out of here." She grabbed her purse and stood up so fast she knocked her drink over and it spilled down the front of her dress. "Shit," she said, sitting back down and trying to sop up the wet mess with a napkin. I tried to help her, but she angrily slapped my hands away.

I looked over at Rollins and saw that he was about to get up and come over but I put up a hand to stop him, fearing Audrey would try and bolt again if he did. Then I remembered what Dennis had told me about her taking an overdose of sleeping pills the summer after we graduated. Was she distraught enough to do something like that again?

"Audrey, you know that you can talk to me if you need to," I said softly. She looked up abruptly.

"And why the hell would I need to talk to you?" she snapped back.

"I can tell you're very upset. I just want to make sure you're okay and that you don't do anything stupid."

She stared at me like I was insane and then it seemed to hit her. She probably realized I knew what she'd done all those years ago. She got up and left and I followed her out the door.

"Dennis told me about the sleeping pills. Please don't do anything stupid."

She stopped and whirled around to face me. "I don't know what the hell it is you think you know about me. But you need to mind your own fucking business. This doesn't have anything to do with you. And the next time I see that fat bastard, Dennis Kirby, I'm going to tell him the same thing."

I watched her hurry off down the street and went back inside the restaurant and was headed back to my table when a voice stopped me.

"So, what's the deal, Clayton? You thinkin' 'bout switchin' to the all girl team?" said Joy Owens, one of the other hostesses that works at Estelle's.

Though Joy looked like a juvenile delinquent, she was actually twenty-three and had recently graduated with an art degree from Kingford College. She was easily one of the most graceless people I knew. When artistic talent had been handed out, Joy got a double helping, but she'd bypassed the line that handed out charm. She was also a lesbian, hence her comment, though to be honest I could never figure out what her past girlfriends had seen in her. She must have mad game when it came to the ladies.

"Are you talking to me?" I asked with a sigh. I looked over and saw that Rollins was still cooling his heels waiting for me at our table.

"You don't see nobody else named Clayton standin' here do you?" Her arms were crossed and she was rolling her neck with attitude.

"Bye, Joy." I started to walk past her but she blocked the way.

"Is blondie your friend?"

"More like an acquaintance and she's not your type, Joy. She's married with kids," I said laughing.

"You're right, she ain't my type. A little too much meat on her bones and I never was into blondes. But just 'cause she ain't *my* type don't mean I ain't *her* type. She's definitely into chocolate." She grinned.

"What?" I asked.

"I seen blondie and her girlfriend at a club I bartend part-time over in Dayton 'bout a month ago. They was all over each other."

"You mean the woman she was just in here with?"

"Yeah. I thought they was gonna have to call the fire department to pry blondie's tongue outta ole' girl's mouth." Joy started laughing.

"You must have made a mistake. It had to have been some other woman you saw," I told her shaking my head in disbelief. Joy was not anyone whose word I'd take on faith alone. I still remembered back to a few months ago when she had me running around the neighboring city of Springfield like a fool looking for my best friend Lynette who'd gone AWOL days before her wedding.

"Naw, it was her all right. She was tossin' back virgin Margarita's like they was goin' outta style. You say she's got kids?"

I nodded.

"She's got five kids, right? I know this 'cause she showed me pictures of them kids. They all got names that start with C. Colleen, Callie, Cassidy, Christopher, and Cory." Joy said the last name with a grimace because her ex-girlfriend's name was Cory and she'd backed over Joy with her car a year ago. Talk about a relationship killer. Exactly how does one keep love alive when you've seen the underside of your sweetie's car?

Having heard the names, I knew she couldn't have made it up and you could have blown on me and I'd have fallen over. Audrey Grant, former cheerleading queen bee of the Springmont High Class of 1986 and married, stay-at-home mom to five kids, was a lesbian. Now, I'd officially heard everything.

Later, Rollins walked me to my door. I stared at him shyly, half expecting him to kiss me, because he usually wanted to. Instead, he gave me a tame peck on the cheek.

"What's wrong?" I asked, suddenly worried that I'd offended him somehow.

"Let's just say I finally get it," he said, chuckling softly. I opened my mouth to speak but he held up a hand to stop me.

"You love Carl. I get it now. I thought maybe you might develop feelings for me. But I was wrong. I can't keep being satisfied with the little bits of attention and occasional kisses you toss my way. It's not fair to either one of us and it's certainly not fair to Carl. I need to move on. I hope you'll let me," he said softly.

I was startled but couldn't deny the truth of what he was saying. I nodded in agreement and was surprised to feel my eyes filling with tears.

"We're still friends, right?" I asked in a small voice, unable to look at him.

"Always." He gave my hand a firm squeeze and was gone.

The emergency meeting of the reunion committee was scheduled for that next evening. But all that next day at work, I couldn't help but wonder who Ms. Flack knew that was getting out of prison soon and why she was so upset about it. Who was this

Vermillion person? Was it a man or a woman? My supreme nosiness was prodding me to find out. So, when I got off from work, I headed over to the records office at Kingford College to talk to someone who might be able to help me.

Myra Gaines had a line of about six students in front of her age scarred wooden counter. Myra was my uncle Alex's girlfriend Gwen Robins's best friend and had been the registrar at Kingford College for twenty plus years. And lucky for me, Myra also had a boyfriend named Bone who called the London Correctional Institution home. It was a long shot, since Ohio had a dozen prisons, but I was hoping Myra could ask him if he might know a fellow inmate by the last name of Vermillion who was getting out soon. I waved to her as I got in the end of the line. By the time I reached the counter, we were alone in the office. At the mention of Bone's name, Myra called a student worker from the filing room to cover for her, and we went outside to sit on a nearby bench on the college green to talk. The August sun was scorching hot that day and I was grateful we were able to find a place in the shade to sit.

"Sorry, Kendra," she said, pushing her glasses up on her nose and looking around. "I don't want anybody I work with knowing my man is incarcerated. You know how it is with folks around here. These

129

academic types can be so damned uppity like ain't none of them ever made a mistake." She lit up a cigarette, took a long drag, and blew the smoke away from me.

I'd never been real clear on just why Bone was in prison, since he was already an inmate when Myra met him on the prison's pen pal website. But Gwen had told me was serving a twenty year sentence. So it must have been one hell of a mistake. I filled her in on what I wanted to know but left out Ms. Flack's name instead telling her it was something to do with a student of mine.

"No problem. I'll be talking to him tonight." Her face lit up like a Christmas tree. "I'll ask him and then give you a call, okay?"

I thanked her then we chatted a bit. "And how's that fine lawyer of yours?" she asked after stubbing out her cigarette and tossing it in the trash basket next to the bench. "What's his name again, Clark?"

"It's Carl and he's fine." I tried hard to keep the sarcasm out of my voice and wished I were telling the truth. Myra was lucky in one respect. At least she knew where Bone was every night.

To my surprise I was the last one to arrive at the high school for the meeting that night. Even Detective Trish Harmon, looking as serene as a coma patient, and her chubby partner, Charles Mercer, looking well fed and cheerful as usual, were there standing off to one side of the room watching everyone. My fellow committee members were already sitting at the round table. No one spoke. Ms. Flack was looking down at her lap. Dennis sat stony faced with his arms crossed. Gerald was leaning back in his seat with one leg crossed over the other drumming his fingers impatiently on the table. Audrey looked tired and sad and sat slouched in her chair staring into space. The only one who looked like she didn't have a care in the world was Cherisse. She gave me a smile as I sat down next to her.

"Is this everyone?" Harmon asked Ms. Flack. She nodded silently and Harmon and Mercer joined us at the table.

"It is our understanding that the members of this committee have been experiencing some strange incidents. I've already talked to Ms. Clayton and Ms. Flack; we need to hear everyone else's stories," said Charles Mercer, while his partner observed everyone. I could tell Harmon still thought the whole thing was just a big joke. No one spoke up.

"We don't have to do this in front of everyone. We can speak to each of you privately," Mercer said when he saw that he might not get any takers.

"I'll go first if no one else will," Cherisse finally

said, standing up. Harmon and Mercer led her to a table on the other side of the cafeteria.

"This is the biggest waste of time. Why would anyone be after me? I haven't lived in Willow since graduation. I've only been back here for six months." Dennis glared at me.

"And I was supposed to be with my kids tonight." Gerald looked at me like I was dirt.

"And I've got a splitting headache and should be in bed, not sitting here because of someone's overactive imagination," whined Audrey, rubbing her temples. She looked over at me and shook her head.

Ms. Flack got up from the table and walked away like the meeting hadn't been her idea. I was on my own and for a split second I felt like I was back in high school. But high school was a long time ago and I wasn't the same scared little teenager anymore. Funny how time leveled the playing field.

"And you know what?" I said through gritted teeth. "I'd rather be shoveling shit than sitting here listening to you assholes bitch and moan. You can give me all the dirty looks you want, but something weird is going on and the police need to know about it so they can investigate before one of your sorry asses turns up dead." It was my turn to glare and I stared each one of them down. I could tell they weren't expecting this kind of outburst from me and I enjoyed their discomfort.

Feeling a little too powerful for my own good, I continued on. "As for what you've done to make anyone target any of you, all you have to do is think back to high school and all the kids whose lives you made miserable with all your teasing, tormenting, and bullying. That's motive enough right there." As soon as it was out of my mouth I regretted it because all of their attention turned to the opposite side of the room, where Cherisse was giving her statement to Harmon and Mercer. Suspicion etched itself across each of their faces. I could see the wheels turning and knew they thought Cherisse must be the culprit.

"You may as well look at me, too," I added quickly. "If you'll recall, I'm the reason you all passed Mr. Fields's science final. You guys were pretty persuasive in getting me to change my mind about getting that test for you, remember?"

Audrey at least had the nerve to look ashamed, but remorse wasn't something Dennis was familiar with.

"High school was a long time ago. Man, you really need to get rid of that chip on your shoulder. Just get over it. Hey, Teddy loved you. Wasn't that enough?" he said, laughing loudly. I could see Gerald's lips twitch in an effort to keep from laughing. But surprisingly Audrey wasn't laughing.

133

"If anyone needs to let it go, it's you, Dennis. You're the same loudmouthed, mullet-wearing clown you were back in high school. Still living in Julian's shadow. But you'll never fill his shoes, will you? Even your own parents preferred him over you, their own son," Audrey said, shocking the hell out of me.

Dennis puffed up angrily and his mouth opened and closed rapidly in an unintentional impersonation of a large mouthed bass. He started to stand up, but Gerald put his hand on his arm and gave him a warning look urging him to sit down and shut up, which he did with great reluctance. Instead, he sat there breathing heavily and giving Audrey murderous looks.

No one else said a word and when Cherisse returned to her seat, Dennis jumped up and went over to give his statement.

"Kendra, do you really think someone is after us because of stuff we did in high school?" Audrey asked in a small voice.

"I don't know. It was just a suggestion." The anger I'd felt towards my former high school tormentor had suddenly evaporated. It felt good to have unloaded all the stuff that I'd had been pent up inside me for eleven years.

"Maybe we're all looking at this the wrong way," said Ms. Flack, who'd been sitting a couple tables away from us silently watching the drama. She got up and came back over to the round table. "Maybe whoever is doing this isn't targeting the class as a whole. Think about it. Kendra and Cherisse weren't a part of any popular clique in high school and I was a staff member."

It was a plausible theory. But I didn't know if I bought it. What about the vengence1986 e-mail address? I wanted to say something but knew Gerald would immediately know that I'd snooped through his e-mail.

"So what are you saying?" asked Cherisse.

"I'm saying maybe we're being targeted for something we each may have done individually. Can anyone think of anything they've done that someone might want revenge for?" Ms. Flack said.

The only person I could think of who'd want revenge against me was Stephanie Preston, the woman I was set to testify against at her upcoming murder trial. Though she was a very sick woman, I supposed she could have had someone else do her dirty work. But that still didn't explain everyone else's accidents.

"I accidentally killed a dog a few weeks ago. He just ran right out in front of my car before I could stop. His owner was pretty upset. I felt horrible," said Audrey.

"I might have a few pissed off clients whose

investments lost money, not to mention three disgruntled ex-wives." Gerald laughed. I had a feeling whatever his clients had lost ended up in Gerald's pocket.

"It's no secret that quite a few people hold me responsible for Julian's death." Cherisse looked around the table defiantly.

"What about you, Ms. Flack?" I asked. She opened her mouth to speak but Dennis returned to the table.

"You're up next, Prozac Queen," he said to Audrey, who got up from the table and stalked back to where Harmon and Mercer were waiting.

Gerald filled Dennis in on Ms. Flack's theory, which made Dennis laugh though there wasn't a trace of amusement in it.

"Man. What have I done recently that someone would want revenge for? That's an easy one. I'm still alive while my so-much-better-than-me cousin, Julian, is dead." He laughed a harsh angry laugh.

But no one disagreed with him.

ANGELA HENRY

Chapter Nine

THE MEETING ENDED TWENTY minutes later. I was relieved that the police now knew about what had been going on. But I had no faith that they'd make looking into the matter a priority.

"Is that it?" I asked, hurrying to catch up with Harmon and Mercer in the parking lot. Harmon gave me an annoyed look, while Mercer looked like it was past his dinner time and he wasn't happy about it.

"We've taken statements from everyone and we'll be looking into the matter. What more do you want us to do?" said Harmon.

"At least tell me if I should be worried. Someone is definitely targeting us, right?" I persisted.

"So it would seem," Harmon said, opening the car door.

"And please call us if you get anymore messages or anything else strange happens," Mercer added. They got in their unmarked Crown Victoria and took off, leaving me feeling anything but reassured.

Instead of going home, I headed over to the Kingford College library to talk to the custodian on duty. I was hoping it would be the same one who was working the night the stone planter fell, or more likely was pushed, off the roof and almost killed me. After inquiring at the information desk, I was directed to the basement of the library where they kept the archives and books that no longer circulated. The hallway in the basement was narrow and dimly lit and lined with shelves filled with box after box of old books. It smelled a little dank and moldy and I suppressed a sneeze. I could see a light on in an office at the end of the hall. When I got to the doorway of the office, I saw a man who must be the custodian seated behind a gray metal desk playing a game of solitaire on the computer. A large cork message board covered in pushpins and Post-it notes was attached to the wall behind the computer, while the top of the desk was covered in dark rusted rings that must have been left behind by the cracked green Kingford College coffee mug sitting next to the computer's keyboard. Shelving along the back wall held cleaning supplies. When he saw me standing there watching him, he jumped and then quickly clicked on the mouse making the game disappear.

"Students ain't s'posed to be down here," he said testily. He was a heavyset middle-aged man with graying red, slicked back hair. His brown uniform pants looked a little snug around the waist and the sleeves of his tan work shirt were rolled up exposing muscular forearms covered with thick reddish brown hair. The name sewn onto the front pocket of his shirt read: Harlan.

"Sorry to bother you, sir, but I was the one who almost got killed when that planter fell from the roof the other night and I was wondering if you found out how it came loose?"

"I can't talk to you if you've filed a lawsuit against the college. Could lose my job." He eyed me suspiciously.

"Oh no," I assured him. "I was just curious. I'm not planning to sue. I promise."

He continued to stare at me like he didn't quite believe me then took a swig from his coffee mug and cleared his throat. "What is it you need to know?"

"I just wondered how such a heavy planter could have fallen from the roof? Was it loose?"

"Those planters are pretty old and fallin' apart. It wouldn't take much to knock one over, which is why we don't let people up there. I must have changed the lock on the door to that roof a dozen times, but they always manage to get up there somehow. My guess would be that some students were up there messin' around and accidentally knocked that planter off the roof. I'm always findin' condom wrappers and whatnot up there." He shook his head in disgust and took another loud slurp of his coffee.

"Were you working that night? Did you find anything up there after the planter fell from the roof?" I asked.

"Yeah, I was here all right. They called and interrupted my dinner break to come clean up that mess. Went up to the roof afterwards and all I found was some empty pop cans and these," he said opening his desk drawer and pulling out two small white shiny objects and tossing them on his desk. I walked over to his desk to take a look.

I could tell he didn't know what they were, but I recognized them immediately. They were fake fingernails. The cheap press-on kind you can get at any drugstore. They were pearl white in color and oval shaped. Dirt was caked onto the sticky adhesive on the back of each one. Could the person who pushed that planter off the roof have been a woman and a couple of her fake nails had popped off in the process? Or was the custodian right and it had just been some students fooling around. No telling how long the nails had been up there. I told the custodian what they were and he wrinkled his nose in disgust and swept them off his desk into the wastebasket.

"I thought they were guitar picks," he said still frowning. I thanked him and left.

Five minutes after I got home there was a soft knock at the door. It was Carl. I silently stood aside and he walked in. It felt like I hadn't seen him in months. I was tired, too tired to fight with him about Vanessa. She wasn't worth the toll it was taking on our relationship. Carl looked tired, too.

"Kendra, I'm—" he began before I silenced him with a kiss.

We kissed for a long time and clung to each other. It was like we couldn't kiss deep enough or press close enough together. We kissed and shed clothes all the way to my bedroom. I lay down on the bed and pulled him on top of me. I reached between his legs and stroked his erection and guided him between my legs. One sudden hard thrust and he was deep inside me, causing me to shudder and cry out in pleasure that bordered on pain.

We lay there not moving with him inside me for several long minutes then I flipped him over until I was straddling him and started riding him slowly, exquisitely slow, maddeningly slow. Slow is good. Soon we were both breathing heavily and sweating. I started to moan and he rolled me over onto my back, quickening his pace until I climaxed. Then he came and collapsed on top of me. It was the shrill chirp of the telephone that woke me later. I squinted at the clock as I reached for the cordless. It was close to

141

midnight. I pressed the talk button.

"Hello?"

"Kendra, it's me, Myra. Sorry it's so late. Did I wake you up?"

I looked over at Carl to see if the phone had woken him up. He pulled the cover up under his chin and rolled onto his side. I took the phone and went into the living room.

"Did you talk to Bone?" I asked anxiously.

"Yeah, I would have called earlier but I—"

"That's okay. I was still up," I lied so she'd hurry up and tell me what I wanted to know.

"Good cause you know I don't usually call no one past eleven o'clock. I'm real polite like that but I figured you'd want to hear what Bone told me."

"What did he say?" I was sitting on the edge of my rocking chair with the phone gripped tightly in my hand.

"He said there's a guy named Calvin Lee Vermillion who's at London with him. Bone said he's been in the joint for thirty years. He's 'bout to get released next week."

"Why's he in prison?"

"Bone said he was a white supremacist. He killed a brotha back in the sixties. Now, ain't that some shit?"

"You ain't never lied," I whispered, more to

myself than Myra.

The next day after work, I headed over to Ms. Flack's house to talk to her about Calvin Lee Vermillion, though I'd yet to figure out just how I was going to bring up the subject. I couldn't shake the feeling that she was in some kind of danger because of this Vermillion guy and wondered if maybe he could somehow be behind all the weird stuff happening to the reunion committee.

Ivy Flack lived in a blue and gray fifties craftsman style bungalow on Hewitt Street. I pulled up in front of her house and noticed her car wasn't in the driveway but got out and knocked on her door anyway on the off chance her car was parked in the detached garage. No one answered the door but I could hear faint meowing sounds coming from inside the house before a large black and white cat appeared in the big picture window perched on the back of a sofa that sat in front of the window. This must be Tamsin. She looked at me curiously with large yellow eyes that seemed to be telepathically trying to tell me what I'd already figured out, the mistress of the house wasn't at home. Tamsin and I stared at each other for a few seconds more before I turned to head back to my car. As I stepped off the porch, I heard a crash that startled me and looked over to see that a scrawny stray dog had knocked over Ms. Flack's aluminum trashcan and was eating something it had found amongst the garbage. When the dog spotted me, it took its prize, which looked like a chicken leg bone, and ran away to hide under the neighbor's bushes. I could hear it crunching on the bone in the distance as I approached the fallen trashcan.

Knowing that if the trash wasn't picked up it would end up all over Ms. Flack's yard and the street, I bent down to clean up the mess. It was mostly empty pop cans, newspapers, detergent boxes, fast food containers, and the rest of the chicken carcass the dog had gotten a hold of. But something amongst the debris caught my eye and made me stop short. I picked it up. It was a package of fake press-on fingernails in pearl white. The exact same kind the custodian had found near the planter that had almost killed me. Only two were missing, which, of course, were the two the custodian had found on the roof. I knew Ms. Flack got manicures on a regular basis, but I did remember her telling me, when I'd run into her on campus last week, about breaking a couple of nails and not being able to get in to see her manicurist right away. In the meantime, she must have resorted to using the fake nails. I stuffed the package of fake nails in my purse. I rooted through the rest of the trash and also found a half empty can of red spray paint. Hadn't

Dennis said that his garage had been spray painted with graffiti?

I stood up too fast and felt dizzy. I sat down on the stoop of my Ms. Flack's side door and thought about how easy it would have been for her to have spiked Audrey's pop with alcohol at the meeting. Audrey was the only one who drank diet pop. Plus, it was no wonder she'd refused my offer to take her to the hospital after she fell down the steps. She'd only pretended to fall. She could have set Gerald's curtains on fire and tampered with Dennis's vacuum. Had she tried to run Cherisse down as well? I didn't recognize the car that almost hit Cherisse that night. I looked over at the detached garage. It was a small one car garage and there were windows on each side as well as a side door. I went over to take a peek and was frustrated to find the curtains were closed. I tried the door. It, too, was locked. I went around the side of the garage to look in the other set of windows.

The side of the garage was right next to the chain link fence that separated Ms. Flack's yard from her neighbor's. I held my breath and squeezed between the garage and the fence. It was a very tight fit. I inched my way over to the window and looked in. Lucky for me, the curtains were open just enough for me to see a dark colored car inside. It was too dark for me to tell if the car was blue or black. But I could tell it was a

145

much older and larger model than the car Ms. Flack usually drove. It certainly could have been the one that I'd seen that night, though I couldn't be positive.

Anger and confusion made me feel almost sick. How could she have done this to us? What reason could Ms. Flack have for wanting to hurt and scare us? What did she want us to pay for? Unfortunately, I didn't have a lot of time to ponder these questions. I had a more pressing concern, which I quickly discovered when I tried to move. I was stuck. Great! Somehow I had managed to snag the button on the back pocket of my denim skirt on the fence behind me. I was stuck fast and I couldn't turn around, not that there was much room to move anyway. I wiggled around trying without success to pull free of the fence. It was such a tight squeeze that I couldn't even reach behind me to extricate myself.

The only thing my efforts accomplished was to shake the fence and make the stray dog, that was still hiding under the bushes on the other side, start barking frantically at me. He barked and snarled, baring his teeth. I couldn't figure out why the hell the damned dog was being so cranky until I noticed its hanging teats and spied two tiny puppies curled up together under the bush. He was a *she*, and she was protecting her pups. When I failed to move, the dog ran around the fence and came charging at me. Being a smaller dog, she was easily able to navigate the tight space and sank her teeth into the hem of my skirt and started pulling. I was worried about what would happen once the dog got tired of a mouthful of skirt and wanted my flesh. I had some cookies in my purse I knew the dog would be interested in. Unfortunately, I'd left my purse sitting by Ms. Flack's side door. I looked around but there was no one who could help me. And how would I explain what I'd been doing peeking into Ms. Flack's garage?

I could feel myself starting to panic. I was desperate, hot, scared, and highly annoyed. I finally realized there was no place to go but up. I managed to lift my arms, scraping them against the side of the garage in the process, and pushed with all my might against the window in front of me. It opened swinging inward and I almost cried with relief. I calculated that there should be just enough room for me to fit through the window. I unbuttoned and unzipped my skirt in the front, quickly wriggling out of it, braced my palms on the windowsill, hoisted myself up, and slid through the window leaving my skirt behind. I landed on the hard, dirty floor of the garage. I quickly got up, dusted myself off, and reached out of the window to grab my skirt. But with me no longer it, the skirt had come loose from the fence and fallen to the ground. To my supreme horror, I watched the dog run, with my skirt hanging from her jaws, back under the bush to her puppies. Damn!

I groped around the semi-dark garage until I found a light switch and flipped it, filling the garage with dim lighting. It smelled like motor oil and bug spray. Besides the car, which I could now see was actually dark brown, there was a lawn mower, hedge clippers, a rake, and a shovel arranged neatly along one wall. There was a small table in one corner that had two large boxes sitting on top of it. I got excited hoping there would be some pants or shorts I could put on. I tore the lid off one box and rummaged around inside. It was filled with old books. A fat black spider scuttled up my arm and I shrieked and slapped at my arm knocking the box off the table in the process. I picked up the books, briefly glancing inside an old copy of Alice in Wonderland and saw it had the name Alice Rivers written inside. The second box held what looked to be junk including vacation pictures of Ms. Flack as a skinny teenaged girl with her family. It looked like they were in Hawaii. There was also a dried out coconut, a dusty lei, and something brown and bushy at the bottom of the box. At first, I thought it was a dead rat and jumped back. Upon closer inspection, I discovered it was an old matted grass skirt.

I scoured the entire garage but could find nothing

to wear, not even an old sheet or a tablecloth. I realized that even if I'd found some clothing, Ms. Flack was a size six and I was a size twelve on a good day. The only way I'd be able to wear anything of hers was if I wrapped it around my head. There was only one thing to left to do. After shaking it out to make sure there were no spiders nesting in it, I reluctantly wrapped the dried out grass skirt around me. It was actually too big and almost wrapped around me twice. I quickly left the garage through the side door. I grabbed my purse and sprinted towards my car. Predictably, the dog came chasing after me. I ran and almost made it. But the dog jumped up and ripped a large piece of the grass skirt from my backside, it's sharp little teeth grazing my right butt cheek. I angrily ripped off the skirt and beat the dog back with it before jumping in my car and taking off.

After going home, showering, and changing, not to mention enduring the pointing, stares, and laughter of some neighborhood kids out riding their bikes upon seeing me in my pink cotton undies with the red hearts, I headed over to the high school to confront Ms. Flack. Summer school was out for the day, but I knew she always stayed at least an hour past dismissal time. I wasn't wrong. Her office door was open and since Mavis looked to be gone for the day, I walked right in.

"Is there something you want to tell me?" I tossed the package of press-on nails on her desk. Her eyes got big but when she looked up at me her expression was infuriatingly neutral.

"Those things are crap. They don't stay on worth a damn," she said with nervous little laugh.

"Oh, I know that. They popped off when you pushed that planter off the library roof and tried to kill me, didn't they?"

She didn't say a word. Just looked down at her lap.

"And don't try to deny it because I found these in your trash can. You're the one behind all the accidents we've all been having, and the threatening messages, too. I'd just like to know why?" I continued before she could protest.

"I'm not sure what's gotten into you. Maybe you need to go home and lie down. You don't look well." She shook her head slowly and looked at me like I was someone to be pitied.

"You're right. I'm not feeling too good. I just found out someone I've known and trusted since high school, someone I respected, has been playing some kind of sick game."

"I don't have time for your issues. I'm going home." She pulled her purse from her desk drawer and stood up abruptly then marched past me out of her office. I was right on her heels.

"What is it you want us to pay for? What did any of us ever do to you?" I persisted as I trailed her down the hall. She turned and gave me a dirty look. It wasn't until we'd gotten to her car that she turned to address me.

"Look, I don't know what your problem is. I have no idea what you're talking about and if you keep harassing me like this on my job, I'm getting a restraining order." She opened her car door.

"Do you have a restraining order against Calvin Lee Vermillion, too?" I asked. She froze and then turned to stare at me. Her expression had changed from angry indignation to one of sheer terror. She looked around quickly like she was afraid someone would overhear what she was about to say.

"Get in," she commanded, jerking her head towards her car before hopping in herself. I got in on the passenger side. Ms. Flack had her head buried in the steering wheel. When she finally looked up, she had tears in her eyes.

"I swear I never meant for anyone to get hurt. But I was desperate," she exclaimed.

"Why?"

"Because if he finds me, he's going to kill me." She looked half crazed.

"Who, Calvin Vermillion?"

She simply nodded.

"What's he got to do with what you've been doing to the reunion committee?" I asked incredulous.

She sighed and her shoulders sagged. "He's someone I knew a long time ago. Someone I wish to God I could forget." She looked at me pitifully.

I nodded urging her to continue.

"It was thirty years ago when I was fifteen. My family and I lived over in Urbana. I was a typical teenager. Whatever my parents wanted me to do, I wanted to do the exact opposite. I started seeing Calvin Lee just to piss off my parents. He was twenty-five and I thought he was cool. My parents forbid me to see him. But I would sneak out of the house at night and hang out with him and his friends. I knew Calvin Lee and his friends hated black people but I never really thought about the wrong of their beliefs. I was only fifteen. I was just happy he liked me. God! I was so stupid." She buried her face in her hands.

"Go on," I prodded gently. She looked up and gave me a tearful nod.

"Calvin Lee was a white supremacist. He and his friend's called themselves the Righteous Whites. One night I was hanging out with them. We'd been drinking heavily. Calvin Lee was driving and he rear-ended another car. The owner got out to inspect the damage to his car. When Calvin Lee and his friends saw that the man was black, they got out and beat that poor man to death. Kicked him until they caved his head in. I saw the whole thing. I still have nightmares about it." She broke off, unable to continue.

"I still don't understand what this has to do with you stalking the reunion committee," I said in exasperation.

"That night Calvin Lee told me if I ever told anyone what he'd done, he'd kill me. And I didn't tell. But what we didn't know at the time was that a woman was on the road walking her dog that night. She saw Calvin Lee's car and got a good look at us. The police tracked me down and told me if I didn't testify against Calvin Lee and his friends, I'd go to prison, too. So, of course, I testified. Calvin Lee got thirty years to life. I'll never forget the look on his face when they led him out of the courtroom. He started screaming that he'd kill me if it was the last thing he ever did."

"And now he's getting out?" I asked, though I already knew.

"I got a letter from the Ohio board of corrections about a month ago informing me that Calvin Lee was being released on parole. I've been married and widowed since I last saw Calvin Lee. He knew me as Alice Rivers. After I married my late husband Stewart, I started going by my middle name, Ivy. But I'm sure it won't take him long to find out that Alice Ivy Rivers is now Ivy Flack. I had to get away from here but I was afraid he'd find me. That's when I got the idea to fake my own death."

My mouth must have fallen open because she quickly continued before I could interrupt her.

"I caused the accidents and sent the messages so everyone would think someone was stalking us. The accidents would then culminate in my death—"

"How?" I asked, unable to contain my curiosity any longer.

"I was planning to sabotage one of the paddle boats at Lake Mead and fake my own drowning at the reunion picnic. You know how deep that lake is. People have drowned and their bodies have never been found. I needed to have witnesses, which is why I involved the reunion committee. Then I was going to go to Mexico to start a new life where Calvin Lee would never find me."

"So, you're the one who took the reunion fund money? So, you could force the committee to have a picnic at the lake instead of a catered dinner?"

"No, I swear I didn't take the money. But I've

154

known it was gone for almost a year. And, yes, I was going to use the missing money as an excuse to have the reunion picnic at Lake Mead."

"You could have killed one of us," I said angrily.

"That was never my intention. I was the one who yelled for you to get out of the way when I pushed the planter from the roof. I only injected a little alcohol into Audrey's Diet Coke can. I fixed Dennis's vacuum so it would just short out and give him a small shock. I set fire to Gerald's kitchen curtains because I could see he had a smoke alarm in that room, and I never planned to actually hit Cherisse. I really wasn't going that fast. I thought I was giving her enough time to get out of the way. I didn't realize she'd freeze up like that."

"That's the problem. Despite your intentions, people did get hurt. Audrey was in the hospital for two days. Dennis sprained his wrist and bumped his head. Gerald was asleep on his couch when you started that fire. What if he'd been overcome by smoke before he woke up? And, if I hadn't been there to push her out of the way, you would have run Cherisse down like a chipmunk in the road." My voice got louder and more irate with each sentence because the blank, clueless expression on Ms. Flack's face told me that she truly

155

didn't understand what she'd done wrong.

"What are you going to do?" she asked in a terse whisper.

"I'm not going to do anything. You're going to the police and tell them what you did, and if you don't, I will."

"Why?" she exclaimed. "No one was killed. What would it accomplish for me to go to the police? I'll stop. I swear. No more accidents and no more messages. Please, I'm begging you not to tell on me. Calvin Lee will be out soon. I'll be arrested and what I did will be all over the papers around here. He'll know where I am and he'll wait until I make bail and then kill me just like he killed that man thirty years ago." She started sobbing and I could feel myself start to waver.

She did have a point, sort of. Luckily, no one on the reunion committee was killed or hurt too badly. If this Vermillion guy was truly looking to kill her for testifying against him, then could I really blame her for resorting to extreme measures to try and get away from him, given that she'd already witnessed him brutally murder someone?

"How do you know he's still looking for revenge? It's been thirty years. People can change after all that time," I reasoned. She shook her head so vigorously I thought her earrings might fall out.

"Not Calvin Lee! He's the most hateful man I've ever known. A while ago someone did a documentary about him and the other Righteous Whites and he blamed everyone for him being in prison but himself. He even blamed his victim. He never said my name, but he swore if he ever got out he'd make the bitch who testified against him pay!" I looked at her red tear stained face and let out a breath.

"Okay. I won't tell the police. But this little plan to fake your death is over. If you want to disappear, then you need to do it without involving anybody else. And if Harmon and Mercer figure out you were the one behind all this, don't you dare mention my name and that I knew what you were up to, got it?"

"Oh, yes, I got it. Thank you. Thank you." I'm sure the sigh of relief she let out could be heard in the next county. She pulled out a silver compact with her initials engraved on it and started checking her makeup and fixing her runny mascara.

"That's a beautiful compact," I commented.

"Thanks. My husband gave it to me," she replied absently.

I continued to stare at her. Looking at the polished, put-together woman sitting next to me, I'd have never guessed that she had something so horrible in her past.

"Please don't look at me like that. I know what you're thinking." She snapped the compact shut and tossed it into her purse. "We all have secrets. It's just some of us know how to hide them better than others."

"So, what are you going to do now?" I asked cautiously, ignoring that last comment.

She looked startled and slightly shocked like the answer to that question should be obvious. "I'm getting the hell out of here," she said, in such a chillingly calm voice that the hair on the back of my neck stood up.

Chapter Ten

THE HEAT IN MY SWELTERING apartment chased me from my bed early Saturday morning. It was much cooler outside than in. So I opened all the windows and had my ceiling fan on full blast as I sat on my couch and nursed a soggy bowl of Capt N' Crunch. There was nothing on TV but cartoons, infomercials for fitness equipment, and the news. Not in the mood to be amused, or made to feel bad about my less than toned thighs, I watched the six o'clock news. There wasn't much going on in the world except for the usual crime, famine, and corruption. But when blonde, big-haired, news reporter Tracey Ripkey, on the air earlier than her usual time slot, started reporting on the early release of Urbana, Ohio, native, and white supremacist, Calvin Lee Vermillion from prison, I sat up abruptly, dumping my cereal bowl all over my oriental rug.

The camera showed a frail, gaunt old man walking out the gates of London Correctional Institute being met by a small handful of family and friends. In the background I could see a throng of protesters shouting and waving signs. According to Ripkey,

159

Vermillion was suffering from liver cancer and had been released a week early to seek treatment. The camera then panned to one of the protestors, an attractive, well-dressed, middle-aged black woman named Ramona Chapman, the daughter of Maurice Groves, the man Vermillion killed.

"Where is the justice? That man should have been given the death penalty for what he did to my father. Now, he's been let out early to seek treatment to prolong his worthless life? What kind of world are we living in? Calvin Lee Vermillion didn't just kill my father, he killed my mother, too. She died of a broken heart a year later, and that left me and my brothers and sisters orphans!" Her voice broke off with a sob and she had to be comforted by a man who was identified as her husband.

Next Ripkey interviewed Vermillion's sister, Mildred Perry, a tall, thin woman with gray-streaked, brown hair who's big blue eyes were bloodshot from crying. A large cross pendant on a thick chain hung from her neck and rested against her almost flat chest. She had her back to the protestors and I could see her flinch every time one of them hurled an insult at her brother.

"My brother has served his time!" She had to shout to be heard over the protestors. "He's spent the last thirty years getting to know Jesus and accepting

160

him as his Lord and Savior. Nothing anyone could do to my brother will bring back poor Maurice Groves. My heart goes out to his family. But Calvin Lee has paid for his crime and should be allowed to live out whatever time he has left with his family."

The last person Ripkey interviewed was the man of the hour, Calvin Lee Vermillion. He looked so haggard and frail I thought he might drop dead on the spot. I calculated his age to be late fifties, but he looked much much older. He certainly didn't look like anyone Ms. Flack had reason to be afraid of anymore. He could barely walk unassisted.

"Mr. Vermillion, how does it feel to be a free man?" asked Ripkey.

"Like a dream come true. I'm so blessed to be back amongst my family," he responded in a weak voice. He might be a dying man, but that didn't keep him from appreciating Tracy Ripkey's blonde good looks and cleavage. I could also tell he was enjoying the limelight, at least until Ripkey asked her next question.

"Mr. Vermillion, do you still keep in touch with the other members of the Righteous Whites?"

Vermillion's lip curled in distain, and he gave the pretty blonde reporter a look that could have curdled milk. It wasn't until that moment that I could see the hatefulness that Ms. Flack had spoken of. Vermillion turned away from the camera, and his sister answered the question for him.

"My brother is a different man than he was thirty years ago." She turned to help her brother into a waiting car.

I called Ms. Flack to see if she'd seen the news. There was no answer. After cleaning up the spilled cereal, I turned off the TV, showered, dressed, and headed out the door to Ms. Flack's house. Surely after she heard what a sick, broken, old man Calvin Lee had become, she wouldn't be afraid of him anymore and could get on with her life.

By the time I got to her house it was almost 8 o'clock; still early, but I figured she might be up packing, that is if she hadn't skipped town yet. I wanted to catch her before she foolishly left everything behind to get away from a man who'd be dead soon. Her car was parked in the driveway in front of the detached garage. I was happy to see no signs of the stray dog from the day before but still kept half an eye on the neighbor's bushes. There were lights on in Ms. Flack's house, but no one came to the door when I rang the bell multiple times. I didn't even see her cat perched on the sofa in front of the window. Figuring the doorbell was broken, I pounded on the front door and it swung open. I walked in.

"Hello! Ms. Flack, are you home?" No answer.

The stillness in the house unnerved me as I walked through the neat and modestly decorated living room. The only sound was the hum of the central air-conditioning. I'd only been in Ms. Flack's house a couple of times, the last time being several years ago, and it hadn't changed at all. There was a tiny dining room that led into a large kitchen. She wasn't in the kitchen, which was also neat as a pin and painted in a soft yellow that made it look bright and cheerful. There was an empty cat carrier sitting on a large butcher block table sitting in the middle of the kitchen, but no Tamsin, and more importantly, no Ms. Flack. I headed out of the kitchen and down the short hallway.

"Ms. Flack, it's Kendra. Are you here?" Still no answer. I could see the bathroom at the end of the hall. The door was half open and I knocked and walked in.

Ms. Flack was in the bathtub, though I needn't have worried about embarrassing her because except for her bare feet, she was fully dressed. Unfortunately, she was also dead. I was rooted to the spot while my body tried to decide whether to flee or faint. I finally pulled myself together enough to press my trembling fingers to her neck to feel for a pulse, even though her open mouth and cloudy, staring eyes told me she was long gone. Her skin was ice cold and I quickly snatched my hand away. I let out a huge breath, that I didn't realize I was holding, and sat down on the toilet.

Ms. Flack was dressed in what looked to be the same clothes she had on when I'd seen her yesterday. I got up and forced myself to look into the tub again. I'd been solely focusing on the body in the tub and hadn't noticed the cord that was plugged into a blackened outlet on the wall by the sink that was attached to an object floating in the tub by her leg. It was a blow dryer. She'd been electrocuted. I quickly left the bathroom, pulled out my cell phone, and called the police.

After giving the 911 operator all the pertinent details, I had planned to wait for the police outside in my car. But I remembered Ms. Flack's bedroom was accessible through the bathroom as well as the hall and went back. Strangely, the door between the two rooms was closed. If she'd been running bathwater, why would she close the door that led to her bedroom? I opened the door and walked through to Ms. Flack's room. The room was a mess. It looked like she'd been packing in a hurry. Two large suitcases were open on the bed and stuffed with clothes. Her closet door was open and the closet was half full of clothes. The bottom of the closet was strewn with empty shoeboxes and garment bags. There was a one-way plane ticket to Mexico City, Mexico, on her dresser, along with a monthly bank statement showing a balance of almost twenty thousand dollars. A closer look at the statement revealed that several large deposits had recently been made to her account. She hadn't been kidding when she said she was getting the hell out of dodge. The cat carrier sitting on the dining room table told me she'd been planning to take her cat as well, though I'd still seen no sign of the cat and wondered where it was hiding.

I saw that the window closest to the closet was open by about three inches, which was strange because the air-conditioning was on. I walked over and examined the window. There was some dirt on the white carpet directly underneath the window. I also noticed that the dust on the windowsill had been disturbed. There was another window on the other side of the bed and I went to look at it. The other window was locked and the sill was covered in dust. It looked to me like someone had gotten into the house through the window and that that same someone could still be in the house. I practically flew out the front door just as the police, sirens wailing, pulled up in front of the house.

Chapter Eleven

"YOU DIDN'T TOUCH ANYTHING, did you?" asked Harmon testily, after I explained what I'd seen in the house. Her partner, Charles Mercer, had gone inside where a couple of uniformed officers were already checking out the scene.

"I checked Ms. Flack for a pulse and I probably touched some stuff when I first went in the house. How was I supposed to know she was dead?" I replied, shocked to realize I was about to cry.

It had finally hit me. Ms. Flack was dead. We hadn't exactly been best friends but I'd liked and admired her a lot, at least until I'd found out about what she'd been doing to the reunion committee. Harmon was eyeing me suspiciously, and I quickly filled her in on Ms. Flack's past involvement with Calvin Lee Vermillion, being the one behind the reunion committee's accidents and threatening messages, and her plan to fake her death and leave town. Predictably, Harmon was not pleased. Her face got red and her lips went tight and white with anger. She opened her mouth to speak but was interrupted when Mercer emerged from the house.

"Looks to me like she'd run bathwater and accidentally fell into the tub, pulled the blow dryer in with her, and got electrocuted," he said shrugging.

"But why would the blow dryer have even been plugged in if she hadn't yet taken a bath or washed her hair?" I asked, looking from Mercer to Harmon.

"Maybe she'd already taken a bath and gotten dressed and just forgot to let out the bathwater," Harmon offered.

It was certainly possible. But she was still dressed in the same clothes she had on yesterday and most people let the water out either right before or right after stepping out of the tub. Pulling the stopper to let the bathwater out is the first thing I do before getting out of the tub.

"Well, what about the open window and the dirt? Why would she have opened the window with the air-conditioning running? I think someone may have killed her," I said. Harmon gave her partner a weary look and then wordlessly headed into the house to check out the scene for herself.

"How long do you think she's been dead?" I asked Mercer.

"Hard to say until the medical examiner gets here. But since you said she was still in the clothes she was wearing yesterday, and the lights are still on in the house from last night, I'd guess between eight and twelve hours at least."

"Do you need me for anything else?" I was trying hard to block out the image of poor Ms. Flack laying cold and dead in that tub for twelve hours. I was more than ready to leave.

"You know the drill. We'll be in touch if we have any more questions." I watched as he headed back into the house.

I got in my car and was pulling away as the medical examiner arrived in his tan station wagon. I headed to work at Estelle's wondering where the hell Ms. Flack's cat, Tamsin, was.

By lunchtime, news of Ms. Flack's death was all over town. Estelle's was hopping, as it is every Saturday, and everyone there was talking about Ms. Flack. And as usual, everything I was hearing was wrong.

"They say she was found nude in her bathtub, dead of an overdose." I overheard one elderly woman telling her companions. They all shook their heads like it was a shame, but I couldn't help but notice the excitement glittering in their eyes.

"I heard she was in the bathtub with her wrists slit. They say blood was everywhere," claimed a man casually to the woman he was dining with. The woman put an angry finger to her lips to shush the man and gestured towards a boy of about six sitting next to her in their booth. But the kid just ignored them both and continued to roll a little blue racecar around the rim of his plate.

"You hear about that dead principal?" asked Gwen Robins, my uncle Alex's girlfriend of almost a decade. Gwen was a statuesque 5'10" and wore wigs to suit her many moods. Today she must have been channeling her inner fool because she was wearing a light brown wig that was spiky on top with long straight hair that hung down her back. She looked like Tina Turner's big evil twin. I had to resist the urge to remind her that Halloween was in October.

"You knew her, right?" she continued, when I didn't answer her right away.

Until then, no one had asked me anything about Ms. Flack, which meant that no one knew I'd been the one to find her, at least not yet. It would be on the news tonight and in the Sunday paper tomorrow, and I was dreading the grilling I was going to get, especially from Mama.

I pulled Gwen aside, well away from the diners, and told her about finding the body.

"Damn, girlfriend. Why is it every time there's a dead body you got to be the one finding it?" She walked away from me shaking her head. I got back to work, determined to keep my mouth shut if anyone asked me about Ms. Flack.

But that didn't keep me from thinking about her all day long while I worked seating the steady stream of diners that poured through the restaurant's doors. The one thing that kept popping into my head was the irony of Ms. Flack's plan to fake her own drowning at the reunion picnic only to die in water for real. I had a hard time believing that her death had been an accident. Someone had murdered her. But I also had a hard time envisioning the man she was so terrified of, Calvin Lee Vermillion, climbing through her bedroom window in his frail condition and tossing her into a tub full of water with her blow dryer. From what she'd told me about him, electrocuting someone wasn't his style. Calvin Vermillion would most likely use his fists and his feet to settle any score he had with Ms. Flack. Besides, he'd just been released from prison that morning. Ms. Flack had been dead since last night. So, who had killed her, and more importantly, why?

By three o'clock I was beat. I had a late lunch of a piping hot chicken potpie in the restaurant's kitchen before I took off for home. I was heading past the public library when it occurred to me that Calvin Lee Vermillion wasn't the only one Ms. Flack had testified against. What about the other three members of the Righteous Whites? Where were they now? Could one or all of them have been responsible for Ms. Flack's

170

murder? In order to find out, I'd needed to know their names. I pulled into the library's parking lot and hesitated before getting out. Back in the Spring I'd been banned from the library for sixty days. I'd been falsely accused of looking at porn on the Internet by two geeky teenaged boys who were mad at me when I didn't give up my terminal so they could sit together. It so happened that one of the boy's mothers was one of the reference librarians. I'd been unceremoniously booted out on my ass and hadn't been back since.

I toyed with the idea of going over to the Kingford College library. In the end, I got out and headed inside. I wasn't about to let some creepy kids keep me away from a place my tax dollars helped to run. I headed back to the periodicals section trying hard not to look over to where the computers were for fear of seeing the boys in question. When I got back to the desk, I was disappointed to see the same librarian who'd kicked me out three months ago manning the desk. Great.

"Can I help you?" she asked giving me a strange look. I could tell she was trying to remember where she'd seen me. She, on the other hand, looked just the same as she had three months ago. She still had the same thick bangs that hung in her face like a sheep dog, hair her troublemaking son had inherited from her.

"I'm looking for information on a crime that was committed about 30 years ago in Urbana. A black man was murdered by a white supremacist group called the Righteous Whites."

"Hmm. That would have been the late sixties and we don't have the Urbana paper on microfilm before nineteen seventy. But, I'm pretty sure the *Willow News-Gazette* probably covered the story. Do you know what month it happened?" she asked, still looking at me strangely.

"I'm not really sure. Can I have microfilm for nineteen sixty-six through nineteen sixty-nine?" I replied smiling at her sweetly and hoping I could get the info I needed before she recognized me as the pervert she chased away back in the Spring.

"I'll be right back." She returned minutes later with 3 rolls of microfilm.

I settled in at one of the microfilm readers and got to work searching through nineteen sixty-six. It took me almost an hour to slowly scroll through the film. I didn't find anything and loaded the film for sixty-seven. I had eyestrain and a roaring headache as I viewed the second roll of film. Lucky for me I found the story with the headline, "Urbana Man Found Beaten To Death," after twenty minutes. The murder had occurred July 9, 1967. I skimmed through the article and read the details of thirty-six-year-old

Maurice Groves's brutally beaten body being found next to his car by a passing motorist.

But there was no mention of any suspects or arrests in the murder. So, I scrolled through the rest of the roll. Except for articles about Maurice Groves's funeral, and the outcry from the local NAACP that the police weren't doing enough to solve Groves's murder, I didn't find another article until almost the end of the roll. It was dated December 28th with the headline, "Arrests Made in Groves Murder". According to the article, a witness to the murder had come forward and identified multiple perpetrators that had led to the arrests of Calvin Lee Vermillion aged 25, Shane Powers aged 24, Donnie Boone aged 24, and his brother, Ricky Boone, aged 22. The four had been charged with second-degree murder. A large picture of a younger, heavier Calvin Vermillion grinning at the camera was below the headline. His look of proud defiance turned my stomach. In contrast, a smaller picture of the Boone brothers and Shane Powers showed three young men who looked terrified. Shane Powers, in particular, looked like he might be sick.

I was rewinding both rolls of film when I felt a hand on my shoulder. It was the shaggy librarian. Looking quite contrite, I might add, and holding a video cassette.

"Ma'am, it just occurred to me who you are and

I'd really like to apologize for what happened back in May," she said, turning slightly red.

"Really?" I said not meaning to sound so huffy. She cleared her throat nervously and continued.

"Yes. My son, Wayne, had no right to do what he did to you. I'm so sorry. You're not the only one he's pulled that nasty little trick on. My husband and I are so upset over his behavior we've packed him off to military camp this summer. Three months of fresh air and exercise with no computers or television will do him a world of good," she said beaming. Thinking back on my unpleasant encounter with her son, I seriously doubted it but smiled at her anyway.

"Is that for me?" I nodded toward the tape in her hand.

"Oh, yes, I almost forgot," she said, holding out the video. "This is a documentary that was made by one of the sociology professors at Kingford. It's about that white supremacist group you mentioned. The Righteous Whites? It's about twelve years old. But I thought you might find it useful."

This must be the documentary Ms. Flack had mentioned when I'd confronted her at work yesterday. I'd forgotten all about it. The name on the video case was Righteous Lies. I was so excited it took everything in me not to snatch it out of her hand.

Once I got home I eagerly put the tape in my VCR and spent the next twenty minutes watching Calvin Lee Vermillion spouting hatred for every race that wasn't white. He'd been interviewed at London Correctional Institution in 1985 and was dressed in faded prison garb. He obviously hadn't been missing any meals behind bars and had made use of the prison's weight room. He was muscular and heavily tattooed with his gray-streaked dark hair slicked back from his forehead. He was also missing one of his front teeth. According to Calvin Lee, the mud people, as he referred to minorities, were responsible for everything from inflation, wars, drugs, and illegitimacy. He also, just as Ms. Flack claimed, blamed his victim, Maurice Groves, for being out on the road that night. Predictably, Calvin Lee was a high-ranking member of London Correctional Institution's Aryan brotherhood. The interviewer, a doctor of sociology named Ben Brock, asked Calvin Lee what he would do if and when he was let out of prison.

"Kill the lying little bitch that helped put me in here," he responded, point blank, scowling at the camera. That certainly verified what Ms. Flack had told me. Did Calvin Lee's cohorts, Shane Powers, Donnie and Ricky Boone feel the same way?

More than a little tired of listening to Calvin Lee's

ignorant ass, I fast-forwarded through the tape to the interviews with the other three Righteous Whites. But at the beginning of Shane Powers's interview the tape suddenly stopped. I tried to fast-forward it, but it wouldn't budge. Fearing my VCR had eaten the tape, I quickly hit the eject button. I was relieved to see my VCR readily spit the tape out. I examined it closely and saw that the film was twisted and knotted inside the case. I tried unsuccessfully to unravel it. There was only one thing left to do. I called the Kingford College operator and asked to be connected to Dr. Ben Brock's office in the sociology department. I didn't really expect professor Brock to be in his office on a Saturday and he wasn't. His voice mail said he was only in his office on Monday and Wednesday afternoons. I left him a message to call me regarding his documentary. Now all I could do was wait.

I spent the rest of my Saturday cleaning and doing laundry. Afterwards, I took a nap and was awakened from a frightening nightmare where I was naked and being chased through the woods by an angry torch-wielding mob that included Audrey Grant, and the rest of the round table crew, and Ms. Flack and the Righteous Whites, by a loud knocking on my door. It was Carl and he'd brought a large pizza with him. Smart man. I gave him an awkward smile and stood aside to let him in. Even though we'd pretty much made up, there was still some lingering tension between us.

"I got pepperoni and extra cheese on one half for you and the works on the other half for me," he said, setting the box down on the trunk in front of my couch that served as a coffee table.

I got paper plates, napkins, and a two liter of Coke from my fridge and we dug in. I told him all about finding Ms. Flack's body, and he had pretty much the same reaction as Gwen. I was rapidly becoming known as a corpse magnet to my family and friends. We ate in silence for a while. I didn't want to start a fight, but I had to know.

"How's Vanessa?" I asked cautiously. Carl just shrugged.

"I guess she's fine. I haven't talked to her in a couple of days." He wiped his greasy fingers on a napkin before pulling off another piece of pizza.

"Has her husband accepted the fact that he's going to be a daddy yet?"

"I think so. That's probably why I haven't heard from her. Dude found out she was crying on my shoulder and suddenly everything changed. Last time I talked to her they were going shopping for stuff for the nursery." He laughed.

"She wanted to make him jealous so he would

think he might lose her. So, I was right." I shook my head. "She *was* using you, just not in the way I thought."

"It's what she does. I was married to her, remember? I know how she operates. She never had any real interest in me. I tried to tell you that."

"And you don't mind?" I asked trying hard not to get pissed when I thought about all the trouble she'd caused between us.

"Not really. I'm not interested in going down that road again. Despite what you think, I've never forgotten what she put me through. But she can't hurt me anymore because I don't love her. I love you. Do you love me?" He cocked his head to the side. He looked like a little boy, and I felt my heart swell with love and affection.

"Yes, I do." I leaned in to give him a pepperoni flavored kiss.

"Good because I think we should take the next step." He was grinning at me and it took a few seconds to grasp what he was saying.

"Huh?" was all I could get out.

"You know. Get married and start a family of our own. Have some little Carls and Kendras running around. I'm ready to be a daddy. I've been ready for a long time. What do you think?" he asked eagerly.

What did I think? I stared at him in shock and felt the love and affection swelling in my heart evaporate like water drops on a hot griddle.

178

Chapter Twelve

I WAS IN A WEIRD mood when Monday arrived. And was it any wonder? Carl had proposed to me. I still couldn't believe it. I also couldn't believe my reaction. I'd told him I'd think about it. Why the hell had I done that? I wasn't ready for marriage. I damned sure wasn't ready for babies. I can barely get my ass out of bed to get ready for work everyday. How was I going to get up every couple of hours to feed a baby? Then there was the question of breast-feeding versus bottle-feeding. Would I be a stay-at-home mom or would I work? Would Carl expect me to move to Columbus to be with him or would he move to Willow to be with me? Then there was the question of why I was even having these thoughts because I knew I wasn't ready for marriage and babies. I couldn't even commit to a pet or a potted plant. How the hell could I get married? Plus, I suspected that Carl, though I knew he loved me, really wanted to be a father more than he wanted to be a husband.

I was at work grading papers when Iris Reynolds, the program secretary, came to the classroom. Iris was dressed in a sleeveless beige dress with a navy blue satin ribbon laced into the bodice. It was a pretty dress, but on Iris it looked like a sack and did nothing to brighten her sallow complexion. I was happy that she'd recently gone back to her natural brown hair color from the unflattering blonde she'd been sporting for a year. She gave me a smile, and I felt bad for the unkind thoughts about her dress. Iris is one of the nicest people I know, even if she has absolutely no tact and isn't afraid to talk about anything. No subject is taboo to Iris.

"You have a phone call from a Dr. Brock. Do you want to talk to him or should I take a message?"

"I'll take it. Thanks." I followed her back to the office, happy that I'd left my work number as well as my cell phone number.

"Dr. Brock, this is Kendra Clayton. Thanks for calling me back," I said into the receiver. I tried to turn away so Iris couldn't hear my conversation.

"Since your message said this was about my Righteous Lies documentary, can I assume that this has to do with Calvin Lee Vermillion's recent release from prison?" Ben Brock's slightly nasal voice sounded amused.

I told him it was. Not really wanting to get into my specific reasons on the phone, I asked Dr. Brock if I could stop by his office later that afternoon before my dreaded class.

"I shall await your arrival with bated breath," replied the sociology professor, who hung up on me before I could thank him for his time.

I turned to hang up the phone and caught Iris enthusiastically sniffing her armpits. She caught me watching her and held up both her arms.

"I think my deodorant stopped working. What do you think? Can you smell me?" she asked, getting up and coming over to me, arms still raised over her head.

I almost broke my neck getting back to my classroom.

Ben Brock's office was located in Oliver Hall on the second floor. It was a dark, cramped corner office with a filmy cracked window and a blurry view of the side of Floyd Library. A large rolltop desk took up most of the office. Ben Brock took up most of what was left. He was a tall white man and large, but not so much fat as hefty, with a shock of brown, curly hair that hung over his collar, with a red bulbous nose that looked like it was always stuffed up. I guessed his age to be late forties. He was wearing faded jeans and an untucked denim chambray shirt. The worn leather sandals on his large feet, which were propped up on a corner of the desk, looked like relics from the sixties. I noticed a woven hemp bracelet on his right wrist. I could hear what sounded like rap music coming from a small boom box by his chair.

"Miss Clayton?" he asked looking up.

"Please, call me Kendra."

Dr. Brock reached down and switched off the boom box. "Love that Wu Tang Clan, don't you?" He gave me a sheepish smile. I laughed and he gestured towards a chair by the door. I sat.

The office smelled a little funny and I soon realized it was a combination of Vicks Vapo Rub and the spicy mustard slathered all over the large deli sandwich sitting on his desk in front of a wedding picture of him and his beautiful wife, a cinnamon-colored sister with long bead-laden braids and a nose ring.

"I'm sorry if I've interrupted your dinner, professor."

"More like a late lunch, and, no, you're not interrupting me at all. And, it's Ben." He swung his long legs down from the desk and sat up to give me his full attention. "Now, what can I do for you, Kendra. I'm all ears."

I explained I wanted to know about the other three Righteous Whites. He blew his nose loudly before answering me.

"Sorry. Summer cold's got me all stopped up. Anyway, the Righteous Whites," he laughed. "A sorrier bunch I have never seen. The real power behind the group was, of course, Calvin Vermillion. Those other three idiots were just stupid and unlucky. Lazy, unemployed losers who had nothing better to do than drink and follow Vermillion around. I never got the impression that they seriously subscribed to his views."

"What happened to them?" I asked.

"Shane Powers died of a massive heart attack back in eighty-five not two weeks after I interviewed him. Donnie and Ricky Boone each got ten years less than Vermillion and Powers. Their lawyers claimed they were both borderline retarded, which I'm inclined to agree with. They got paroled within a few months of each other about five years after I interviewed them. Last I heard, Donnie's a preacher out in California. Got married and has a houseful of kids. Ricky, on the other hand, got blinded in a prison fight and lives with their younger sister and her husband, a cop."

"Neither one of them has been in any trouble since they got released?"

"What kind of trouble?" he asked, clearly curious as to what I was getting at.

"Does the name Alice Ivy Rivers mean anything to you?" I asked.

"Of course. She was Calvin Lee's girlfriend and the other person involved in the murder of Maurice Groves." He took a big bite of his sandwich.

"No. She was a witness." I corrected him. But Dr. Brock shook his head vigorously. I had to wait until he finished chewing his mouthful of sandwich for him to elaborate.

"Not according to Calvin Lee. He's maintained all along that Alice Rivers was an active participant in what they did to Maurice Groves. He claims they knocked Groves down and Alice Rivers was the one who started kicking him first."

I almost fell out of my chair. Ms. Flack a murderer? Was it possible?

"And you believed him? He's a racist and convicted murderer," I needlessly pointed out.

"The only people who know for sure are the people who were there that night. But, Shane Powers, and the Boone brothers, also backed up what Calvin Lee told me. The three of them had a falling out with Vermillion and he was no longer speaking to them months before they were all arrested. They had no reason to back up his story unless it was true."

"But why in the world wasn't she charged with murder?" I still wasn't sure I believed anything a man like Vermillion said. I'd known Ms. Flack for more than a decade, and until recently, she'd never seemed anything but caring and helpful.

"Miss Clayton, you already answered that question. Who was a jury going to believe, an innocent looking fifteen-year-old girl or a racist who had a rap sheet as long as my arm? Besides, there was a lot of pressure on the district attorney's office by community leaders to get a conviction and put an end to the boiling racial tensions in the town. They needed Alice Rivers to testify against the other four. My guess would be that the DA figured sending four out of five people to prison was better than not getting any convictions. I bet they offered her immunity for her testimony."

I filled him in on Ms. Flack aka Alice Ivy Rivers's probable murder and her fear of Calvin Vermillion finding out where she was. Now it was his turn to be shocked.

"Wow. I saw that on the news. I didn't know it was her. Is that why you asked me about Powers and the Boone brothers? You thought one of them could have killed her?"

"Seemed logical to me that one of them could have finally tracked her down and made her pay for sending them to prison while she was scott free. If they didn't do it, then Calvin Lee could have paid someone to kill her and make it look like an accident," I said.

"Not if he thought she was already dead," he replied.

"What?" I leaned so far forward in my chair I

almost fell out. Dr. Brock laughed when he saw the shocked look on my face.

"Two years ago, Calvin Lee's sister, Mildred Perry, contacted me and asked if I'd be willing to do another follow-up documentary on her brother's conversion to Christianity. Seems after my original documentary aired, Mrs. Perry was consumed with saving her brother's soul. Calvin Lee was obsessed with getting revenge on Alice Rivers. It's what he was living for, and his sister knew it would ruin his chance for parole. Mildred claimed she did the only thing she could do to get him to let go of his hatred. She lied and told him Alice Rivers was killed in a car accident. Since Calvin Lee's illiterate, it was unlikely he would find out otherwise. He believed what his sister told him. As for the Boone brothers, I seriously doubt either one of them killed her. If you'd met them, you'd know what I mean. Emotionally, they were a lot like children. They didn't hold grudges."

But if none of the Righteous Whites killed Ms. Flack, then who did? It was getting late. I thanked Ben Brock for his time and headed off to class.

"What was it like?" Cherisse Craig asked me later that evening at dinner. She'd been waiting for me at my car when I'd gotten out of class.

I was so conflicted about Ms. Flack's supposed

involvement in the Groves murder that I wasn't really in the mood for company and tried to politely put her off. But she said she needed to talk to me. When she offered to buy me dinner, and since I'm not about to turn down a free meal, we ended up at Estelle's.

"I've never seen a dead body before. How bad was it? Did she look like she suffered?" I was a little freaked out by her morbid interest in the state of Ms. Flack's body. Maybe if we hadn't known the woman I'd have been more eager to share.

"She just looked like she was sleeping." I took a long sip of my chocolate milkshake to hide my annoyance. I could tell she didn't believe me. But at least she dropped the subject. I was still no closer to finding out why she wanted me to have dinner with her.

"What did you want to talk to me about?" I finally asked. She stopped eating her taco salad and wiped her mouth before speaking.

"Ms. Flack was the one who got me the job with Julian," she said bluntly, watching for my reaction.

"Really," I said slowly. I suddenly remembered her telling me that the woman Julian was seeing had helped her get her job with him. Ms. Flack and Julian Spicer had been a couple? Cherisse nodded knowingly when she knew I'd figured it out.

"They were seeing each other? For how long?"

"About a year," she said. "They tried to hide it. But I knew. Hell, I couldn't help but know. She would come by and they'd have these long two hour lunches in his office. But, girl, the noises coming out of that office weren't anything G-rated. He had her ass speaking in tongues."

Eew! I hadn't wanted to think about Ms. Flack's dead body, but I really didn't want to think about her spread and ready on Julian Spicer's desk, either.

"They were both grown folks. It shouldn't have mattered that they were an item. It wasn't anybody's business," I said. Cherisse rolled her eyes.

"All I know is it's not fair that everybody thinks that Julian missing out on that contract was the only reason he was upset and fell off his roof. He broke up with Ms. Flack the day before he died. I'm not the only one he was mad at; of course, no one knew about them so I got all the blame. And you know what?" she asked lowering her voice and leaning forward.

"What?" I asked, leaning in, too.

"I wouldn't be surprised if she pushed him off that roof."

"Why would she have killed Julian? Because he dumped her?" I asked wearily. I wasn't so sure I wanted to hear more negative things about a woman I'd so recently admired.

188

"Julian was planning on being a big contributor to her campaign for mayor. But I think he must have found something out about her because he not only broke up with her, he cut ties to her campaign. The day before he died I heard them arguing in his office. Ms. Flack was crying and begging him to believe her about something. Julian threw her out of his office and told me that he wouldn't be taking any more of her calls."

Could Julian have found out about her past? I told Cherisse about Ms. Flack's connection to the Righteous Whites but left out what Ben Brock had told me. I still couldn't believe it. I could barely finish what I was saying before Cherisse cut me off.

"See. I told you so," she whispered excitedly, waving her napkin in the air. "I knew it. He must have found out. Kendra, she was planning to run for mayor. If people knew she'd been involved with a white supremacist who killed someone, she could not only kiss her chances of becoming mayor goodbye, she might have been fired from her job as well. I bet she pushed Julian off the roof to keep him from telling everyone." Cherisse sat back in the booth looking excited.

I couldn't argue with her logic and didn't try. It just opened another big can of worms. If Julian had found out about her past, who told him? And did whoever told him kill Ms. Flack? Cherisse excused herself to go to the bathroom, and I finished up my burger and fries, eager to get home so I could be alone to think.

"Well, if it isn't Nancy Drew. I thought that was you over here," said a sarcastic voice near my ear. I turned and looked into the doughy face of Dennis Kirby and rolled my eyes. I knew he could tell I didn't want him to sit down but he did anyway.

"I'm about to leave."

"Well, Cherry's plate is still plenty full." He gestured towards Cherisse's half-eaten salad. "What's wrong? Is the food here bad? Is she in the bathroom puking?" He laughed loudly when he saw the pissed look on my face.

"Please go away. Your sense of humor wasn't funny back in high school and now it's just pathetic." He looked like I'd slapped him and for some strange reason I instantly felt bad.

"Man, I was just kidding. Just trying to lighten the mood. I...oh forget it," he mumbled and got up to go.

"I'm sorry." I said stopping him. He grinned and sat back down. I noticed that his wrist was still bandaged from the accident in his garage.

"Hey, I'm sorry, too. I saw you and Cherry, ah,

Cherisse through the window when I was walking by and I figured you guys were probably talking about Ms. Flack. Heard you were the one to find her. That must have been awful, huh?"

Not wanting to get into any details, I simply nodded.

"I was the one who had to identify Julian after his accident. My folks were too broken up to do it," he said in a gruff voice. "It's not anything you ever forget." I could see the start of tears glistening in his eyes and looked away. This wasn't a side of Dennis I was used to seeing.

"How are your parents doing?" I pushed my empty plate aside to give him my full attention.

"They're okay. Mom's arthritis is getting worse and Dad's heart is bad. I got a line on a job as an assistant athletic trainer with the Kingford College baseball team. If I get it, I'll be busy working and traveling with the team and won't be able to keep an eye on them. I'm trying to talk my folks into moving into a smaller house all on one floor. But so far they aren't going for it." I knew firsthand from my dealings with Mama just how stubborn older people could be and couldn't offer any advice.

"Dennis, could you do me a favor?"

191

"What?" He gave me a surprised and suspicious look.

"Don't get me wrong. I think what happened to Julian was horrible. But I don't think it's fair that you, Audrey, and Gerald are blaming Cherisse. You shouldn't be making her a scapegoat for what happened to your cousin. It's bad enough you guys made her life miserable in high school. Can't you just cut her a break?"

He gave me a blank look then started laughing hysterically.

"What's so damned funny?" I snapped.

"Oh, sorry, I was just thinking about how different Cherry is from her sister. What was her name, Selena?

"Serena." I gave up all hope of ever having a serious conversation with Dennis Kirby.

"What ever happened to her? Do you know if she's married?" he asked with such avid interest that I didn't have the heart to tell him that she was still missing, and married or not, he wasn't her type. I just shrugged and looked at my watch.

"Even with her fancy new clothes, Cherry's no match for her sister. Now, Serena Craig was my kinda woman hot, wild, and tattooed. Serena's a hothouse flower while Cherisse is a dandelion." Dennis laughed and pounded on the table so hard that his fist landed on Cherisse's fork, launching the salsa-drenched lettuce resting on it into his face.

I burst out laughing but a loud gasp behind me made me turn. It was Cherisse and she was in tears. She was staring at us with such a hurt look on her face that I realized she must have overheard what Dennis said and thought I was laughing with him and not at him.

"Cherisse, I wasn't—" I began, trying to explain. She grabbed her purse from under the table and ran out the door before I could stop her.

"Man, what's her problem?" Dennis wiped his face.

I just glared at him.

Chapter Thirteen

"LORD, YES, I REMEMBER that terrible murder," exclaimed Mama the next day. I'd stopped by her house on my way to work the next morning, and she'd insisted on fixing me breakfast. While she whipped up the waffle batter, I asked her about the Groves murder.

"Did you know Maurice Groves?" I had to be at work in a half hour and was trying to wolf down the piping hot waffle quickly. However, the waffle had other plans. The warm maple syrup, and melted butter dripping from it, were forcing me to slow down and savor my meal.

"No. I didn't know him. I knew some folks from church who did, though. Heard he was a hardworking man who took good care of his family. Are you sure Ivy Flack was mixed up in his murder? I remember meeting her back when you were in school and she seemed so nice."

Mama took a sip of her coffee and glanced at the glaring headline of that morning's paper, which declared: "Dead Principle Linked to 1967 Race Murder" Ms. Flack's secret was out. The picture that

194

accompanied the story showed a teenaged Ms. Flack, identified by her former name, Alice Ivy Rivers, being escorted from the courthouse after having testified against the four members of the Righteous Whites.

I looked closely at the picture, trying hard to see if I could detect any traces of violence in the teen that had become Ivy Flack. Despite what Ben Brock had told me, I still had a hard time believing she'd had a hand in Maurice Groves's grisly fate. But all I could see was a skinny teenaged girl with thick bangs, wearing cat-eyed glasses and a winter coat that looked too big. She was accompanied by her parents who were identified as Sharon and Fred Rivers, both of whom looked shell-shocked and wore expressions that practically screamed, *Why did this happen to us*?

"You're upset, aren't you, baby?" Mama asked, lightly squeezing my arm.

"I thought I knew her," I said in disgust after taking a sip of milk.

"Don't judge her too harshly. Are you still the same person you were when you were fifteen?"

"I hope not," I replied.

"Me, too," she said. "Cause I seem to recall a certain fifteen year old who was so lazy when it came to doing her schoolwork because she was too busy reading romance novels that she almost flunked the tenth grade. Remember her?"

"Yeah, but look how she turned out," I smiled smugly, causing Mama to chuckle.

"And I also remember that same fifteen year old who snuck out of the house when she was grounded because of those pitiful grades to go to a party because some little bumpy-faced boy she liked was going to be there, and he didn't even pay her any attention and spent the whole evening dancing with some other girl. Remember her?"

"It's not just about her past." I said, instead of pointing out that Conrad Franklin's face hadn't been that bumpy and he only danced with Rita Baker because she was a ho. "She did some other stuff, too." I told her about the stalking of the reunion committee and the plan to fake her death.

She let out a deep breath. "I swear I don't know why I bother watching the soaps. Those people in Hollywood could never make up mess as good as this."

I agreed with her, shoved the last forkful of waffle into my mouth, and rushed out the door to get to work.

After work I had a free afternoon and, on a whim, headed over to Urbana. I located an address for an M. Perry in the Urbana phone book at work and, assuming it was Calvin Lee's sister, planned to pay her a visit. Urbana was a small town on the other side of

196

ANGELA HENRY

Springfield, Ohio, a mere fifteen minute drive from
Willow. M. Perry lived on Logan, a street that dead-
ended next to a set of railroad tracks. I drove slowly
until I found the address and then pulled up in front of
a two-story white house with black shutters and a
slightly sagging porch. There was a large tree in the
middle of the mostly dirt and weed-filled front yard
with an overweight beagle lying on its side
underneath. I though for a minute the dog might be
dead until it got up and lumbered across the yard to
finish its nap on the porch. There was a brand new
green Ford pickup truck in the driveway. But I had the
feeling that no one was home, or maybe it was just
wishful thinking.

I sat in my car and contemplated the wisdom of
coming to see Mildred Perry. I wasn't buying for a
minute that Calvin Lee Vermillion had truly changed
his beliefs. The timing seemed a little too convenient
to me. Did Mildred Perry share her brother's views on
race? Would she even open her door if she saw a black
woman standing on her porch? From what I'd seen on
television, and heard from Ben Brock, Mildred Perry
was a religious woman. Just how far did her
devoutness go? It's been my experience that too many
people tended to pick and choose the parts of the Bible
that appealed to them the most, and often it was the
parts that allowed them to feel superior to other folks,

197

morally or otherwise.

I was so caught up in my thoughts that the tap on my driver's side window almost sent me the through the roof of my car. I looked over and saw that a tiny elderly man, of indeterminate race, whose tanned wrinkled face reminded me of a golden raisin, was smiling at me. The street had been totally deserted a minute ago and I figured he must have come out of one of the neighboring houses. I rolled down my window and he leaned into the car.

"Hi there. You here for the Bible study meetin'," he asked providing me with an excellent excuse.

"Yes, I am. Do you know if Mrs. Perry's at home?" I leaned back a little and hoped he would notice he was trespassing in my personal space. No such luck. He leaned in even further.

"No, ma'am. Millie's brother took sick early this morning. She rode over to the hospital in the ambulance with him. He's got that cancer real bad. She's still not back so I been tryin' to catch everybody to let 'em know Bible study's been cancelled. Ain't seen you here before. You new?"

"Yes. This was going to be my first meeting." I tried to look and sound disappointed.

"Well, if you're a friend a Millie's, you might wanna go on over to the hospital and see if she needs anything. She ain't got nobody but that brother a hers since her husband died. Never did have no kids. I'd go myself but I'm so old, and got so much wrong with me, I'm afraid if I walked in there they'd keep me," he said with a chuckle. I thanked him and headed over to the hospital.

Urbana had one hospital, Mercy Memorial. I pulled into the half-full parking lot and hoped the media hadn't gotten wind of Calvin Lee being rushed to the hospital. I looked around before going inside and was relieved to see there were no news vans anywhere to be seen. Calvin Lee was apparently yesterday's news. It didn't take me long to locate Mildred Perry. I found her talking, or sobbing to be more precise, on a pay phone near the emergency room waiting area. I watched as she finished her conversation and went back to sit down on a nearby couch. I hated to intrude on her misery, but she did look like she could use a friend. I pulled a tissue from my purse and offered it to her.

"Are you okay, Mrs. Perry? Is there anything I can get you?" I asked gently. She gave me a startled look and cautiously took the tissue and blew her nose before replying. The tears in her blue eyes made them look even brighter. She looked like a woman who'd almost been pretty but never quite made it. She was wearing the same large cross pendant that I'd seen her wearing on the news, as well as a pair of brown polyester shorts that came to her knees and a blue sleeveless blouse with wet stains down the front, probably from her tears. Her gray-streaked, brown hair was longer than most women her age wore it, but it looked thick and healthy and hung down her back.

"My brother just died. I'm waiting for my pastor to come help me with the details." She looked away then realized I knew her name and added, "Do I know you?" She looked at my face and then my clothes. I could tell she was trying to figure out if I worked for the hospital. I could have lied but I just didn't have the energy to deceive her.

"No, ma'am. We've never met. But I think we have a mutual friend, Alice Ivy Rivers?" At the mention of Alice River's name, Mildred Perry's thin frame tensed up, and her hands curled into fists.

"Alice Ivy Rivers is no friend of mine. And if you were smart, she wouldn't be your friend, either." She got up and walked over to look out the window. I followed.

"That's the problem, Mrs. Perry. I thought she was a friend of mine but I realize now that I never really knew her. Ben Brock told me that you told your brother she was dead. Is that true?"

"Yes," she said blowing her nose again. "At one time my brother's sole purpose in life was to get even with that girl. It was eating him alive. He needed a new outlook, a new focus to redirect all that passion. I felt it would do him a world of good to get involved in the church and redirect his life towards Jesus. Rid himself of all the hate that ruined his life and took the life of another man. Alice came to me and begged me to tell him she was dead because he found out where she was and had other inmates calling her and sending her threatening letters. It would have ruined his chance at parole if they found out he was behind it. So I lied to him and told him Alice was killed in a car crash. I didn't do it for her, mind you. I did it so my brother could move on. When he found out she was dead, he eventually joined the prison ministry," she said proudly.

"Alice knew Calvin Lee thought she was dead?" I asked. Mildred Perry nodded.

I sank down in a nearby chair. Ms. Flack had lied to me. How could I have been so stupid? Hadn't Ben Brock told me she'd been involved in Maurice Groves's murder? Why had I been so reluctant to believe it?

"Don't feel bad, honey." She sat down next to me and patted my hand. "She has everybody fooled."

"Mrs. Perry, do you believe what your brother said about Alice Rivers having participated in Maurice Groves's murder?"

"I have to admit that I didn't at first. Calvin was a

201

liar. But what always gave him away was that he could never keep his lies straight. I thought he was just trying to blame others for what he'd done to that man. But in the thirty years he was in prison, his story about what happened that night Groves was killed never changed. Calvin told me Maurice Groves worked as a janitor at the same factory as Alice Rivers's daddy. She was afraid he was going to tell her father he'd seen her out with Calvin after her parents had told her to keep away from him. She didn't want to get in trouble. She attacked him first, and since my brother didn't like blacks anyway, he and the others followed her lead."

I felt sick to my stomach and couldn't speak.

"I was with Calvin when he died and I asked him if there was anything he wanted to get off his conscious before he died. He told me no. I think if he'd have lied about Alice Rivers, he'd have said so."

I thanked Mildred Perry and got up to leave, but she had something else to say.

"You tell Alice Rivers, or whatever she's calling herself these days, that I meant what I told her," she said vehemently.

I turned to look at her. Having been busy taking care of her sick brother, she obviously had no idea the former Miss Rivers was dead. I filled her in and the news took the remaining wind from her sails. More tears streamed down her face but they were angry tears this time.

"What did you tell her?" I asked, sitting back down next to her. She wiped at her eyes and I gave her another tissue.

"I guess it doesn't matter now," she said, looking down at the floor.

"I'd really like to know." I tried hard not to sound like I was pleading but I could tell she picked up on my anxiousness. Dangling a juicy piece of information in front of a nosy person's face was like teasing a tiger with lamb kabob. I waited. She sighed heavily.

"I read an article about her in the paper last year. It made me so sick to think that she was the principal of a high school, while my brother spent his whole adult life in prison. I went to see her. I told her that confession was good for the soul and that she needed to tell the truth about what happened to Maurice Groves. She told me to go to hell." She stopped to catch her breath before continuing.

"I figured if she wasn't going to tell the truth, then everyone in her life needed to know what kind of person she really was. I started following her. I saw her with a handsome young black fella. I could tell he must be her boyfriend, even though she was almost old enough to be his mother. I found out who he was and called him and told him all about her past," she said indignantly.

"How'd he take the news?"

"I couldn't tell if he believed me or not. He was very polite and thanked me for calling but asked me to please not call him again." Poor Julian. He must not have known what the hell to think.

"Did you tell anyone else?"

"No," she said, shoulders slumping. "I found out he died in an accident a few days later and I got scared thinking maybe he confronted her and she killed him. I felt so horrible I decided to just let it go. My pastor had been telling me all along that vengeance belongs to the Lord. I didn't listen and that poor man's death could be my fault."

I put a comforting arm around her and she gave me a teary smile.

"I've still got problems with letting my anger get the best of me because when I found out my brother's cancer was beyond medical help, and he wouldn't get to enjoy much of his freedom, I got so angry over the unfairness of it all that I called Alice again and told her that she had up until the day Calvin Lee was released to set the record straight or I was going to the newspapers and the TV stations. I know there's no proof of what she did, but the attention alone would have ruined her."

"What did she say to that?"

"First, she offered me money to keep quiet. When

I didn't bite, she said she needed time to get her affairs in order and find a good lawyer." We both knew she had no intentions of confessing to anything.

"And you weren't scared she might come after you? If she did kill her boyfriend, then getting rid of you, too, wouldn't have been any big deal."

"I slept with my husband's pistol underneath my pillow. I don't know if I would have been able to use it if it came to that, but it sure helped me sleep a whole lot better."

There wasn't much more to say. I sat with her until her pastor, a ruddy-faced man with a bushy grey beard, arrived then said my good-byes.

On the way home I stopped at Young's Dairy and got a large strawberry sundae, made with strawberry ice cream and loaded with whipped cream. I sat outside at one of the wooden picnic benches to eat it. I needed something to do to calm my jumpy nerves and help sort out my thoughts. Some people knit when they need to calm down, others clean, some take a drive, or get a drink. I eat. It has yet to fail me. This time was no different.

Ivy Flack, formerly Alice Rivers, had been a fraud. As a teen she'd run around with a smarmy, racist, older man that her parents had forbade her to see. She'd lashed out at poor Maurice Groves, the innocent man she thought might blow the whistle on her, with deadly results. Thirty years hadn't changed her much. She was still conniving and dangerous. She hadn't been trying to fake her own death because she feared Calvin Lee Vermillion. She'd been trying to get out of town because his sister was about to tell the world about her, and she was going to lose everything, possibly even her freedom because immunity can always be revoked and she could still be tried for Maurice Groves's murder.

I thought about everything that had happened during the time the committee had started meeting: the accidents, the messages, and everyone's reluctance in getting the police involved. Why? Then the image of Ms. Flack's bank statement lying on her dresser popped into my head. She had twenty thousand dollars in her account with several large deposits made recently. Then I remembered running into her on campus the day she'd had flyers for her campaign made and how she talked about how broke she was because of home repairs and having to buy a new car. Where had the twenty thousand dollars come from? She'd told me she'd received the letter about Vermillion's release last month, meaning she'd known for at least a month prior to her death that Mildred Perry was going to go to the press about her past. How had she been planning to finance her new life in

Mexico?

And then it hit me. Why hadn't I seen it before? The messages she sent to the reunion committee had said: "You will pay for what you did". I'd been thinking the messages had meant *pay* with our lives. But they'd meant *pay* as in money. Ms. Flack hadn't been stalking the reunion committee at all. She'd been blackmailing us to get money to go into hiding before Calvin Lee was released and Mildred Perry blew the whistle on her. I didn't really know in what order the messages and accidents occurred. She must have sent the messages first then caused the accidents to prove she was serious. That's why none of the other committee members had wanted the police involved.

She must have contacted them again and they must have paid her, which meant that Audrey, Gerald, Dennis, and Cherisse all had something to hide that they were willing to pay to keep quiet. I'd received a message, too. Only I wasn't contacted again because I was the only one who'd called the police. I don't have anything to hide and no money to pay anyone off if I did. That told me she must have just been fishing. Hoping that, like her, we all had something we wouldn't want anyone to know about, and would be willing to pay to keep quiet. That must have been what she'd been referring to during our last conversation when she'd said, everyone had secrets but some people were better than others at hiding them. And she'd been right. They'd paid her, and in turn, she'd paid with her life because her killer thought she'd really known their secret.

She must have been able to keep her identity secret from the people she was blackmailing. However, I'd been able to figure out she was behind it all. Someone else on the committee must have, too. There was certainly a karmic justice in Ms. Flack's death. I wondered why I even cared who killed her. To be honest, I don't think I did. But she had remained free for a crime she should have gone to prison for. Whoever killed her should go to prison as well. Now, the next question was, which one of my fellow reunion committee members killed her? And how was I going to find out?

Chapter Fourteen

LATER THAT EVENING, A surprise rainstorm brought some relief from the relentless heat. Instead of being out someplace enjoying the cooler weather, I was sitting in the Coffee Break Café with, of all people, Detective Trish Harmon. I'd called her to talk about Ms. Flack and my suspicion that she had been a blackmailer, and was subsequently killed for it. She was on her way home and said she had a little time to talk and suggested we meet for coffee. The cool air must have been having a positive affect on her because she was not only listening to me but wasn't treating me like I was a bad rash. I also noticed she was dressed a little better than usual in a slim khaki skirt and a peach colored V-neck shirt that brightened her complexion and made her look almost ten years younger.   But cool air or not, she still wasn't convinced Ms. Flack had been murdered.

"That's one hell of a theory. You honestly believe that Ivy Flack was murdered because she was blackmailing the reunion committee? But she was bluffing about actually knowing their secrets? That's pretty ballsy."

"She was desperate, Detective Harmon, she needed money to get out of town and start a new life."

"But we still haven't found any evidence pointing to Ivy Flack having been murdered. There was no bruising on the body, no skin under her fingernails, no ligature marks, nothing to suggest a struggle of any kind. The dirt on the carpet underneath her bedroom window was also found on the bottoms of a pair of her sandals that were found near the bed. The only fingerprints we found on the open window in her bedroom were hers. We didn't find any other evidence of a forced entry."

"All that means is that she knew her attacker. She must have let the person in."

"Or it means she wasn't murdered," she countered.

"Well, I bet you found a large amount of money in her bank account, right?" Harmon didn't confirm or deny it; she just looked at me with her thin eyebrows arched in surprise.

"Don't you wonder where it came from? Isn't that proof that someone paid her off?"

Harmon took a sip of her iced cappuccino, grimaced, and added a pack of sugar to it. "They never make this sweet enough for me." I waited for her to answer my question, which she didn't do until she'd taste tested her drink for the correct amount of sweetness.

"There's a perfectly good reason for the large amount of money in her account."

"Which is?"

"She cashed out a teacher's retirement fund she had from a previous job in Illinois. A teaching job she got right after college a couple of years before she started working for Springmont High. We found the check stub in her purse and checked it out."

"Okay," I said, unwilling to concede defeat. "That accounts for one of the large deposits I saw on her bank statement. What about the others?"

Harmon's cappuccino stopped halfway to her mouth. Her face tightened slightly and I realized I'd ruined the brief rapport that we'd been enjoying.

"You did go snooping through her room after you found the body, didn't you?"

"And this surprises you how?" I asked. She took a sip of her drink and then looked at her watch.

"I'll tell you what, Miss Clayton," she stood up and slung her purse over her shoulder. "If you can come up with any evidence at all to prove that Ivy Flack was blackmailing anyone, I'll look into it. I promise. Normally, I wouldn't condone you conducting your own investigation. But I know you'll just do what you want anyway, and I honestly don't think you're going to find anything. All those other

211

deposits to her account that you're so suspicious of were cash and therefore untraceable." She turned to walk away, and I called out one last question before she got out the door.

"Did you ever find her cat?"

"No," she said chuckling. "Maybe the cat's the one you should be looking for. Maybe the cat did it."

Everyone's a damned comedian.

I called in sick to work the next day. I lay in bed trying to figure out what to do next. I kept picturing that shit-eating grin on Harmon's face last night and desperately wanted to wipe it off. I was also trying to figure out what I was going to tell Carl. He'd asked me not to keep him waiting too long for an answer to his marriage proposal. Luckily, he was going to be tied up in a trial the rest of the week and I wouldn't see him until the weekend. What was I going to tell him? I wondered what my life would be like married with children. I had a sneaking suspicion it would involve me needing a lot of chocolate. My best friend, Lynette, who'd gotten married back in May, was so busy these days with her job, two kids, a new house, and new husband that I hardly ever got to see her any more.

Marriage and motherhood made me think of Audrey Grant, married mother of five, who, according to Joy Owens, was also gay. I had to admit it did look like a lover's spat I'd witnessed between her and that woman at Estelle's last week. But just because Joy knew Audrey's kid's names doesn't mean she wasn't lying about seeing her kissing another woman. A lot of straight people go to gay bars. If it were true, however, keeping something like that secret from her husband, who might divorce her and try and take her kids away, would be something she might be willing to kill for. I guess I knew how I was going to be spending my morning. I was going to pay Audrey a little visit.

Audrey answered the door of her red, brick, two-story Colonial looking tired, harassed, and covered in what looked like dried puke. She had a runny-nosed, blonde boy, who looked about a year old, perched on one hip, while another crying tow-headed little girl of about four clung to her leg and wailed. I looked past Audrey into the house and saw the only child of hers that I'd met, Cassidy, sitting on the steps of a circular staircase coloring in her Barney pajamas. Another little boy, who looked older than the one on Audrey's hip, but younger than his still wailing sister, was running down the hallway wearing a juice-stained undershirt, and nothing else, because he'd taken off his diaper and put it on his head. I only saw four kids, but the fifth one made its presence known when the loud angry cry of an infant came from somewhere in the back of the house.

Audrey took one look at me and burst into tears. The little girl clinging to her was so startled she stopped crying and stared up at her mother.

"Mommy's sad. She and daddy had a fight," lisped Cassidy, who'd finally looked up from her coloring book and noticed me.

"Cassidy!" said Audrey so sharply the little girl jumped. "Take Colleen into the kitchen to watch cartoons." Cassidy sulkily did as she was told and led away her little sister who had started wailing again.

"I'm sorry, Kendra, but as you can see, I'm in the middle of a meltdown. Is there a reason you came by?"

Before I could reply, Cassidy's shrill little girl screech of, "Mommy! Chris flushed his diaper down the toilet again!" caused Audrey to shove the other little boy she was holding, whose named turned out to be Cory, into my arms and go tearing off down the hall.

I followed her back to a large kitchen with dirty dishes pilled high in the sink. The kitchen opened into an even larger, messier family room. Cassidy, Colleen, and Chris, who had pulled his juice-stained shirt over his face in an attempt to hide, were standing in the doorway of a small bathroom right off the kitchen. The floor was flooded and when we looked into the toilet, we could only see part of the diaper. The rest of it was wedged deep into the toilet. There was also a sock in the toilet, along with what I first thought was a brown crayon, but turned out to be poop. Eew! Audrey lost it.

"Christopher Grant! How many times have I told you to stay away from this toilet?" She bellowed.

Colleen ran and hid under the kitchen table, Cassidy started sucking her finger; the infant, Callie, whose name I deduced by process of elimination, started crying again. I looked over at the bassinet on the floor by the couch and saw her little arms flailing. Cory, the kid I was holding, had miraculously fallen asleep with his little head resting on my shoulder. As for the culprit, Chris, he pulled his undershirt down from his face and started babbling, "I sorry, Mommy. I sorry."

"I can't take this anymore," Audrey said, looking hopelessly lost. She walked into the kitchen, leaned against the counter, and sobbed. I laid Cory on the couch.

"Come on, Audrey. I don't have anyplace to be this morning. Let me help you out." It was as if I'd said the magic word: *help*. Audrey instantly straightened up and gave me a grateful look.

During the next couple of hours we managed to get the toilet unstopped, all five kids bathed and dressed, the family room straightened up, and the breakfast dishes washed. There was little conversation, as Audrey was clearly still upset, which is why I didn't bother pointing out the smiley faces drawn on the wall behind the couch in magic marker, for fear of another meltdown. Was this how she spent every day? How did she do it? What would have happened if I hadn't shown up to help her?

By ten o'clock, Cassidy had been picked up for day camp, Chris and Colleen were intently watching *The Lion King* on DVD, Cory was happily playing with a set of blocks in his playpen, and baby Callie, who was two months old, was asleep. I, on the other hand, besides wishing I'd taken my ass to work, was exhausted. I sat down on the couch next to Audrey.

"Thanks for helping me. You saved the day." She put her feet up on the coffee table.

"I don't know how you do it. I'm worn out and it's only ten o'clock."

She laughed. "Believe it or not, it's not always this bad. I usually have a better handle on things. It's been a bad morning. Glen, my husband, and I had a huge argument this morning and it was downhill from there."

I'd never met Audrey's husband. I looked over at the family picture on the side table by the couch and saw that Audrey's husband was a serious-looking, short, stocky man with thick brown hair and glasses.

216

He was the only one in the picture not smiling. I knew he was an electrical engineer. He wasn't the pretty-boy type Audrey had favored in high school, though if Joy was right, then apparently her taste had changed dramatically, which brought me back to why I had come over in the first place.

"Have you had time to follow the news?"

"You mean about Ms. Flack?" She got up from the couch. She opened the fridge and pulled out two cans of diet pop and handed me one. I hate diet pop but popped the tab and took a drink anyway.

"I still can't believe it. You know, I don't mean to be insensitive, but this is the second time the head of the reunion committee has died in a freak accident. I was supposed to be the head of the committee this time around but I'd just had Callie when they were talking about starting up the committee again. I'm so glad I said no."

"If people knew what I knew about Ms. Flack, they might think she got what she deserved," I said bluntly. No need to beat around the bush. Her eyes got big for a few seconds then she looked away.

"Why?" she asked lightly, glancing over at her children to make sure they weren't listening. They weren't.

I toyed with the idea of just telling her I'd figured out Ms. Flack was blackmailing her but decided she probably wouldn't confide in me unless she thought I'd been a victim, too.

"Someone contacted me about a week ago. This person told me they knew about something I did years ago, something I don't want anyone to know about. They wanted five thousand dollars to keep quiet about it." I looked over at Audrey. She looked like she'd stopped breathing and all the color had gone out of her face.

"What did you do?" she finally asked in a whisper.

"Well, since I didn't have five thousand dollars, I decided to do a little detective work to see if I could find out who this person was. It was Ms. Flack."

"What!" she said so loudly the kids turned to stare at her. "Are you sure?"

"One hundred percent," I replied.

Audrey angrily jumped up from the couch and started frantically pacing back and forth and talking to herself, "That bitch! I can't believe it!"

"Audrey, calm down; you're scaring the kids." Colleen and Christopher were staring at their mother with wide eyes. Baby Callie stirred in her sleep but didn't wake up. Cory was picking his nose and eating the boogers.

I got up and headed into the kitchen and gestured for her to follow me. She practically stepped on the backs of my shoes in her haste to get out of hearing range of her kids.

"So, I guess I wasn't the only one she was blackmailing?" I watched her closely. Audrey hesitated. I could see the uncertainty in her eyes and decided to put her out of her misery.

"Look. I don't want to know what she had on you. I don't care. I just want to know if there were other people besides me she was blackmailing."

She nodded solemnly.

"Did you pay her?" Her eyes filled with tears and she nodded again.

"How much did she get you for?"

"Forty-five hundred dollars. I had to take it out of the kids' college fund." She looked like she might die of shame.

"And you had no idea it was her?"

"The person who called me was disguising their voice. But I could still tell it was a woman. I just thought it was an old girl—," she stopped abruptly and looked flustered when she realized what she'd almost said. She was going to say an old girlfriend. Joy had told the truth for once in her life. I gave her a blank look and pretended not to notice.

"I thought it was a friend playing a joke on me," she concluded.

"Would you be willing to tell the police?"

"Are you insane? If my husband finds out about any of this, he'll kill me. I'm already trying to figure out how I'm going to replace that money before he notices the account is short. Promise me you won't tell anyone, please." She'd grabbed my arm and was squeezing so hard I knew I'd be bruised.

"Okay," I said, shaking off her hand. "Okay. I won't say anything. But if the police find out Ms. Flack was blackmailing people, then who do you think they're going to be looking to arrest for her murder? You didn't pay her with a check, did you?"

"Murder? They said it was an accident on the news."

"I'm the one who found her body. Believe me. It was no accident and I wouldn't want the police looking at you if it gets out she was a blackmailer. You didn't pay her with a check, did you? "

"No, I gave her cash."

"Good. There's nothing to link back to you unless—," I said, eyeing her suspiciously.

"Unless, what?" she asked looking frantic. I leaned in close. I was aware that I was getting carried away with this little game I was playing but I couldn't stop now.

"Unless you killed her. Audrey, you didn't kill Ms. Flack, did you?"

In retrospect, looking down at my torn shirt on the drive home, I was lucky she hadn't blacked my eye. The moment after the words had come out of my mouth she'd grabbed me by the front of my shirt, dragged me wordlessly to the front door, opened it, pushed me out, and slammed the door behind me. I was standing on the porch in shock when the door opened again and she threw my purse at me. I hurried to my car with my ripped shirt hanging open and exposing my bra, oblivious to the stares of a couple of the neighbors who were working in their yards. She was damned lucky it had been an old shirt.

After I went home and changed, and not wanting anyone from work to see me out when I was supposed to be home sick, I had an early lunch at Wendy's. I sat in my car and ate trying to figure out my next move because I was fairly certain Audrey hadn't killed Ms. Flack, not that she wasn't capable of it. Anybody who'd almost had a nervous breakdown over a diaper that had been flushed down the toilet might be upset enough to kill over being blackmailed. But she'd seemed genuinely shocked when I told her Ms. Flack

221

was the blackmailer. I was rummaging around in my purse for an extra napkin to wipe up some spilled Frosty when I came across the pink message slip from Clair Easton that I'd swiped from Gerald Tate's wastebasket. I'd forgotten all about it. The message was in regards to her account. On a whim I pulled out my cell phone and dialed the number on the slip. A woman's voice answered on the third ring.

"Hello." The voice sounded efficient and no nonsense, like a woman who didn't take any mess.

"Ms. Easton?" I said, trying to match her tone.

"Speaking."

"Ms. Easton this is…" I struggled to quickly come up with a name. My eyes latched on to my empty fast food bag. "This is Wendy Burger. I'm with the stock regulatory commission of Ohio and I'd like to ask you a few questions about Gerald Tate if—"

"That bastard! I'll tell you everything I know. When can you come over?" I certainly wasn't expecting an invitation. And because I usually I had to pry info out of people, I was at a loss for words.

"Hello? Ms. Burger, are you still there?"

"Yes. Sorry, Ms. Easton, I was consulting my calendar. I'm free this afternoon at 2. Are you available then?"

Clair Easton agreed to meet me later that afternoon and gave me her address. I recognized the street as one of the more expensive neighborhoods in the affluent Pine Knoll area of Willow. I'd have to change into something more professional looking than the shorts and tank top I was wearing before the meeting, which was still almost three hours away. I couldn't wait to hear what she had to tell me about Gerald. Until then, I wondered what other trouble I could get into. It didn't take me long to think of something.

Chapter Fifteen

THE KINGFORD COLLEGE STUDENT union was where I found Dennis Kirby, who had just settled down to a lunch of a chili cheese dog and greasy fries. I'd gone to the bookstore to see him but was told by one of his coworkers that he was at lunch. His coworker also warned me that he didn't get the trainer job he'd applied for and was in a foul mood. Dennis was oblivious to anything other than the plate in front of him and didn't notice me until I sat down at his table. He didn't look especially thrilled to have company and reminded me of a dog who thought his food was about to be taken away.

"Aw, my feelings are hurt, Dennis. You don't look very happy to see me." Dennis grunted and wiped chili sauce from his chin.

"That's because I'm trying to figure out what you want," he replied grumpily.

"I talked to Audrey this morning and—"

"You accused her of murdering Ms. Flack. Yeah, I know. She called Gerald and me after she threw you out of her house. That's pretty wack. Audrey's really upset."

224

I had to press my lips together to keep my mouth from falling open. Audrey had called Dennis and Gerald and told them about my visit? An unnerving sense of déjà vu caused my spine to stiffen with apprehension.

"Wow. I didn't realize you and Audrey were still so close. You two have been giving each other dirty looks at every reunion committee meeting."

"Audrey can be annoying as hell, but we're still friends. She told us all about your little visit, about how you helped her out with the kids and then turned around and accused her of murdering Ms. Flack."

"I didn't—" I started to protest but he wouldn't let me finish.

"Don't try and pull a fast one on me and don't even think about trying to talk to Audrey again. Stay the hell away from her," he growled, not bothering to look up from his plate.

"Can I assume that you and Gerald were being blackmailed, too?" I asked on the off chance he might want to spill. He didn't.

"Know what I think?" he asked, wiping his fingers and not waiting for my reply. "I think you made up this whole thing about Ms. Flack being a blackmailer. The woman was never anything but nice to us and here you are trashing her, and she's not even here to defend herself. I think you're the one who's been blackmailing us. 'Cause by the looks of you, I can tell you can't be making much money as a teacher. And we all know from your little outburst at the last committee meeting that you're still bitter about being a fucking loser in high school. This is probably all about revenge, isn't it? Now you're just pretending to be a victim too so you can cover your tracks. And I'm telling you now, it ain't gonna work. You're not getting another dime from us. It's over!"

"Are you serious?" I asked, laughing.

He didn't answer, just glared at me and took another big bite of his chili dog.

"You think I just made all this shit up so I could get even with your little clique?"

"Hey, you said it, not me."

"Dennis, I hate to break it to you, buddy, but high school was eleven years ago and you idiots are the last people I've been thinking about. You really need to move on, starting with that ridiculous mullet." I got up and started to walk away.

Dennis called out after me. "Stay away from us, Kendra. Remember what happened the last time!"

I hurried back to my car. I was furious, and a little scared. They'd closed ranks on me and I was either too stupid, or too naive, to see it coming. Of course they were going to stick together. It was in their best interest to do so. The old round table crew was back in action. I wasn't going to be getting any more info out of Gerald or Dennis, but I still had my meeting with Clair Easton to look forward to. I tried not to think about the hell they had put me through back in high school. But I couldn't help wonder what they'd do to me when they found out I was still looking into Ms. Flack's death.

I also wondered why Dennis hadn't gotten the job with Kingford's baseball team. He was certainly qualified. I knew someone who could find out for me. I got on my cell phone and called the records office, asking Myra Gaines if she knew anyone in the human resources department who might know why Dennis Kirby was passed over for the trainer position.

"You're gonna owe me big time, girlfriend," she replied.

"That depends on if you can get me the info."

"Are you kidding? Ain't much that goes on around this college that I either don't already know about or can't find out," she bragged.

"And?" I asked, calling her bluff.

"And, I heard that Kirby dude got passed over because he lied on his application about his last job. He didn't resign from that job. He was fired. Guess his dumb ass didn't think anyone would check his references, 'cause his daddy's a former trustee."

"Really?"

"Yep. And before you ask me why they let him go, I don't know. My source didn't know that much."

I thanked Myra and promised her a free lunch at Estelle's. I wanted to keep *my* source happy.

I called information and got the number for Bellbrook College in San Diego, the place Dennis Kirby had worked as an athletic trainer before moving home. I dialed the number and asked the receptionist to connect me to the college's director of athletics. The phone was answered quickly on the first ring.

"This is Mark Weber. How may I help you?" asked the man so fast I almost didn't catch what he was saying.

"Mr. Weber, I'm calling from Ohio College. One of your previous employees, Dennis Kirby, is applying for an athletic trainer position and listed you as a reference." I heard Mark Weber swear softly under his breath.

"What was that, Mr. Weber? I didn't quite catch what you said."

"Who did you say this was?" He sounded highly annoyed.

"Oh, I'm sorry. This is Audrey Grant calling from Ohio College in Cleveland about your former employee, Dennis Kirby. Can you tell me what kind of an employee he was?"

Mark Weber sighed again before replying. "Frankly, I can't imagine why the in world Dennis Kirby keeps using me as a reference when I was the one who fired him."

"Really? Can you tell me why you let him go?" There was a long pause. At first I thought he'd hung up until he finally spoke again.

"You didn't hear this from me, you got it?"

"Of course. We never had this conversation," I assured him.

"There were allegations made by some players that Mr. Kirby was supplying members of the baseball team certain performance enhancing drugs," he said in a flat voice.

"Steroids?"

"Among others," he replied stiffly.

"Was there an investigation?"

"The college handled the matter internally. We fired Mr. Kirby and expelled the players involved. Now, I don't mean to be rude, but I have to get to a meeting. Do yourself a favor and don't hire Dennis Kirby." He hung up on me.

Dennis was fired for supplying college athletes with drugs, and Audrey was a closet lesbian. That just left Gerald and Cherisse. I had a pretty good idea what Gerald was hiding. I just needed confirmation from

Clair Easton. But I still had an hour to kill before my appointment with her. It was time I talked to Cherisse.

Cherisse Craig still lived in the same house on Bird Lane that she'd grown up in with her parents and twin sister, Serena. It was a small house on a slab with a flat roof that made it look like a shed, with a carport instead of a garage. All the houses on her street were similar in design, the only differences being the color of each home. Many were white but with different trim on the windows and doors. But some of the homeowners had gone to extremes in trying to achieve some semblance of individuality. One person had opted for Pepto Bismo pink, another neon yellow, and yet another a deep dark blue that looked almost purple. Cherisse's house was brown with black shutters. I was happy to see her car parked in the driveway.

I was hoping that she wasn't still mad at me about the conversation she overheard between Dennis and me the other night and would buy my excuse that I was there to apologize. Actually, I really did need to explain that I hadn't been laughing at what Dennis had said about her being a dandelion compared to her hothouse flower of a sister. Having a gorgeous sister, myself, I knew all too well how hurtful it was to be compared unfavorably to her.

I walked up to Cherisse's house. I didn't need to

knock because as soon as I walked past the wind chime hanging from a hook on her porch, the tinkling sound immediately brought her to the door. She was dressed in a red and gold silk Kimono style robe. Her dreads were held back from her face with a scarf. She opened her screen door and looked past me, up and down the street before even addressing me. I quickly turned to see what she was looking at and saw nothing, except some kids playing in the yard across the street. When she finally looked at me, I could see her eyes looked a little swollen and puffy. Could she still be upset by what Dennis had said?

"Cherisse, are you okay?" I asked.

"I'm fine," she said quickly but looked far from it. She looked bleary-eyed. "What are you doing here?"

"I'm sorry to bother you. I didn't mean to wake you. I just needed to talk to you."

"No. No. I've been up for a while. Come on in." She stepped aside so I could enter.

I walked in and immediately noticed how cold it was in the house. Her air conditioner must have been turned up full blast. I could feel the chill bumps pop up on my bare arms and legs. Cherisse flopped down on the black leather couch where she must have been lying when she heard the wind chime. The house was dark, the only light coming from the front window, and it smelled faintly of garlic.

I'd only ever been to Cherisse's house once before and that had been to study for a history test back in high school. I remembered Cherisse and me sitting in the kitchen quizzing each other on the places, dates, and prominent figures of the French Revolution, while her parents sat watching TV in the living room. They seemed really happy to have me over. Her mother served us cookies, chips, and cream soda and would periodically poke her head through the kitchen door to see if we needed anything, her father made corny jokes that I could tell really embarrassed her. It never occurred to me at the time that they must have thought that Cherisse had finally found a friend.

Cherisse and I weren't friends. I had been mad at my best friend, Lynette, who was busy being in love with the guy who would eventually become her first husband. When she had bailed on our plans to study for the test together, so she could sneak off and see her boyfriend, I'd impulsively asked Cherisse if she wanted to study together. I had been trying to prove that I didn't need Lynette, and possibly piss her off in the process. In short, I had used Cherisse. I had had a nice enough time at her house, despite witnessing a hellacious fight between her parents and her sister, Serena, who had come home glassy-eyed and reeking of marijuana. But I had no intentions of ever going back. By the next day, Lynette and I were cool again,

232

and my study session with Cherisse was forgotten. Thinking about that long ago visit embarrassed me. In retrospect, maybe I wasn't a whole lot different from Audrey Grant and her crew.

I sat down at the other end of the couch, and Cherisse watched me through hooded eyes. The coffee table in front on the couch was littered with wadded up tissue. I noticed a prescription bottle of nasal spray and a box of Kleenex sitting on the table next to a glass of iced tea.

"Are you sure this is a good time? I can come back later if you don't feel well." She shook her head no.

"It's just my allergies acting up. My doctor put me on some new medicine and it's not working worth a damn. The only thing it does is knock me out. I just took some about twenty minutes ago, so whatever you need to talk to me about you need to make it quick." She pulled another tissue from the pocket of her robe and blew her nose again.

"Well, first off I wanted to let you know that I wasn't laughing at you the other night at dinner. Dennis— "

"Is going to get what he has coming to him," said Cherisse, interrupting me. She was looking grim and determined and I couldn't tell if she was kidding or not.

"Huh?"

"He's such an asshole." She shrugged sleepily. "People like him always get what they deserve eventually, and that's a fact. Trust me. He *will* be getting what he deserves."

"What about Ms. Flack? Do you think she got what she deserved?" She looked at me like she could barely keep her eyes open.

"Ms. Flack? Well, yeah. I guess so. Why?" she asked before lapsing into a sudden sneezing fit. I realized I needed to make this quick.

"I think someone killed Ms. Flack. I don't think her death was an accident."

"Huh? Why?"

"Cherisse were you being blackmailed?" That at least seemed to wake her up a little. She pulled herself up to a semi-sitting position.

"How did you—?" she began before I held up my hand cutting her off.

"Just answer the question, please. Were you being blackmailed?"

"Yeah," she said in a small voice. "Were you?"

I explained my theory about Ms. Flack's need for money and about Audrey Grant's confession that she was being blackmailed. Cherisse looked like she might cry.

"I trusted that bitch. Are you sure she's the one who was behind it all?" I just nodded.

"You paid, right?" I asked. She nodded.

"She knew all about why I left the job I got right after high school. That's why she helped me get that job with Julian. She knew about me having an affair with my boss. He's married. I ran into her at the post office one day last year right after I left my job after I finally realized he would never leave his wife. I was upset and she asked me what was wrong. I only told her because I needed someone to talk to. I don't have many friends." She looked down at her lap. I felt guilty again.

I knew Audrey used to be a legal assistant with the DA's office. If she'd had an affair with one of the DA's she worked for, it could ruin his career, not to mention his marriage. For Cherisse to have paid a blackmailer must mean she was still in love with her boss and didn't want to cause him any pain. It also blew my theory about Ms. Flack not knowing what everyone's secrets were. If she knew about Cherisse's married lover, then she must have also known about what the rest of the reunion committee's secrets were. But, why try and blackmail me? What did she think she had on me?

"And you never knew it was her?"

"I thought it was someone I used to work with at the DA's office. The person who called me said there was a videotape of my boss and me making love in his office and if I didn't pay, they'd give it to the media, and his wife. I had no idea it was her. I swear." She had another sneezing fit and reached for the box of Kleenex. It was empty and she started to push herself up from the couch.

"You just lie still. I'll get you some more tissues. Where are they?"

"Bathroom." She pointed down the hallway.

I headed down the hall and quickly located the tiny bathroom. There was an unopened box of tissues sitting on the back of the pink toilet on top of a crocheted doily. I grabbed it and accidentally knocked a wicker basket that was sitting on the counter by the sink onto the floor, spilling the contents everywhere.

"What was that?" I heard Cherisse call out from the living room.

"Nothing. Be right there," I replied and quickly started picking up the contents of the basket.

I got down on all fours and picked up a couple of tubes of lipstick, a bottle of foundation in a color called ginger snap, a cheap bangle bracelet with flaking gold vermielle, a black plastic hair clip, tweezers, a nail file, a bottle of magic magenta nail polish, and something that stopped me in my tracks: a sterling silver compact with the initials "I F" engraved on the lid. It was Ms. Flack's compact. The one I'd seen her using in the car the very last time I talked to her on the day she died. What the hell was Cherisse doing with it?

I took the compact and headed back into the living room, forgetting to bring the box of tissue with me.

"Where did you get this?" I asked as I stood over her. All I got was a loud snore as a response. She was fast asleep.

"Cherisse." I tried to shake her awake. "Cherisse, wake up. This is important." But she was down for the count, and not even tossing a handful of water in her face could wake her up.

It was getting late, I put the compact in my purse and planned to ask her about it when I saw her after class later that evening.

Chapter Sixteen

I WENT HOME AND quickly changed into a slim grey skirt and a cream-colored, short-sleeved cotton blouse for my meeting with Clair Easton. I rummaged around in my dresser until I found a pair of sheer black hose that didn't have a run in them. I hunted under my bed for some decent dress shoes, finally locating a pair of low-heeled black pumps. After surveying my appearance, and deciding I looked a little washed out, I added a touch of plum lipstick. As an afterthought, I put on a pair of glasses that I thought made me look business-like and left for my appointment.

Clair lived on Scotch Pine Drive in a large Tudor-style home that looked liked it had been plucked out of medieval England. The house was white and heavily decorated with half timbers of exposed brown beams. About a dozen tall narrow windows covered the front of the house giving, multiple views of the street. The front lawn was large and a lush green. As I headed up the brick paved driveway, I could see a Hispanic man, wearing the uniform of a landscaping company called Diaz Lawn

& Landscape, trimming the large bushes that flanked the front door. Everything in the yard was varying shades of green, and there were no flowers that I could see anywhere on the property. That told me that Clair Easton must not be a fan of anything as frivolous as flowers, or she was too cheap to have them planted. The man trimming the bushes nodded and smiled at me as I rang the doorbell. I could hear the fast click of approaching heels and seconds later the door swung open and I looked up at a tall, masculine-looking woman with short reddish hair and pale green eyes. She looked to be in her late fifties, though her plaid polyester skirt and high-necked ruffled blouse made her look like an old lady.

"Ms. Easton? I'm Wendy Burger." I held out my hand, willing it not to tremble.

"Do you have some identification, Ms. Burger? One can't be too careful these days," she said primly, looking me up and down.

Crap. I didn't have any ID that identified me as anyone other than Kendra Clayton. I nodded and smiled dumbly as I reached into my purse praying for either a distraction, or that Clair Easton was blind as a bat and wouldn't be able to see that my name didn't match my license. I was toying with the idea of running back to my car and taking off when I got the distraction. While Clair Easton stared at me

239

impatiently as I fumbled through my purse, we heard a loud cry that made us both jump. We turned to see the man who was trimming the bushes clutching his forearm as blood flowed from between his fingers. Ms. Easton shoved me aside as she rushed to his aid.

"The kitchen's down the hall. Run and get me the first aid kit. It's in the cabinet under the sink."

I ran inside the dark foyer, and my eyes had to adjust to the gloom before I saw the narrow hallway that led to the kitchen. Along the way, I couldn't help but notice how outdated the house was. There may have been no flowers in the yard, but the walls were covered in the ugliest green and blue flowered wallpaper that I'd ever seen. There was thick beige shag carpet on the floor of the hallway that opened into a large kitchen with cracked yellow linoleum on the floor. The appliances looked like props from a seventies sitcom as did a red vinyl dinette set that looked like the chairs were missing some stuffing. I looked under the rust-stained porcelain sink and located a banged-up white metal box, with paint flaking from the red cross painted on top, and ran it outside to Ms. Easton.

"It's not as bad as it looks, Miss Easton," claimed the man in heavily accented English. He'd taken off his shirt and had it wrapped around his arm, but blood had seeped through. Clair Easton wasn't listening,

240

however. She was too busy rummaging through an assortment of old dried-out Band-aids and bandages and a roll of formerly white and no longer sterile-looking gauze, trying to find something to cover the gash.

"Nonsense, Mr. Diaz. I'll have your arm all bandaged in no time. Now hold still," she commanded, pulling the bloody shirt from his arm and tossing it at me. I cursed softly as some drops of blood from the shirt spattered my blouse and smeared the waistband of my skirt. Today was just not a good day for my clothes.

Clair Easton was a big woman, not fat, just bigger than poor Mr. Diaz. She grabbed him firmly by the arm with one hand and pulled him close to bind his wound. Mr. Diaz and I looked at each other in horror. No telling what kind of bacteria would be introduced into his wound if she insisted on using gauze that looked like it had last been used to wrap mummies in ancient Egypt. I opened my mouth to protest when she stopped abruptly.

"Oh, good," she said, leaning down over his arm to get a better look. "It looks like it's stopped bleeding." She snapped her fingers at me, which I assumed meant she wanted the shirt back. I tossed it to Mr. Diaz instead. He caught it and took off running to his van.

"Oh, wait," I called out when I noticed he'd left his hedge clippers behind. I grabbed the clippers and waved them. But Mr. Diaz had already pulled off.

"I hope he's going to the hospital. Blood loss is a dangerous thing," she said, heading back in the house. I was hot on her heels.

"How did he cut himself?" I followed her inside the house and propped the clippers by the door.

"Said he laid his hedge trimmers on top of the bush he was working on to wipe sweat from his eyes and they slid off and gashed his arm. Everyone is so careless these days." She made a disgusted clucking sound with her tongue as she closed the door behind us. Much to my relief, she seemed to have forgotten that I never showed her my ID.

I followed her into a large dimly lit living room, sparsely furnished with cheap, lumpy brown furniture. Thankfully the walls were minus the wallpaper from the hallway, but the same beige shag covered the floor. I'd bet money there were beautiful hardwood floors underneath all that horrible shag carpet. The room's only saving grace was a large arched brick fireplace that dominated almost half of one wall. It reminded me of the fireplaces I'd seen in pictures of hunting lodges. And just like in a hunting lodge, there was a large moose head hanging over the mantle staring at us with dull and dusty glass eyes. There was also a golden retriever, curled up with its head near its tail, on the floor next to the fireplace. I reached down to pet the dog but snatched my hand away when my fingers encountered stiff, hard fur. The dog was stuffed. My hostess laughed heartily.

"That's Jeeves. He was such a good dog. Weren't you, boy," she said in exaggerated baby talk as she gazed lovingly at the preserved pooch. "He died last weekend. I loved him so much I just couldn't bear to part with him. I just got him back from the taxidermist this morning. It was a super rush job and worth every penny. He did a wonderful job, wouldn't you agree?"

All I could do was nod and smile and wonder how badly the taxidermist had ripped this poor woman off since the dog's fur felt like the bristles on a hair brush.

"When I die I hope we'll be laid to rest together," she said matter-of-factly. She reached down and plucked a piece of lint from Jeeves's forever-glossy coat.

"That's...so...nice," I said and decided then and there to make this a quick visit. Poor Jeeves. I'm sure he didn't plan on spending his afterlife collecting dust and sniffing his own butt for all eternity.

"Please have a seat." Claire Easton gestured towards the lumpy couch. I sat and she took a seat across from me in a lopsided recliner. "Can I get you anything to drink? A soda perhaps?" I could tell by her eager-to-please demeanor that she must not get much company.

"No, thank you. I'm fine," I said quickly. Thinking back on the state of that first aid kit, I didn't want to speculate on how long past the sell-by date any beverages she had would be.

"I guess we can start then," she said, settling into her chair.

"Do you mind if I tape this conversation," I asked, pulling a small tape recorder I sometimes used in class from my purse. She eyed it for a moment and blinked rapidly a few times before slowly nodding her head in agreement. I switched on the recorder and sat it on the coffee table between us.

"Okay. Please state your name for the record," I told her, mimicking what I'd seen during interrogation scenes on *Law & Order*. I had no idea if there even was a Stock Regulatory Commission of Ohio, but I was fairly certain that if there was one, they didn't interrogate people. But ignorance is bliss, right?

She sat up straight in her chair, like the tape recorder could see her, and said, "Clair Lenore Easton."

"All right, Ms. Easton. Can you please tell me how long Gerald Tate has been your financial consultant?"

"Two years. He first became my consultant when

he worked for Wiley and Richards. When he left to join Wheatley Financial, I followed him," she replied without hesitation. She apparently didn't know that Gerald had been forced to resign from his last job for stealing from his clients.

"And when did you notice inaccuracies with your account?"

"About a month ago. I had a one hundred fifty thousand dollar annuity that Gerald sold me last year. I know I have this big fancy house, but the money in that annuity was all the cash I had in the world," she said her voice quavering for a second.

"Was? Is it all gone?"

"Not all of it. I still have almost one hundred thousand dollars. But over fifty thousand dollars is missing from that annuity, and I didn't spend it. And to make matters worse, now I'm going to owe taxes and surcharges on that money." She slapped her thigh indignantly.

"And how does Ger...ah Mr. Tate explain this missing money?"

"He had the nerve to insist that I authorized the use of that money for some high risk investments that didn't pan out. He's trying to make it seem like I'm just mad because I lost my money and I'm trying to blame him."

"Wouldn't you have had to authorize the use of

that money with a form or signature or something? Were you shown documented proof that you authorized him to invest that money?"

She stared at me hard and cocked her head to the side. "You don't seem to know much about policies and procedures for someone who works for the Stock Regulatory Commission, young lady. Are you new?"

"Yes, I am. Does it show?" I asked, laughing nervously. "This is the first inquiry they've let me head up on my own."

"Well," she said shrugging her shoulders, "I guess you have to start somewhere. How did you hear about my case?" She looked slightly confused.

"We got an anonymous tip," I told her, not quite able to look her in the eye. I was suddenly feeling really guilty for deceiving this woman. But if Clair Easton was telling the truth, and I thought she was, Gerald had stolen a lot of money from her.

This must be what Gerald was being blackmailed about. Did he find out Ms. Flack was the blackmailer and kill her? If Audrey was right about Julian Spicer having used the reunion fund money to help get Gerald out of a jam on his last job, then he must have only had to pay back a few thousand dollars. Chump change compared to the fifty thousand dollars he'd stolen from Clair Easton. Gerald was looking at jail time if Wheatley Financial had him prosecuted. I seriously doubted they'd just fire him.

"Who else have you contacted at Wheatley Financial about your account?"

"I've contacted several people and all they tell me is that they're going to look into it. Until you called I thought they were just telling me what I wanted to hear to shut me up. I'm so relieved to hear that someone is taking this seriously enough to report it because I was about to call the company president, John Howard Wheatley, himself."

"I'd give him a call anyway, Ms. Easton. He may not even know about your missing money. I can't imagine that he'd let this go without looking into it personally. His company's reputation is stake."

"But what are you and the stock commission planning to do?" She was nervously clenching and unclenching her hands in her lap. I felt awful. It was time for me to go.

"Well, this interview is the first step in a very long process. Someone will be in touch with you about the next step." I stopped the tape recorder and gathered up my things to make a hasty retreat. I stood up to go and Clair Easton jumped out of her chair, too.

"Do you have any idea if I'll get my money back?" she asked, standing in front of me and blocking my way. She was looking down at me with such fierce intensity that I realized I'd made a big mistake in coming to see this woman. Just how big a mistake I wouldn't find out until later. Clair Easton wasn't wrapped too tight and the theft of her money must have caused her to unravel even further.

"Ms. Easton, if Gerald Tate stole your money, then not only will he be prosecuted, but he'll be made to make restitution. He'll have to pay every dime of your money back." I stepped around her and headed for the front door.

"What do you mean *if* he stole my money?" she shouted as she followed me down the hall. I quickly pulled the door open but she slammed it shut before I could get out. Uh oh!

"Ms. Easton, you really need to calm down. I understand you must be very upset. But I need to go now." I spoke to her as calmly as I could, hoping she in turn would calm down as well. She didn't.

"You said *if* he stole my money. You don't believe me, do you? I can tell you think I made it all up, don't you?" She was red in the face and ringing her hands. Suddenly, she grabbed me by my shoulders and leaned down so close to my face that I could tell she'd had something with onions on it for lunch. I held my breath and leaned back.

"Let me go, Ms. Easton." I pulled out of her grasp and reached around her to grab the doorknob. "Of course I believe you. Now, as I've told you, someone will contact you. Have a nice day." I managed to get the door open, shove past her, and rush outside into the fresh air and sunshine.

"I'm not a liar! He did steal my money! He did! Where are you going? Come back here! I'm not finished with you!" She screamed at me as I practically ran back to my car.

I almost collided with an older couple walking past the house. They looked vaguely familiar. But I couldn't figure out where I'd seen them. I hopped in my car and took off, leaving them staring from me to Clair Easton who was still screaming at me from her front door.

Later that evening, after my class, I waited around for Cherisse so I could ask her about Ms. Flack's compact, which was still burning a hole in my purse. But she never showed up. I picked up a turkey sandwich from a nearby deli and headed home, resolving to go see her first thing in the morning. After I'd eaten, I poured myself a big glass of wine and settled myself in front of the TV. I was flipping aimlessly through the channels when there was a loud pounding at the door. Knowing it couldn't be Carl, I opened the door just a crack. Detective Trish Harmon shoved the door open all the way and came in uninvited followed by her partner, Charles Mercer. Both were grim faced.

"What the hell is this all about? What are you doing here?"

Instead of answering me, Harmon nodded towards the pile of clothing that I'd worn earlier to see Clair Easton. I'd shed the bloodstained clothes as soon as I'd gotten home after my disturbing encounter with the crazy woman and hadn't had time to toss them in the hamper before leaving for my class. Mercer picked them up and pointed out the bloodstains to Harmon.

"Are these your clothes?" Mercer asked.

"Who else's would they be?"

"Ms. Clayton, you'll need to come down to the station with us," she said, grabbing my upper arm firmly. I yanked out of her grasp.

"Why? What is this about?" I backed away from them.

"We need to talk to you about Clair Easton," said Harmon, reaching out to grab me again.

Crap! She must have reported me to the police. But I wondered how she'd found out my real name.

I accompanied them to their car, thanking God that Mrs. Carson wasn't home to witness me being placed into the back of a police car and wondering how much trouble I was in.

Chapter Seventeen

AFTER ARRIVING AT THE Willow Police Department, Harmon and Mercer left me cooling my jets in a police station interrogation room for almost an hour before they finally came in. Mercer sat an ice-filled Styrofoam cup and a can of Coke in front of me. He gave me a friendly smile that I wasn't buying for a minute. I'd watched enough crime shows to know that they were trying to fill me full of liquids so I'd have to pee, then refuse to take me to the bathroom until I gave them what they wanted—a confession. They weren't about to get to me though my bladder. I pushed the can away and glared at them.

"Well, Ms. Clayton, I can't say that I'm surprised. I knew you'd end up here one day," said Harmon. She looked so smug I was surprised she hadn't rubbed her hands together in delight. After all, she'd fulfilled a dream by dragging me down here.

"Were you at Clair Easton's house earlier today?" asked Mercer, managing to look much more neutral than his partner.

"Obviously you know that I was or I wouldn't be

here," I snapped.

"Why did you go to see Ms. Easton?" Mercer again.

"Ask your partner." I smiled at Harmon. I was happy to see the smirk vanish from her face. "She's the one who told me that if I could find any evidence that pointed to Ivy Flack having been a blackmailer that she'd look into it. That's what I was doing, looking for evidence. You told me I could, remember?"

Mercer looked at his partner with a raised eyebrow and Harmon flushed. "What I told you, Miss Clayton, was that I knew you would do what you wanted regardless of what I said, or thought, which is why you're here."

We glared at each other and I again noticed that she was looking much more put together than usual. She was wearing an expensive-looking navy pinstriped pantsuit, that I'd never seen before, with a grey silk shell and high heeled pumps. She was also wearing makeup, and she'd dyed her short hair a rich brown. But it wasn't just the new clothes and the dye job that were different about her. She seemed much more alive and vibrant than I'd ever seen her. Unlike her usual gloom and doom expression, she actually looked happy, and not just about having dragged me into the station. I didn't have much time to speculate on the reason for her transformation because Mercer was talking to me again.

"And just what did Clair Easton have to do with your theory that Ivy Flack was a blackmailer?" he asked calmly, always playing the good cop to Harmon's bad one.

"And why were your fingerprints found on the pair of hedge clippers that were used to stab her to death?" interjected Harmon, before I could say a word, causing Mercer to sigh and sit back in his chair and cross his arms.

I, on the other hand, sat bolt upright in my chair. I opened my mouth to speak, but the only thing that came out was a loud gasp. Clair Easton was dead? Killed with hedge clippers? The only hedge clippers I'd seen were the ones Mr. Diaz had left behind. The same hedge clippers that I'd picked up and carried into her house. My fingerprints were on those clippers and were on file at the police station because of another murder case I'd been involved with last year. Plus, I had bloodstains on the clothes I wore to her house. No wonder they thought I'd killed her. I had to clear this up and quick.

I filled them in on the details of my visit. I explained why I'd gone to see her. I told about Mr. Diaz cutting himself, his blood staining my clothes, and why I'd touched the clippers. I explained Clair

253

Easton had told me that Gerald Tate had stolen money from her, about her getting upset when she thought I didn't believe her, and her screaming at me as I left her house. My mouth was dry and I was out of breath when I finished. I opened the Coke and poured it over the half-melted ice and took a long drink, while Harmon and Mercer looked at each other.

"Do I need a lawyer?" I asked after draining the Styrofoam cup. I poured in the remaining Coke and took another sip.

"I don't know. Do you think you need a lawyer, Ms. Clayton?" replied Harmon.

"I didn't kill Clair Easton. When I left her house, she was alive. There was a couple walking past the house that saw her yelling at me as I left. The person you need to talk to is Gerald Tate. I had no reason to want Clair Easton dead," I insisted.

Harmon opened her mouth to speak when the door to the interrogation room opened and a chubby, balding, black uniformed officer poked his head inside the room and gestured for them to come out. I saw that he had a piece of paper in his hand. Mercer got up and walked out of the room, and with great reluctance, Harmon started to follow him. Before she could get out of the room, I stopped her as an all too familiar, and extremely unwanted, sensation crept up on me.

"Hey! I need to go to the restroom," I told her.

"Tough," she said, sailing out of the room, smirk firmly intact.

Damn. They got me.

Two hours later, I was finally allowed to go home after Mr. Diaz had been questioned and backed up my story of cutting himself and his leaving his clippers at the house, and the couple that had seen me leaving the Easton house had confirmed that Ms. Easton was alive and screaming when I left. Of course, during this time, I had to pee so bad I'd have confessed to anything at that point, including shooting Tupac…and Biggie. I wondered how long it actually took them to find out the information they needed to clear me. I suspected they'd left me in that room for two hours on purpose, which is why I ultimately grabbed the empty Styrofoam cup, crouched in a corner and took a whiz in it.

I left the cup in the center of the table. When Harmon came in and told me I was free to go, she grabbed the cup too quickly and the warm contents sloshed on the sleeve of her pretty new suit. She got the strangest look on her face and I high-tailed it out of the room before she realized what was in the cup. I heard her loud exclamation of, "Jesus H. Christ!" all the way down the hall as I practically ran out of the station wondering if assaulting a police detective with pee was a felony or a misdemeanor?

I didn't have my car with me and was on my cell phone calling for a cab when I saw the couple that had been walking past Clair Easton's house and witnessed her screaming at me. They were going to their car. They had another younger man with them and I suddenly remembered why the couple looked so familiar. They were Dennis Kirby's parents, and the man with them was Dennis. Great. I quickly headed in the opposite direction for the bus stop when I heard Dennis call my name. I stopped and turned to see him lumbering across the parking lot towards me.

"Do you need a ride?" he asked, shocking the shit out of me. Was this the same man who had threatened me earlier? I even looked around thinking he must be talking to someone else.

"No. I'm serious. You don't need to take the bus. I can give you a ride home."

"Why would you want to give a blackmailer a ride home?" I asked, trying hard not to sound pissed.

"I'm sorry, okay. I was just mad about not getting that trainer job I applied for. Then Audrey called and was crying on my shoulder about you accusing her of killing Ms. Flack. Then you showed up and I just took it all out on you. I'm sorry. I really am. Honestly, I didn't mean any of that shit I said." I had to admit he did look contrite. I hoped it wasn't just an act for his parents, who were watching us from the car.

"I never accused Audrey of murdering Ms. Flack," I said indignantly, though technically I think I had. "And I'm no blackmailer!"

"Okay, I believe you." He held up his hands. I noticed his wrist was still bandaged. It must have been a really bad sprain to still be bandaged almost two weeks later. "I know better than anybody what a drama queen Audrey is and I know you'd never blackmail anybody."

"Did you and your parents know Clair Easton?"

"Not really. She was always the neighborhood crackpot. Sometimes she would speak to you and be friendly, and other times she'd look at you like she'd never seen you before. How'd you know her?"

"Long story," I said. He was waiting for me to elaborate but I wouldn't. "Did you know Gerald was Clair Easton's financial consultant?"

"Why would I? Gerald doesn't discuss his clients with me." I couldn't be sure, but I got the feeling he was lying to me. He may not have been serious about what he'd said during our last conversation, but his loyalties were still with Audrey and Gerald.

"And you didn't know that she claimed he stole fifty thousand dollars from him?"

"So, what, now you think Gerald killed that Easton woman? Man, you sure don't think very highly of us." He laughed. I just stared at him. Pissing him off wasn't the way to get the info I needed.

"I think I'll take that ride," I said, giving him a big smile.

I sat in the backseat of Dennis's black Lexus with his mother, Emma Kirby, who was still a very pretty, petite, blonde woman in her early fifties. Ellis Kirby, Dennis's father, sat in the front seat. Both of the Kirby's were polite, especially Emma, who was thrilled to discover that I was the granddaughter of Estelle Mays, who used to work for her family.

"How is Estelle? It's been years since I've seen her," said Emma Kirby. Up until that point, she hadn't really paid much attention to me beyond the bounds of common courtesy.

"She's fine. I'll tell her you said hello."

"Since you're a friend of Dennis's from high school, you must have known Julian, right?" asked Ellis Kirby partially turning in his seat. I could see Dennis's jaw clench briefly and wondered if it was due to his father's assumption that we were friends, or the mention of his deceased cousin.

I also couldn't help but notice that Dennis didn't look much like his refined and cultured parents, both of whom were immaculately and expensively dressed in contrast to Dennis's wrinkled Polo shirt and chinos.

Beyond the blue eyes he shared with his mother and the cleft in his chin he got from his father, Dennis didn't seem to fit. He was like an ostrich in the nest of a pair of swans.

"Well, we didn't have the same friends. But, yes, I knew him," I replied politely.

"Kendra was a good girl, Dad, too good to hang with the likes of Julian and me. We were wild men," chuckled Dennis. His father gave him a tight smile.

"You mean *you* were a wild man, Denny. I suspect Julian just got dragged along for the ride," replied Emma Kirby coolly. Ellis Kirby chuckled his agreement.

I could have easily contradicted that statement but kept my mouth shut because apparently the Kirbys didn't want to hear anything remotely unflattering about their nephew. Poor Dennis. Thinking back on Audrey's comments at the last reunion committee meeting about Dennis playing second fiddle to his cousin Julian, it was no wonder he was such a loudmouth. He was looking for attention.

"Why were you at Clair Easton's house? Did you know her?" asked Emma, turning towards me. Even in the dark car, I could see the curiosity in her eyes.

"I was conducting a marketing survey," I replied quickly. I met Dennis's eyes in the rearview mirror and his smirk told me he knew I was lying. His mother

259

seemed to buy it, though.

"Poor Clair. She was always odd but when her dog died last weekend she went off the deep end."

"Did she find out what killed him?" Dennis's father asked.

"Jeeves was killed?" I said more to myself then anyone. I wondered why Clair Easton hadn't mentioned that fact during our meeting.

"She found him dead in her backyard last Saturday night. He must have gotten into some rat poison that she kept in her garden shed," replied Emma Kirby.

"Man, when she found him you could hear her screaming like she'd been shot. I bet you could hear her from six blocks away," Dennis said, shaking his head sadly.

"That dog was all she had. She never married or had children or anything. She was alone. It was so sad," Emma Kirby replied, pulling the sweater of her Kelly green twinset closed to ward off the chill of the air conditioning. I noticed she was wearing a gorgeous pearl drop bracelet. Before I could compliment her on it, Ellis Kirby spoke up.

"Then she should have kept the damned dog inside. She let it roam all over the neighborhood. It dug up my azaleas." Ellis Kirby sounded highly put out.

"They're both dead, dear. I think your flowers are quite safe now." The sarcasm in Emma Kirby's voice cut her husband to the quick and he gave her an embarrassed look before fiddling with the radio dial.

"Dad does have a point, Mom," said Dennis in an attempt to lighten the mood. "She used to walk that dog at all hours. I've come home at three in the morning and passed her walking Jeeves. He was so hyper she was running through everyone's yards trying to catch him. It was the funniest damned thing I ever saw." Ellis Kirby chuckled heartily, but Emma remained silent.

The rest of the drive was silent. Dennis dropped off his parents first. I was surprised that they only lived four doors down from Claire Easton in a salmon-colored, three story, art deco house that sat up on a hill. I'd have figured them for a nice sedate Cape Cod. As we were pulling out of the steep driveway, Dennis indicated that he lived in the old caretaker's cottage at the back of his parent's property.

"Much as I love the folks, I can't be in the same house with them. I like having my own place and they don't want me in the house anyway. I'm a slob," he said, laughing.

"Was Julian a slob?" Dennis looked over at me. His expression was unreadable.

"I guess you picked up the fact that my parents think Julian was a saint."

"Doesn't that bother you?"

"Not like it used to. That's why I moved to the West Coast. I thought if I put some distance between us they'd miss me and appreciate me more."

"Did they?"

"Yeah, they did. But only as long I was on the West Coast. Once I moved back home, it was the same old story." He shrugged his thick shoulders. "Where to?" he asked, changing the subject. I told him where I lived and we were silent for a few minutes.

"Did you know Julian gave the reunion fund money to Gerald to help him out of a bind on his last job?"

"Audrey told me after the last committee meeting. I guess I'm not surprised. Julian was like that. Always helping out a friend."

"I never got to know that side of him," I replied, trying to keep the bitterness out of my voice. He glanced over at me but didn't comment.

"Kendra, I lied to you back in the parking lot when you asked me if I knew that Clair Easton was Gerald's client."

I swung around to face him. "Why?"

"Because I didn't want to discuss what I'm about to say with my parents nearby."

"Sounds serious."

"It is. Julian was Clair Easton's accountant. He

was the one who recommended her to Gerald in the first place. When Audrey told me Julian had given the reunion fund money to Gerald, I was worried that Julian may have also dipped into one of Clair Easton's accounts. She wouldn't have noticed a few hundred missing here or there. It would just kill my folks if they thought he was stealing."

"But why would he have stolen from Clair Easton?"

"Julian was in a lot of debt. His business was in trouble, which was why he freaked out when he lost out on that account thanks to Cherry. And he'd bought the old Bridges house out on Faucet Road and was sinking a ton of money into it to get it all fixed up. He was planning to turn it into a real show place and thought he would make a huge profit and use the money for his business. Even doing most of the work himself, the cost of materials was eating him alive."

"He was trying to flip the old Bridges place?" The house Dennis was referring to had been an old abandoned house where he and his round table cronies used to get drunk and smoke weed. I had no idea that Julian had bought the place.

"Flip? Oh, yeah that's what they call it. Yeah, he was trying to flip it. But it flipped him instead," he said referring to the fact that Julian had fallen to his death from the roof of the house.

"Why didn't he just get the money he needed

from your parents?"

"Because they loaned him the money to start up his business. My folks adored Julian. But they're both real big on initiative and making your own luck. They don't believe in having anything handed to you. Their big thing is that hard work never hurt anybody. But hard work didn't do a damned thing for Julian."

"You don't think Julian could have actually stolen money from Clair Easton, do you?"

"Naw, probably not. But Gerald's another story. He's as broke as Julian was and ten times shadier. I mean, don't get me wrong. I love the guy to death. But he owes child support for four kids and is still paying his first wife alimony. He's seriously tapped out and refuses to live within his means. You saw that car he drives, didn't you?" I nodded. I could have pointed out that a Lexus wasn't the kind of car most college bookstore managers drove but didn't bother. He must have bought the car when he'd had his last job.

"I know he's your friend, Dennis. But if he was desperate enough to steal money from a client, then he may have also—"

"Killed Clair Easton? I hope to hell not. But I guess anything is possible when you're desperate," he said softly.

We were silent again and Dennis turned onto my street. But I still had a lot more questions.

"Did you know your cousin Julian was seeing Ms.

Flack?" Dennis's head whipped around and his mouth fell open.

"No way. Julian was banging Ms. Flack? You gotta be kidding me."

"You really didn't know? I thought you two were close?"

"Not once I moved out West. We were both so busy we just didn't have the time to talk as much as we used to. I can't believe it. Julian and Ms. Flack? You know, now that I think about it, Julian used to do handyman work on the side to earn extra money. He learned all that stuff from his dad. He told me he was seeing someone whose house he'd done work at. He never told me who it was, though. Damn! I had no idea he was into older women."

He pulled up in front of my duplex and I thanked him and got out. I started to walk away when his voice stopped me. I leaned down into the window.

"I'm really sorry about that rumor I started about you back in high school. About you having had a secret abortion and not knowing who the baby's father was. Forgive me?" He was giving me an embarrassed look and I stared at him without speaking for what seemed like an eternity before he repeated his request.

"Can you ever forgive me? I know I was a real asshole."

First an apology from Audrey and now Dennis. I hoped this wasn't a sign of the coming apocalypse.

With great effort I gave him a smile and managed to say, "Don't sweat it. It was a long time ago. You were a different person. We all were."

I watched Dennis pull off and headed into my apartment thinking not about how much that rumor had hurt me, but realizing I now knew what Ivy Flack thought she'd had on me. She'd actually believed that old rumor about me and thought I'd be willing to pay to keep it quiet. If she'd believed it, then someone must have told her it was true. Who disliked me that much?

Chapter Eighteen

MY MOUTH WAS FILLED with buttered toast
and I was rushing around trying to get dressed the next
morning when my phone rang. It was only 7:00. I
didn't have to be at work until 8:30, but I was trying to
catch Cherisse before she left for work. I managed to
answer the phone on the second ring.

"Hello?" I said, trying hard not to choke on half-
chewed food.

"Why are you so out of breath?" asked Carl,
chuckling softly. I quickly swallowed the toast and
washed it down with a gulp of orange juice.

"Hey, sweetie. How's the trial going?"

"That's why I'm calling. Looks like things are
going to wrap up sooner than I thought. So I'll be in
town tomorrow night instead of Saturday afternoon.
Have you been thinking about what we talked about?"

"I've hardly thought of anything else," I replied,
slumping into a nearby kitchen chair.

"Good. Then I bet you have an answer for me. I'll
see you tomorrow night, babe." He hung up and I sat
there holding the receiver, staring off into space.

This was not good. He was going to want an

answer to his marriage proposal and I just wasn't prepared at all for that conversation. I still didn't know what I was going to tell him. I had a sinking feeling that our entire relationship was going to be decided during that little chat. The bleating dial tone startled me and I hung up the phone.

I arrived at Cherisse's house ten minutes later and noticed a familiar car in her driveway. It was a black BMW convertible. It was Gerald Tate's car. I parked across the street. It was still pretty early and her curtains were drawn. There were no signs of life coming from Cherisse's house, which told me that Gerald must have spent the night. I had no idea they were an item. Of course, I could be completely wrong as to why his car would be parked in her driveway before 7:30 in the morning. I tried to keep an open mind. Maybe they were running buddies and hooked up every morning to run. But thinking about the gut Gerald had acquired since high school, the only running he was doing was back and forth to the fridge. Clearly, I needed to get a closer look to verify my suspicions.

Except for a paperboy, who looked about twelve, flinging papers from his bike a few houses down, the block was deserted. I started to open my car door when Cherisse's front door opened suddenly. I

268

quickly slid down in my seat until the only thing showing was the top of my head. I peered through my window and watched as Gerald, dressed only in a towel slung around his middle, opened the screen door and reached down to get the paper that was laying on the doormat. In doing so, the towel slipped off and he caught it just before his privates were exposed to the cool morning air. He turned with the paper in one hand, and the towel in the other, and I got a crystal clear view of a round, brown ass bisected by a hairy butt crack. Eew! So much for them being *running* buddies. But they were buddies all right. The kind that starts with an F and ends with a K.

Gerald was too busy with the towel to notice me and thankfully pulled the front door shut behind him. I got out of my car and quickly crossed the street to Cherisse's front yard and walked around to the side of the house. I was hoping there was a window open so that I could eavesdrop. There were two windows on the side that faced the house next door. The blinds on both windows were closed tight and they were both locked. I moved around to the back of the house. There were two small windows that looked out onto the backyard as well as a concrete patio with green metal patio chairs arranged around a matching glass table with a fringed umbrella. The back door was open and I could hear voices coming from inside the house.

I couldn't really hear what they were saying because of the loud hum of Cherisse's central air-conditioning unit, which I was standing next to. I started to creep towards the back door so I could hear better when the voices got closer. The back door opened. I turned and ran back around the side of the house, slipping on the wet, dew soaked grass, getting grass stains on my white pants and hurting my wrist as I threw my hand down to catch my fall. I had to stifle a moan as I clutched my throbbing wrist to my chest. I looked around the corner into the backyard and saw that Cherisse and Gerald were eating their breakfast at the patio table. I willed my rapidly beating heart to slow down and listened.

"I still can't believe you did it," said Cherisse, spooning what looked like honeydew melon into her mouth. She was dressed in the same red Kimono robe that she'd had on yesterday and didn't sound nearly as congested.

"I told you I was going to. I didn't have a choice, did I? If I didn't stop her, she was going to ruin everything." Gerald had put on sweatpants and a white wifebeater T-Shirt. My ears perked up at that last part. Was he talking about Clair Easton or Ms. Flack?

"I just wish there'd been another way. I mean what you did was so brutal? Don't you feel bad at all?" asked Cherisse.

"Hell no!" replied Gerald vehemently. "She gave me no choice. It was her own damned fault. It needed to be done. I couldn't afford to have her running her mouth to Wheatley. I need my job."

"Do you really think she would have gone to your boss?" Cherisse was pulling apart a croissant and spreading jam on it. Gerald shrugged nonchalantly and shoveled scrambled eggs into his mouth.

"I didn't want to take any chances. I just wanted the bitch gone and now she is," he said grimly after taking a gulp from a large coffee mug.

"Well luck seems to be on your side because you're home free now. But you need to be more careful. Next time you won't be so lucky."

"Hell, lucky is my middle name," said Gerald, laughing nastily. Charisse gave him a sharp look and took another bite of croissant. She started to tell him something that from the look on her face wasn't going to be anything nice, when the cordless phone sitting next to her plate started ringing.

"Hello," she said, cradling the phone between her ear and shoulder. I saw her frown and look around wildly. "What are you talking about?"

"Who is it?" asked Gerald, looking worried.

"Mrs. Grable from across the street. She said there's a woman watching us," Cherisse said, covering the receiver with her hand.

Crap. Someone had seen me. I looked over my shoulder and saw a woman in a green housedress, with fat pink curlers in her hair, watching me from the front porch of the Pepto pink house across the street. She was on the phone babbling and jabbing an accusing finger in my direction. I straightened up and turned back to look at Gerald and Cherisse.

Gerald immediately got up from the table and started looking around the backyard. I hot-footed it across Cherisse's front yard, ran across the street, jumped in my car, and started the ignition just as Gerald ran into the front yard.

"I'm callin' the po po on yo ass. You better run!" The woman I assumed to be Mrs. Grable called out in a gravelly smoker's voice as I pulled away from the curb.

I looked back as I sped away and my eyes met and locked with Gerald's. If the look on his face chilled me to the bone, then the slashing motion he made across his throat after pointing at me, made me almost wet my already dirty pants.

Later that day, during the two-hour break between the morning and afternoon sessions, I sat at my desk in my empty classroom to think things over. Two women were dead and there was one person both women had in common: Gerald Tate. From the conversation I'd overheard, Gerald had done something that Cherisse had described as brutal to some woman. Both Ivy Flack and Clair Easton posed threats to Gerald and both died in violent brutal ways, Ms. Flack by electrocution and Clair Easton by stabbing. Could Gerald have killed them both, or was Cherisse in on it too? Cherisse did have Ms. Flack's silver compact. What was it doing in her bathroom? She had to have taken it after she shoved her into the bathtub with her blow dryer. It must be some kind of trophy.

I felt pain flare up in my wrist as I tossed my empty pop can in the trash. I'd had Iris tape it with an ace bandage from the first aid kit when I'd gotten to work, but even though I knew it wasn't broken, it was still sore and swollen. I should probably see a doctor. And I knew just the one I wanted to see. I took the rest of the afternoon off and headed to the doctor's office where I knew Cherisse worked as a secretary.

The medical practice of Drs. Mann, Freeling and Parks was located on Main Street in a three-story brick building that, in the years since it had been built, had been everything from an insurance office to a secretarial school, and everything in between. When I was a teenager, the ground floor was where my old dentist, Dr. Richman, now deceased, had had his office. It had been home to a medical practice for the past five years. I ought to know. Dr. Irene Freeling was Mama's doctor and I'd brought her to many an appointment. Cherisse worked for Dr. Trent Mann, whose office was on the second floor. I walked into the packed waiting room and spotted Cherisse from across the room. She looked up with a smile when she heard the door to the office open. It immediately left her face when she saw that it was me. She was purposely avoiding my eyes and was pretending to be busy shuffling a stack of papers together as I approached the counter she was sitting behind.

"Can I help you?" she asked, through tight lips coated in peach lip gloss.

"Only if you plan to tell me the truth." I looked around the waiting room to see if anyone was listening. The room was filled with mostly elderly people who were either watching the large TV mounted to the wall, dozing, or reading magazines.

"Are you here to see the doctor?" she asked, nodding towards my bandaged wrist.

"No. I'm here to see you, and I'm sure you know why."

She sighed heavily and scowled at me. "I'm at work. I don't have time for this," she whispered fiercely, looking dramatically around the waiting room. I looked, too. No one was paying us any attention. Apparently, we couldn't compete with Judge

Judy and Reader's Digest.

"Take a break. We really need to talk. I'm not going away until we do."

We stared each other down for a few seconds and then Cherisse got up and stomped off to another room. I overheard her asking someone named Leanne to cover for her while she took a break. She came out from behind the counter and headed towards the doorway to the hallway. I assumed she wanted me to follow her. I did. She walked quickly to the stairwell and down two sets of steps and out the back exit to the parking lot, at which point she rounded on me.

"What the hell do you want?"

Instead of answering her, I pulled the silver compact that I'd found in her bathroom out of my purse and waved it in her face.

"I found this in your bathroom yesterday. It was Ms. Flack's. What were you doing with it?" She reeled back a little like I'd just swung at her and her mouth fell open. No sound came out, though. I pressed on.

"You killed her, didn't you? Or maybe it was Gerald. Did you guys do it together? And what about Clair Easton? Which one of you killed her?"

"Hold up! Are you crazy? I didn't kill anybody! Neither did Gerald."

"Then why do you have Ms. Flack's compact, and who did I overhear you and Gerald talking about this morning?"

She looked truly confused for a minute before breaking out into a grin.

"Is that why you ran off this morning like the police were after you? You thought you overheard us talking about a murder?" She started laughing. It was a harsh condescending little laugh accompanied by the slow deliberate shake of her head meant to mean that she couldn't believe how stupid I was. I could feel my blood start to boil.

"That's what you get for spying on us and dipping into our conversation. All up in our Kool-Aid and don't even know the flavor." She laughed even louder. I just gave her the death stare until she finally shut up and wiped the tears from her eyes.

"We weren't talking about Ms. Flack or that crazy Clair Easton. We were talking about Sunny Abou."

"Sunny who?" I asked. The name did ring a bell. Then it came to me. Sunny Abou was the receptionist at Wheatley Financial. "Sunny the receptionist?" Cherisse nodded.

"Sunny and Gerald had a four-month-long affair. That's why his last marriage ended. Sunny's pregnant. She thought Gerald would marry her."

"And he isn't?"

"Gerald never had any intention of marrying Sunny. He thought she was bluffing about being pregnant. And even if she isn't, he's not about to pay child support for another kid. When she found out, she got nasty and started making threats."

"What kind of threats?"

"Threats to ruin his career."

"How?"

"Sunny runs things in that office. She has keys to everyone's offices and knows everyone's passwords and access codes. She was able to get into Clair Easton's account and routed a bunch of her money into an account in the Cayman Islands with his name on it. She made it look like Gerald stole it. Gerald's been scrambling trying to figure out a way to get Ms. Easton's money back before his boss finds out. Sunny just sat back and started waiting for the phone calls from Clair Easton about her money. Every time she called, Sunny handed Gerald the message and told him he could make it all go way. All he had to do was buy her a ring and set a date."

"What did he do to her that was so brutal?"

"He reported her to the INS. She was here on a student Visa that expired two months ago. Some INS officials showed up at work yesterday and took her into custody. She's being deported."

"Oh my God!"

"Yeah, I feel really bad for her. She just wanted Gerald to do right by her and the baby. Can you imagine what's going to happen to her when she gets home, having been deported with no degree, unmarried, and pregnant?" That took me be surprise. Weren't Cherisse and Gerald an item? She saw the look on my face and answered my unspoken question.

"Gerald isn't my man. We just hook up now and then when we're both between relationships, or in Gerald's case, marriages."

"Even after how he and his friends treated you in high school?"

"It's just sex. It's no big deal. We're just having fun. Besides, I know he respects me more than those other chicks because I'm hip to his game."

"His game?"

"Yeah," she said, laughing. "You know how men are. They'll do and say anything to get laid. They'll pretend to be everything from your savior to your soul mate to get into your pants. It's only after they've gotten what they want, and can't get away from you fast enough, that you realize it was all just a bunch of bullshit. Gerald's no different. He's good at spotting a woman's insecurities and working them to his advantage. But I'm not like Gerald's other chicks. I can see way past all his crap." She laughed like it was a big joke.

However, her slumped shoulders and sad eyes told me the joke was on her. She was in love with him. And had done a pretty good job of convincing herself that she wasn't like all of the others when in fact, she was worse because she was still hanging on hoping for an upgrade in her booty call status. Poor Cherisse.

"That still doesn't explain why this was in your bathroom," I said, holding up the silver compact.

"She must have left it at my house."

"I saw her with this the day she died. The last thing she told me was that she was leaving town in a hurry. Why did she come to see you when she was so hot to get out of town?"

She threw her hands in the air in exasperation. "Can you hear yourself? You honestly believe I could have murdered Ivy Flack? Me?"

I looked at her closely without speaking. She started biting her thumbnail and wouldn't look at me. I was making her awfully nervous for some reason. Only someone who had something to be guilty about would act so nervously. Something wasn't right. I was looking at this all wrong. I thought about that nasty abortion rumor about me in high school. I'd cried on Cherisse's shoulder about it the day I went to study at her house. She'd comforted me because she thought I was going to be her new friend. When she'd asked me if I was okay the next day, I'd blown her off because Lynette and I were friends again and I didn't need her anymore.

"You were helping Ms. Flack, weren't you? You two were in on it together. All that stuff you told me about her blackmailing you over an affair with your old boss and you thinking she pushed Julian off the roof was just a smoke screen so no one would suspect you two were partners, right?" She just stared at the ground. I pressed on.

"You were sleeping with Gerald and he confided everyone's secrets to you, didn't he? And you told her everything he said, including that old rumor about me having had an abortion. For her it was about getting the money to start over someplace else. But for you it was a way to get back at us all for the way we treated you in high school, not to mention everyone thinking you were to blame for Julian's death."

She suddenly smiled and looked quite pleased with herself. She started clapping. "Give that girl a gold star. You figured it all out, didn't you? You're just so damned smart. For your information, Ivy Flack was probably the only real friend I ever had back in high school. I would spend hours crying in her office. She always knew just what to say to cheer me up. My own twin sister ran off and left me, but Ivy was always there for me. We kept in touch after high school. I went to see her at work the day she found out her ex-boyfriend was getting out of prison and she told me his sister was threatening to spread lies that would ruin her."

"My God, Cherisse," I said softly. She didn't hear me and continued on.

"It was my idea for her to fake her death and disappear, but she needed money. So, yeah, I gave Ivy the information to blackmail the reunion committee. I was even the one who made all the phone calls telling them how much they needed to pay to keep their secrets buried and why the hell not? Audrey's husband makes a lot of money, Dennis's family is rich, and Gerald wastes so much money trying to live the good life it wouldn't kill him to give up a few thousand, and then there was you." She gave me a disgusted look that made me flinch.

"But you knew that rumor about me was a lie. Why would you set me up to be blackmailed?"

"I didn't know it was a lie," she replied innocently. "All I had was the word of some chick who used me and pretended to like me, to get back at her best friend. And how reliable is the word of someone like that? I decided a long time ago that the rumor about you must have been true. Your uncle has that nice restaurant. I figured you could get money from him. I never thought you'd go to the police."

I felt sick to my stomach. "Cherisse, I am so sorry about what I did to you. It was so long ago. I was just a thoughtless kid. What's your excuse for the way

281

you're acting now?"

"You're right. It was a long time ago. But the scars will last me a lifetime. Do you know I've been in therapy for years over what happened in high school? But you better believe that I will not be used or made fun of ever again. Do you hear me?" She stepped forward so abruptly I was forced to take a step back. "All the people who wronged me got exactly what they deserved, or soon will," she said cryptically. She turned and walked towards the building.

I called out after her. "Did you kill her? Was she supposed to split the blackmail money with you and didn't? Was she supposed to take you with her and wouldn't?"

She didn't stop walking until she got to the door, then she turned back. "She just came over that day to tell me good-bye. She gave me the compact to remember her. It was a gift. As you've already pointed out, it was never about money for me." She smiled and then turned and walked into the building.

Chapter Nineteen

BEING ON SOMEONE'S SHIT LIST is not fun. However, being on someone's shit list and not knowing it, is even worse. I had no idea Cherisse had been holding a grudge against me for all these years. I could have told her the truth about her so-called friend Ivy Flack, but why bother. If Ms. Flack had been able to comfort her during her dark high school days, then who was I to take that away from her? She had certainly been a better friend to her than I had. Maybe Ms. Flack was trying to make up for what she'd done to Maurice Groves, when she was just a teen herself, by befriending another troubled teen.

As I drove, I tried to decide if I should tell Harmon about what I'd found out. There was absolutely no proof that Cherisse had aided Ms. Flack in her blackmail scheme. And to be honest, I did believe her when she said she didn't kill her, which brought me back to the same questions: who killed Ivy Flack, and was her death related to Clair Easton's murder? Beyond Gerald, I could see no clear connection between the two women, and even that connection wasn't a strong one because of what

283

Cherisse had told me about Sunny Abou being the one who really stole Clair Easton's money. There had to be something else that linked them. But what was it if it wasn't Gerald Tate?

I almost felt sorry for Gerald. Almost. He'd messed with the wrong women. Sunny was being deported and would likely take the account number to the bank account in the Cayman's with her. Even though Clair Easton was dead, all his boss would have to do is follow the trail Sunny left right back to Gerald. And Cherisse may be in love with him, but in a twisted act of passive aggressiveness, she'd helped her friend Ivy Flack blackmail him for something he didn't even do. I'd bet money it wasn't just to get back at him for the way he treated her in high school, either. Most likely it was so he'd cry on her shoulder and make her feel needed. Ain't love grand?

I arrived home tired and cranky. My wrist was still throbbing and I took a couple of ibuprofen and lay down on my couch. A couple of hours later, I was awakened by the sound of movement from down below in my landlady Mrs. Carson's house. My living room was directly over her kitchen. Figuring it was just Mrs. Carson puttering around making her dinner, I turned over and started to go back to sleep. Then, realizing Mrs. Carson was still on her cruise, not due home until Sunday, and it was only Thursday, I sat bolt upright.

I got on the floor and pressed my ear against the Oriental rug by my couch to see if I could hear anything else. After a few seconds of silence, I heard the distinct sound of footsteps in the kitchen down below. Mrs. Carson was not a wealthy woman and had nothing much of monetary value to steal. But she did have a prized sterling silver tea set that had been passed down through her family from her great-great-great-grandmother. If a thief made off with that tea service, it would probably kill her. I should have called the police. But when do I ever do what I'm supposed to do? Instead, I got up and grabbed the keys to Mrs. Carson's house, that she'd left so I could water her plants, and the baseball bat that I kept for protection because I refused to get a gun, and headed out my door.

I crept down my steps all the while peering in the darkened window of Mrs. Carson's kitchen. I saw a shadow move quickly past the thin white cotton curtains. I rushed down the remaining steps with the bat slung over my shoulder like I was about to hit a homerun. I arrived at Mrs. Carson's slightly ajar front door at the same time as the man who was coming out of it. Without even waiting to see who it was, I started screaming and swinging at the man's head like it was a piñata, while he danced around ducking and swooping like a large bird.

"Heifer, are you crazy!" yelled the man, who turned out not to be Mrs. Carson's youngest son, Stevie. Notice I didn't say Stevie wasn't a thief. That's because Stevie Carson's fingers were so sticky he could touch his own head and leave behind a bald spot.

"Stevie? What are you doing here? I thought you were in jail."

Stevie straightened up and looked around nervously. Come to think of it, Stevie always looked nervous and with good reason. Someone was always after him. Sometimes it was the police; most of the time it was people he'd either stolen from, or sold stolen merchandise to. He was a wiry, rail thin, middle-aged man of average height, with a pencil thin mustache that outlined his full upper lip and beady little eyes that darted around so much he never really looked you in the eye. He was dressed in a black sweat suit that was covered in what looked like cat hair, black combat boots, and a fishing hat covered in lures. His thinning Afro was peeking out from the sides of the hat. Mrs. Carson had four other hardworking and law abiding children, but for some reason Stevie was by far her favorite. Go figure.

"Got out two days ago, if you must know." He pulled the hat down further on his head and looked over my shoulder nervously. I turned and looked, too. No one was there.

"Are you staying here?"

"Nope," he said shaking his head vigorously. "Came by to drop off that crazy ass cat. My old lady, you know Sweetie, doncha?" he asked, cocking his head to the side. I shook my head no. Stevie had been living off and on with the same woman for more than twenty years. But since Mrs. Carson automatically hated every woman her favorite son had brought over, Sweetie, had never been welcome in her home.

"I said I'd take care a that cat for my mama while she was gone. She had my sister drop it off at Sweetie's crib before they left on that cruise. By the time I got out a the county lockup that dang cat had clawed up Sweetie's curtains, pissed all over her house, and killed her pet parakeet. She told me it was her or the cat. So, I brought it back home. I'll come by and feed it, but it can't stay with me."

Stevie wasn't the most reliable person in the world. I knew in order to save Mrs. Carson from coming home to a dead pet I'd have to step up even though Mrs. Carson's Siamese cat, Mahalia, and I hated each other with a passion.

"Don't worry about it. I'll feed her until your mother gets back."

"Good lookin' out," he said, grinning at me and

exposing perfect straight white teeth. Stealing and dental hygiene appeared to be the only things Stevie took seriously. He pushed past me on his way down the porch steps.

"Oh, and Stevie," I called out after him. He stopped and looked back nervously.

"My name's not heifer."

"It is when you swingin' a bat at my head."

I guess he did have a point.

I went inside Mrs. Carson's house and flipped on the light switch. That small movement sent searing pain through my wrist, which hadn't felt too bad when I'd been awakened from my nap but was now throbbing again due to my batting practice with Stevie's head. I flexed it and it felt stiff. I was alarmed to see it was also starting to swell. I don't know what I was thinking swinging that bat around like I was Xena Warrior Princess. I'd re-injured my wrist. I looked around for the cat, not bothering to call her because I knew she wouldn't come to me, and finally found her perched on top of Mrs. Carson's china cabinet. She was staring down at me with almond-shaped blue eyes filled with their usual distain.

Instead of trying to coax her down (she could stay up there forever as far as I was concerned), I went into the kitchen and rummaged around the cabinets looking for cat food. I located a half-filled bag of Meow Mix in the pantry and filled her monogrammed food bowl. I also filled her matching water dish to the brim and started to scoop out her fake jewel encrusted litter box but was happy to find it didn't need cleaning. When I went back to the pantry to put the cat food away, I happened upon a flat blue case sitting on the counter. I'm too nosy to resist such temptation and didn't try. I opened it.

Inside was a collection of leather cat collars, one for every day of the week, and each with a different charm hanging from it that read: My name is Mahalia Carson. On the back was Mrs. Carson's address and phone number. I'd never paid enough attention to the little monster to notice she had a whole wardrobe of collars. No wonder Mahalia was such a diva. She was spoiled rotten. I heard loud purring that sounded like a busted carburetor coming from down below and looked to see Mahalia sitting at my feet. She looked up at me and started hissing as if to say, "*Stay out of my shit.*"

"Don't hiss at me you ungrateful fur ball. I'm the only one between you and starvation." I closed the blue case. Mahalia ignored me and started grooming herself.

By now, my wrist had swelled to twice its size. I needed to get to the emergency room. I switched off the lights and headed out the front door, looking back briefly to see the glow of a pair of indignant blue eyes staring at me from the top of the television.

Three hours later I was back at home with a tightly bandaged wrist, an ample supply of ibuprofen, and some gel filled ice packs. Thankfully, my wrist wasn't broken, just badly sprained. I popped two more ibuprofen and slept on my couch so I could keep my wrist elevated by resting it on the back of the couch. I dreamt I was lying curled up on the hearth of a fireplace. I was cold and stiff. I couldn't move. I couldn't scream. I was frozen. All I could see of my surroundings was the inside of the fireplace I was lying next to and a stiff dog tail. I soon realized I was the dog. The tail was mine. And I wasn't just any dog, either. I was Clair Easton's dead dog, Jeeves. I tried to make a sound but couldn't. I heard a voice coming closer. It was Clair Easton's voice.

"Here you go, Jeeves. Here's a nice playmate for you." She bent down near my tail and set something next to me on the hearth.

I could see enough of Clair to see she had a pair of hedge clippers sticking out of the side of her neck. Every time she spoke, blood poured from her mouth. But I couldn't turn away.

"Meet your new little friend." She turned me

around and I was almost cold nose to cold nose with a black and white cat. It was Ms. Flack's missing cat, Tamsin. The cat had been stuffed as well. Its mouth was pulled back over its sharp little teeth in a permanent hiss. But unlike me, the cat could still yowl which it did loudly in my ear.

I woke up with a start and found myself lying on the floor between my couch and the trunk that served as my coffee table. The sound of my alarm clock buzzed loudly from my bedroom. It wasn't until I'd showered and was on my way to work that I realized the significance of dreaming about the pets of two dead women.

It was the one thing that Clair Easton and Ivy Flack had had in common. Both women had been very fond of their pets. Now both Clair Easton and her dog were dead, and Ms. Flack was dead and her cat was missing. It finally hit me that the cat hadn't run away. Ms. Flack's killer must have killed her cat as well. The cat must have attacked the killer and been killed because of it. But the killer couldn't leave a dead cat behind because then everyone would know that Ms. Flack's death hadn't been an accidental electrocution.

But what I couldn't figure out was why in the world was poor Jeeves killed? He died almost a week before his master. The only reason for Jeeves dying first that I could possibly think of would be that whoever killed Clair Easton must have planned her death at least a week in advance and didn't want her dog attacking them or barking and alerting Clair, or her neighbors, to their presence in her house or on her property. Maybe the killer learned their lesson after being attacked by Ms. Flack's cat and didn't want to take any chances the second time around.

Of course I could be completely wrong about all of this, which was probably the case. I knew why Ms. Flack had most likely been killed. But since Gerald hadn't really stolen her money, why would someone kill Clair Easton? Plus, hadn't Emma Kirby claimed that Jeeves had gotten into some rat poison in Clair Easton's garden shed. Not that it wouldn't be easy enough for someone to feed a dog something that had been poisoned. I guess the bigger question was why I cared so much. I really didn't need this added stress. Carl was coming over after work that night and I needed to decide what I was going to tell him. That's what I needed to be worrying about. Not two dead women and their dead pets. I decided then and there that I was going to put it completely out of my mind. After all, it had nothing to do with me. Ah, if it were only that simple.

Fridays are half days at the literacy center. Fridays are also pretty sparsely attended. Today's attendance was worse than usual. It was just me, my coworker and fellow teacher, Rhonda Hammond, and exactly two students. I blamed it on the weather. It was gorgeous outside and for once not too hot. I wanted to be someplace else as well. The county fair had just started and thoughts of funnel cake, cotton candy, and corn dogs on a stick filled my brain. I wanted to leave. Instead, Rhonda and I graded papers and watched the clock. We didn't even talk much. Rhonda wasn't in the best of moods.

"Are you trying to grade that quiz or kill it?" I asked, after watching her stab at the paper with a red marker. Rhonda gave me an annoyed look.

"Why are men so damned stupid?" she asked loudly to no one in particular. One of our two students, thankfully both of them were female, glanced up at us and laughed and nodded in agreement.

"What'd he do this time?" I knew she was talking about her husband, Kevin. Lately, he couldn't do anything right.

"For the last two nights people have been prank calling our house. We answer the phone and someone will ask us what kind of poopies we have. How many poopies do we have? Or what color are our poopies? Are they big poopies or little poopies? I was about to call the police until I saw this." She pulled a copy of the *Willow News-Gazette* out of her desk drawer and tossed it at me. I picked it up and looked. The paper had been turned to the classified section and was folded in half. I couldn't tell what I was supposed to be looking at.

"Okay. Help me out here."

"It's right here." She pointed to an ad in the center of the page.

I read it and almost wet myself. It said: *Beautiful Mixed Breed Poopies. Free to a good home. Poopies are eight weeks old and have had shots.* I could tell she was highly pissed. I laughed anyway.

"It's not funny! Kevin put that ad in the paper. I asked him to make sure to have the person at the paper read it back to him to make sure it was correct. He swore he did. He couldn't have or we wouldn't have idiots calling our house asking about our poopies. We got into the biggest argument last night."

I laughed even harder.

"Whatever. I'm glad you find my misery so funny. I need a damned cigarette." She rubbed the fingertips of her right hand together. Something she always did when she was craving nicotine. She pulled her cigarette case and lighter from her purse and stalked out of the room.

I started reading the rest of the newspaper. One story in particular caught my eye: "Murder Witness Breaks 30 year Silence."

The story was about an 82-year-old Urbana woman named Sybil Myers. Thirty years ago, Sybil Myers had been out late walking her dog and witnessed Maurice Groves's brutal murder at the hands of the Righteous Whites. The article went on to say that despite what she had seen, she'd never spoken about that night to anyone besides the police. There were more details about what Ms. Myers had witnessed, but I'd stopped reading. Not because I couldn't stomach the gory details, but because I'd finally figured out why Clair Easton and Jeeves may have been killed.

Sybil Myers had been out late one night walking her dog and had seen something she wasn't supposed to see. According to Dennis, Clair Easton also had a habit of walking Jeeves at all hours. What if when she was out walking him and saw something? Something that got her killed. I remembered my visit to her house. She'd never mentioned anything about her dog having been poisoned by someone. She was a paranoid woman, but she never mentioned seeing anybody or anything that was a threat to her life. She'd only been interested in getting her money back. Could she have seen something that she didn't even realize she'd seen? Was there something weird going on in her neighborhood late at night? If so, how was Ivy Flack involved? But, again, it wasn't my problem. I needed to be thinking about what I was going to tell Carl that night.

Later that evening, Carl and I sat across the kitchen table from each other eating the Chinese takeout he'd brought over. He was still wearing the suit he'd worn to work and was quiet and subdued. So far he hadn't even mentioned his marriage proposal, which should have made me happy but didn't. I was in the middle of telling him all about how I almost clobbered Mrs. Carson's son, Stevie, with a baseball bat. I was trying to get him to laugh and not having much success, when he made a startling announcement.

"I'm moving to Atlanta."

"Huh?"

"I applied for a job with a law firm in Atlanta a year ago, right after Vanessa left me, before I even met you. I obviously didn't get the job but they were impressed enough with me that when the person they hired quit, they gave me a call this morning and offered me the job."

"And you took it?"

"Yes." He wiped sweet and sour sauce from his mouth. I felt like I'd been kicked in the stomach.

"I thought you liked your job?"

"I do. But I need a change. This law firm takes on

a lot of high profile criminal cases. I'd still be involved in criminal law, only from the other side. And the money is almost three times what I'm making at the prosecutor's office. How could I turn it down?" I sat staring at him, my eyes rapidly filling with tears.

"I know you'll miss your grandmother, but she can come visit us anytime she wants. She can even have her own room," he said when I didn't say anything.

"What are you talking about?" I wiped my eyes with my napkin. He looked as confused as I did.

"You know, after we get married." He was staring at me and all I could do was look down at my half-empty takeout container.

"Sorry. I need to do this the right way, don't I?" He pulled a small black ring box out of his suit pocket and laid it on the table between us.

I reluctantly picked it up and opened it. Inside was a half carat marquis cut diamond engagement ring. Carl reached over and took the ring from the box and got out of his chair, bending down on one knee. He took my left hand and slid the ring onto my ring finger.

"Kendra Clayton, will you marry me?"

I felt like all the air had been sucked out of the room. I was lightheaded. He continued to stare at me expectantly, hope shining in his eyes. I didn't know what to say. I did love Carl and the thought of him moving to Atlanta, and away from me, made me sad. But I didn't know if I was ready to get married, either.

"I just need a little more time, Carl."

Carl's face fell and he slowly got to his feet and started walking to the door. I hurried after him.

"I'm sorry. Please don't be mad. I love you. But I just need more time to think."

"I'm not mad," he snapped, then, hearing how his words came out he grabbed my hand and squeezed it hard. "I just thought we were on the same page. I thought you wanted this, too."

"It's just all happening so fast. Getting married is a huge step and now moving away to a big city where I won't know anybody but you."

"Damn! I'm getting really tired of this small-town mentality of yours. I guess it was asking too much for you to be happy and excited. This could be a whole new beginning for us, a new life. Why are you so hell-bent on staying in this town? It's dead. Nothing's going on here. You don't even have a fulltime job. Don't you want more than this?"

"My small town mentality?" I snatched my hand out of his and took a step back. "Do you hear yourself? You sound just like your uppity mother," I said, referring to the fact that Carl's mother, Martha Brumfield, didn't think too highly of me because I worked two part-time jobs, one of them as a lowly restaurant hostess, thus giving me yet another reason not to want to rush down the aisle with her son.

"Leave my mother out of this!"

"Okay, let me get this straight. So, because I'm not jumping for joy because you're leaving and didn't so much as ask *me*, the woman you claim to love and want to marry, how I feel about you taking a job out of state, I'm un-ambitious? I'm supposed to just blindly follow you wherever you go without question and be damned happy for the invitation? I can't believe you. Here," I pulled the ring off my finger and shoved it into his hand. "I hope you're very happy in Atlanta." I shoved him out the door and slammed it behind him. I could hear him cursing and pacing angrily in front of my door for a few minutes before giving the door a savage kick and leaving. It appeared my decision had been made for me.

Chapter Twenty-One

THREE HOURS LATER, I was sitting in my car parked two doors down from Clair Easton's house. There's nothing like drowning your sorrows by immersing yourself in matters that don't really concern you. I chalked it up to my small-town mentality. There was still yellow crime scene tape across Clair Easton's front door. It was after midnight and the neighborhood was dark and deserted. Most of the houses that I could see had no lights on, indicating that the residents were either asleep or not at home. I got out of my car and looked around briefly before heading up Clair Easton's driveway. I knew I wouldn't be able to get into her house, but her house wasn't really what I'd come to see. It was her garden shed I was interested in. Emma Kirby said that Jeeves had died as a result of getting into some rat poison kept in Clair's garden shed.

I headed to the end of the driveway, stopping in front of a large detached garage. To my left there was a high ivy covered wooden gate leading to the backyard. I tried to push it open, but it was latched from the other side. There was no other entrance to the backyard. I tried to wedge some sticks I found on the ground through the gate to pull up the latch. The first one I tried was too thin and snapped and the next one was too fat to fit through the gap. I looked around and saw a trellis on the side of the garage next to the fence.

I hurried over and started to climb. Once I was level with the top of the fence, I swung my right leg over the top. I got my balance by bracing myself against the fence and the side of the garage. I made sure to put most of the pressure on my non-sprained wrist before swinging my other leg over and jumping down into the backyard. I landed on my ass on top of a pile of compost. I quickly jumped up and brushed grass clippings and fruit peelings off of my pants. I pulled the small flashlight I'd brought with me out of my pocket to make sure it wasn't broken. It wasn't and I switched it on.

The backyard was huge. The grass was a little long but, from what I could see in the dark, it was lush and green. There was a large gazebo with peeling white paint and a peeked roof in the center of the backyard. I shone the flashlight inside but except for mouse droppings, and a broken stone birdbath covered in bird crap lying against one wall, it was empty. The shed was at the back of the yard and was a big gray metal box with a flat roof. There was a large rusty padlock looped through the handles. I doubted very seriously that Jeeves could work a padlock. If he'd gotten into something in the shed, how did he get in there? I jerked hard on the lock, and to my surprise, it opened. I slid open the shed door and winced as a loud metal scraping sound penetrated the darkness.

I hesitated a few seconds before stepping inside. The smell of gas, rust, and manure smacked me in the face. Once inside, I could see there were shelves lining the back of the shed. On the shelves were various sizes and shapes of ceramic pots for plants, an ancient grime covered gasoline can, a large half empty sack of manure enriched lawn fertilizer, a rusted out lawn chair, and a shovel. There was a spray bottle of insecticide, but no rat poison. There was no way Jeeves could have even gotten into the shed let alone gotten into poison. Someone must have given him something poisoned.

I started to leave and head back towards the gate when I heard voices. I crouched down against one side of the open shed door and switched off my flashlight. The voices were getting closer and were coming from the other side of the fence behind the shed. I saw a section of the fence swing outward as another gate, completely hidden by the thick ivy, opened. I remained still as a statue as two figures walked into the backyard right past the shed and me. It wasn't until they'd gotten to the gazebo and walked through a narrow shaft of moonlight that I was able to make out who it was. It was Gerald Tate and Dennis's mother, Emma Kirby. Oh, boy. They went inside the gazebo and I crept closer. I could see them embracing through the gazebo's open latticework. They were pressed together so tightly they looked like one shadowy, pulsating entity. Soon the sound of heavy breathing and moaning joined the sound of crickets.

To get a better look, I shone my flashlight inside and saw that Gerald had Emma Kirby pressed against the wall. His pants were down and her legs were wrapped around his waist. I knew Gerald was a dog but damn! I could not believe he was doing Dennis's mama. They were getting louder and louder. I watched as she unwrapped her legs from his middle and he spun her around and bent her over taking her from behind. He was banging her so hard I thought her head might go right through the wall. They were so into it, they didn't notice the light from my flashlight. Hell, I could have done the electric slide dressed as Smoky the Bear right in front of them and they wouldn't have noticed. I turned the flashlight off.

I wondered how long the two of them had been fooling around in Clair Easton's gazebo? Is this what she'd seen that had gotten her killed? Was Jeeves poisoned in order to keep him from barking and alerting Clair to the presence of illicit fornicators in her backyard? But had she seen them anyway and threatened to tell Emma Kirby's husband? How would Ellis Kirby handle knowing his wife was getting busy with their son's black friend in a neighbor's gazebo? Probably not well considering he'd had a conniption over Jeeves digging up his azaleas. I'm thinking having his wife diddled behind his back might send him over the edge.

This new development also put Gerald back into the mix. Maybe Cherisse hadn't told her buddy Ms. Flack about Gerald stealing from Clair Easton. Maybe, she found out he was screwing Emma Kirby and was hurt and told Ms. Flack who in turn blackmailed him and was killed for it. If that was the case, then Cherisse could have also lied to me about the conversation I'd overheard between her and Gerald about Sunny Abou being deported. I was so lost in thought I didn't realize the noises in the gazebo had stopped. I peeked inside again and saw Emma and Gerald hurriedly fixing their clothes. They kissed passionately and then headed for the door of the gazebo. I crouched down out of sight and watched as they walked across the backyard and disappeared through the hidden gate. As I passed by the entrance to the gazebo, something in the grass glittered in the moonlight and caught my eye. I bent down to pick it up. It was a platinum bracelet with large pearls dangling from it. I recognized it as the bracelet Emma

Kirby was wearing when Dennis had given me a ride home. I thought it only fair that I return it to her.

I arrived at the Kirby home the next morning and sat in my car in front of the house until I saw Ellis Kirby leave in his shiny silver Jaguar, followed about ten minutes later by Dennis in his work clothes. Wanting some time alone with the lady of the house, before the men folk came back, I hurried up the steep driveway and had to catch my breath before ringing the doorbell. The front double doors were high, narrow, arched and made entirely of glass. The center of the doors was decorated in frosted, white geometric designs that kept visitors, both invited and unwanted, from being able to look directly into the house. I had to ring the doorbell a second time before a young and very pretty redhead wearing khaki pants, tennis shoes, and a gold polo style shirt with the words Willow Memorial Hospital stitched over the right breast.

"I'm here to see Mrs. Kirby. Is she at home?" I asked politely.

"Mrs. Kirby is having her physical therapy. Is she expecting you?"

I opened my mouth to lie but the loud crash of broken glass, followed by the sound of Emma Kirby yelling, stopped me cold.

"Ashley! Ashley, come quick!"

The startled young woman rushed off and I followed her into a large, airy dining room with large windows that overlooked the backyard. Emma Kirby was standing over the remains of a broken glass pitcher and a puddle of spilled orange juice on the dining room's parquet floor.

"It just slipped right out of my hand!" she wailed as she clenched and unclenched her fingers. Her knuckles were red and enlarged. Dennis had mentioned she had arthritis. That's why she must be having physical therapy. Emma Kirby looked startled and confused when she saw me come in behind the maid.

"It's okay, Mrs. Kirby," said Ashley with a weary sigh. But Emma Kirby was too busy staring at me and looking agitated.

"Ashley, how many times have I told you that you can't have friends over while you're working?" she told the young woman, obviously not remembering me from the night before when Dennis gave me a ride home.

Ashley looked horrified and opened her mouth to protest. But since I wasn't exactly digging the way Emma Kirby was looking at us like we were about to tie her up and start swinging from the chandelier, and picking our noses with the shrimp forks, I spoke up.

"Mrs. Kirby, I'm sorry to bother you. Remember

me from the other day? I went to school with Dennis."

She was still looking confused. I tried again.

"I'm Estelle Mays's granddaughter. Dennis gave me a ride home from the police station, remember?"

"Oh, yes, of course. It's Kim, right?" Her faced flushed slightly with what I assumed was embarrassment.

"Kendra, actually." I wondered why my name was so hard for some people to remember. "I came by to see Dennis but he's not home. I was just wondering if you knew when he'd be home?"

"Why don't we go in the family room while Ashley cleans up this mess." She waved a dismissive hand at the broken glass on the floor. Ashley gave her evil look before heading to the pantry for a broom. I didn't blame her one bit. She wasn't the maid.

I was tempted to point out to Emma Kirby that it was *her* mess. Instead, I followed her through a spotless gourmet kitchen—heavy on the black granite and stainless steel—into a room just off the kitchen.

The room was large and decorated in soft blues, browns, and greens and though I could tell it had been professionally decorated, was warm, inviting, and comfortable. The same large floor to ceiling windows that had been in the dining room were also in this room. From the windows I could see a beautifully landscaped garden and a small white cottage at the back of the property on the other side of a large kidney-shaped swimming pool. I remembered Dennis telling me he lived in the cottage.

"Now why did you need to see Dennis?" Emma Kirby asked me after we'd settled into comfortable armchairs near the windows. She was casually dressed in tan slacks and a red V-neck shirt. Her mid length ash blonde hair was tied back from her face with a paisley scarf. She had on simple black ballet flats that probably cost more than my whole outfit.

"Um, nothing really important," I said, scrambling to come up with an excuse. I hadn't expected her to ask me why I was there or given much thought to my reason for coming over beyond returning her bracelet and watching her reaction. Now that I was there, I couldn't figure out just how to bring it up without revealing why I'd been lurking around Clair Easton's backyard in the first place. "Just reunion committee business," I finally told her.

"I just assumed the reunion was cancelled."

"Well, we haven't officially decided to cancel it. We all feel really horrible about Ms. Flack, but she wasn't really a member of our graduating class. There's no reason to cancel the reunion."

"Good. Then I guess I'll go ahead and donate that money I was going to donate to the reunion."

Just then Ashley came into the room with two

pills and a glass of water on a tray. Emma Kirby snatched the pills and downed them in one big gulp of water.

"What money?" I asked when Ashley left the room.

"Dennis told me about the reunion fund money going missing. I sent Dennis over to tell Ivy Flack I'd be happy to donate five thousand dollars so you all could have your reunion. Then she died so I just assumed it would be cancelled.

"Wow. That's awfully nice of you. I'm sure that would have made Ms. Flack happy."

"You know, I thought it was really odd that Ivy Flack was even on the committee in the first place. Dennis said she was a lonely woman. I bet he was right. I mean she wasn't married and had no kids. She probably didn't have anything else better to do."

"I wouldn't say that," I said suddenly getting an idea. "She was hardly lonely. I think she probably joined the committee to be near Gerald. They had the hots for each other."

Emma Kirby's face went momentarily slack. Then her eyes narrowed, and her lips tightened. It was a few long seconds before she spoke again. "Really. They were involved?" she asked slowly, looking down at the floor. I should have probably felt guilty about smearing the reputation of a dead woman. Strangely, I didn't. Go figure. Maybe it was because Ivy Flack hadn't been the person I thought she was. As for Gerald, I had no sympathy for him whatsoever.

"I wouldn't exactly say they were dating, if you know what I mean. But one night before one of our committee meetings, I got to the high school early and went to Ms. Flack's office. Her office door wasn't all the way shut and I saw them together. They were all over each other."

Emma's face turned bright red. It never ceased to amaze me how cheaters could get so upset when they found out they'd been cheated on themselves. Surely, she hadn't thought she was the only one Gerald was sleeping with? Could she truly be that naive?

"Maybe you were mistaken. Maybe it wasn't Gerald," she said in a slightly quavering voice.

"No. It was him alright. I've known Gerald since high school. I know him when I see him. Plus, Ms. Flack was his type," I said, plunging the knife in deeper.

"What type would that be?" she asked in a cold flat voice.

"I don't like to gossip," I said, hoping my nose wasn't about to do a Pinocchio. "But you know Gerald's first wife was ten years older than him. I think he's really into older women, especially older women who have money. Gerald has fillet mignon taste on a ground beef budget. Not to mention all those kids and ex-wives to support."

Emma Kirby stood up abruptly. "Dennis had to go into work for a couple of hours. He'll be home later. I'm sorry to be so rude, but I just remembered I have an appointment. Ashley will see you out."

She left the room abruptly. I just sat there wondering what to do next. I was looking out the window when I spotted something odd in the backyard. I got up and walked over to the window for a closer look. Down below, about ten feet from Dennis' cottage, was a flowerbed of azaleas. All the flowers were a beautiful intense pink except an area about a foot and a half wide near the edge of the flowerbed where they were bright orange. It didn't match at all. This must have been the spot that Jeeves had dug up and there must not have been any more pink flowers to replace what he'd destroyed. No wonder Ellis Kirby had been so upset. No wonder Clair Easton hadn't had any flowers in her own yard, with a dog like Jeeves. But it seemed odd to me that Jeeves hadn't dug up the whole garden. Why just that one spot?

I turned to see Ashley silently waiting to escort me out. Once I was behind the wheel of my car, I saw Emma Kirby pulling out of the driveway so fast in her hunter green Range Rover that she backed over the aluminum trash can sitting on the curb. I caught a glimpse of her face before she tore off down the street. She had blood in her eyes. I knew where she was going and followed at a discreet distance.

Minutes later, she arrived at Gerald's two-story town house on nearby Terra Cotta Drive. She pulled into his driveway behind his black Beemer and was out of her car, pounding on his door, before I'd barely turned the corner. I pulled up across the street just as Gerald came to the door looking bewildered. Emma pushed her way into the house. I got out of my car, crossed the street, and stood right outside Gerald's still open front door, looking inside. I couldn't see Gerald and Emma, but just like the night before in the gazebo, I could hear them just fine. I walked into the house and peaked around the corner. The two of them were in the dining room and didn't notice me as I stood on the sidelines watching them.

"What the hell are you talking about?" Gerald said in exasperation.

"You know exactly what I'm talking about, you lying asshole!" screamed Emma.

"Emmy. Calm down. I swear I don't know what you're talking about. I really don't."

"Don't you dare call me Emmy, you bastard! I know all about you and Ivy Flack!"

"Ivy Flack?"

"You were fucking her! And after everything I did to protect you! How could you?" Emma buried her face in her hands and started to sob. Gerald tried to touch her but she jerked away from him.

"Are you crazy? I never fucked Ivy Flack. Who the hell told you that lie?"

"That would be me," I said, speaking up and causing them to turn in my direction. Gerald's mouth fell open, while Emma stabbed an accusing finger in my direction.

"She saw the two of you. She saw you with your hands all over Ivy Flack!"

"She didn't see shit cause I never fucked Ivy Flack! I don't know what the hell you're trying to pull, but you better tell her the truth, Kendra." He took a menacing step towards me. I stood my ground.

"He's right, Mrs. Kirby. I never saw him with Ivy Flack. But, I did see him with you last night in Clair Easton's gazebo."

Emma looked relieved upon hearing I'd lied about her lover then got big-eyed when she realized I knew she had a lover. Gerald got really quiet, probably because he'd suddenly remembered that I also knew about him and Cherisse Craig. I wondered if Cherisse had also informed him that I knew about him and Sunny Abou? Where did the man find the time?

"Why would you tell me such a lie?" Emma

313

looked confused.

"Don't say another word. She doesn't have any proof that we were together last night."

"I have this." I pulled the bracelet from my purse and waved it in the air. "I found it right outside Clair Easton's gazebo last night after the two of you left." Emma gasped and reached out for the bracelet. I stepped back and held it out of her reach.

"That's mine. Give it back at once." She headed towards me. I gave Gerald an I'm-about-to-bust-you-for-real look and he grabbed Emma's arm before she'd taken two steps.

"Hold up. She must want something, right? Is that it? Do you want money to keep quiet?"

I laughed. "Are you offering me Mrs. Kirby's money? Because anyone who knows you knows you don't have any money. No, what I want is information." I twirled the bracelet around my finger.

"About?" asked Emma Kirby, eyeing her bracelet.

"About whether Clair Easton knew the two of you were using her gazebo as a love nest. Is that why she was killed? Did she find out about your affair and threaten to tell your husband, Mrs. Kirby?"

"What?" they both said in unison. Then looked at each other.

"You think one of us killed Clair?" said Emma Kirby. Gerald laughed.

"Dennis warned me about this," he said, shaking his head. "Kendra thinks we're all murderers, don't you? First she accused Audrey Grant and Cherisse Craig of killing Ms. Flack. Now, she's accusing us of killing Clair Easton. You're really pathetic, you know that?"

Emma Kirby ignored her balding boy toy and took a step closer to me. "Why in the world would you think we would hurt Clair?"

"You were the one who told me Clair's dog, Jeeves, got into some rat poison in her garden shed. I looked in her garden shed last night. There was no rat poison in there. Someone poisoned Jeeves, and it was probably the same person who murdered her. She must have seen something that someone wanted to keep her quiet about. Did she see the two of you in her gazebo and threaten to tell your husband?"

"My husband doesn't give a damn what I do. We stopped sleeping together years ago. All he cares about are his precious flowers. He knows I'm sleeping with someone else. He doesn't care. Hasn't said one word to me about it. He got more upset over Jeeves digging up his azaleas. He actually confronted Clair about it," she said bitterly.

"Well, what about the rat poison story? There's no way Jeeves could have gotten into that shed."

"I was just repeating what I'd heard around the neighborhood. That's the rumor that's going around, that Jeeves got into rat poison. And last night was the first and only time we ever used Clair's gazebo. Usually, I walk over here, but Ellis and I got in late from a dinner dance at the club and I didn't feel like walking over here in the dark. I remembered Clair's gazebo. It was closer. She wasn't using it anymore, so why not?"

"Well then what were you talking about when I overheard you saying you protected Gerald?"

"I protected him from getting fired from his job. Gerald's boss, John Howard Wheatley, is an old family friend. When that silly African girl on his job tried to ruin his career, I had a talk with John and got everything straightened out." She grabbed Gerald's hand and smiled lovingly up at him. Gerald gave me a smug look. So much for her not knowing about Sunny. I wanted to puke. The reason for him climbing into bed with Emma Kirby, his friend's mother, was suddenly crystal clear. What a loser.

"You knew about Sunny being deported?"

"I'm the one who suggested it," Emma said sweetly. "It was for her own good. The poor thing was unstable. Why else would she steal Clair Easton's money and try to pin it on Gerald. All because he wouldn't succumb to her advances."

I rolled my eyes. Gerald was looking nervous. He knew that I knew the truth.

"You can give Emma back her bracelet, Kendra,

and then get out of my house before I call the police and tell them you stole it." Gerald put his arm protectively around Emma.

Emma held out her hand, and I reluctantly dropped the bracelet into it and turned to go. When I got to the door, I looked back and saw the two of them wrapped in each other's arms. I shouldn't have done it, but I just couldn't help myself.

"Will you be going to Africa with Gerald to visit his and Sunny's baby, Mrs. Kirby?" I hurried out the door to the sound of Emma Kirby's outraged voice screaming.

"Baby! What baby?"

Chapter Twenty-Two

WHEN I GOT HOME late that afternoon, after having had lunch with Mama and going to the library to study for my test on Monday, there was a burgundy and white Lincoln Town Car parked in front of my house. I didn't know anyone with a car like that, so I didn't pay much attention to it and headed up the steps to my apartment. But a loud blast from the car's horn stopped me in my tracks. I turned to see a vertically challenged, fiftyish black man with permed hair jump out of the driver's side door. It was Lewis Watts and he was a sight to behold dressed in a hot pink three-piece suit trimmed in white leopard printed fur with matching hat, platform shoes, and long white cape. A white cane with what looked like a large crystal doorknob on top was clutched in one chubby fist. I didn't blink an eye. Lewis dressed like this all the time. He was grinning at me at first, then looked me up and down and scowled.

"I knew it! Dammit, Kelly, what the hell are you wearing?"

I looked down at my jean shorts and tank top and then back at him in confusion. Then it hit me and I groaned and leaned against my railing for support before I fainted. I had a date with this fool. I'd forgotten all about it.

"Can't we do this some other time?" I whined and looked up and down the street praying no one was witnessing this.

"Hell no! You ain't gettin' outta this, girl. We had a deal," Lewis said indignantly, slamming the tip of his cane on the sidewalk.

"But I'm not ready."

"We got plenty a time. Now, go git dressed. I'll be in the car. And don't keep me waitin' too long. I got to have my cousin Leon's Lincoln back to him by midnight."

"And what happens if you don't? Will you turn into a pumpkin?" I asked hopefully. He just scowled at me and hopped back into the car.

Wanting nothing more than to get this over with, I went inside, took a quick shower, and changed into a blue silk halter dress I'd bought last year at Déjà Vu thrift shop, and the only pair of truly dressy shoes I owned, a pair of three-inch silver ankle strap sandals. After putting on a sterling and lapis choker and spritzing on some vanilla perfume, I headed out of my apartment with all the enthusiasm of an inmate going to the gas chamber. As I headed down the steps, Lewis jumped out of the car and ran around to the passenger's side to open the door for me, staring hard at my attire in the process with a slight frown on his face.

"Do I pass the test?" I asked him.

"You look real...*nice*," he said, still frowning. His emphasis on the word nice wasn't lost on me. Had he been expecting me to trot out of the house in a bustier and thong?

"This is as good as it gets. Let's go before I change my mind." I got in the car and immediately sank down into the fur-lined front seat. *Lord, don't let anybody see me with this idiot,* I prayed.

Five minutes later, cruising to the soulful sounds of James Brown, we pulled onto Route 70 heading towards Dayton. I was greatly relieved to be going to another city for our date, but something was starting to smell fishy and it wasn't just Lewis's cologne which he wore so heavy I had to crack my window. It was the way he kept giving me sidelong looks and chuckling.

"Where are we going?"

"To a ball, like I told you," he said, keeping his eyes firmly on the road ahead.

"What kind of ball?"

"Relax, Kelly. It's one I go to every year. It's put on by my club, The Distinguished Gents," he said proudly.

"This isn't a formal is it?" I was still getting a

320

weird feeling and Lewis's shit-eating smirk wasn't helping matters any.

"Just sit back and enjoy the ride, okay, baby doll. It'll be fun. You'll see," he said cryptically, laughing outright now. I felt a chill go down my spine.

"What kind of club is The Distinguished Gents?"

"It's a motorcycle club," he said smugly.

"Are you serious? You ride a motorcycle?" I got an instant mental image of Lewis perched atop a Harley with his little feet dangling on either side unable to reach the pedals. I burst out laughing.

"What's so funny?" he said huffily.

"You on a motorcycle."

"I didn't say we rode motorcycles, Miss Snotty. See, that's how much you know."

"You belong to a motorcycle club that doesn't ride motorcycles?"

"Naw. See, Slinky Bledsoe, one of the cats in the club, has a Ducati and we all take turns sittin' on it."

I laughed even harder.

"Cain't none of us actually ride it 'cause we all on disability—or least I used to be. They don't know I got kicked off so don't be blabbin', you hear me?"

"It all depends on how bad you get on my nerves," I warned him.

Half an hour later, we pulled into the back of a crowded parking lot of a VFW hall. Lewis turned nervously to me and then looked quickly around the lot before pulling a brown paper bag from under the front seat and handing it to me.

"Here. You need a little somethin' somethin'. Put this on," he commanded. I snatched the bag out of his hand and opened it. Inside, was a long, curly, white blonde wig.

"What the hell is this?"

"Just put it on, Kelly, please," he pleaded.

"Why?" I asked, craning my neck to try and see the other people who were arriving for the ball. That's when I noticed the attire of the other attendees. My mouth fell open and I got out of the car and headed towards the banquet hall. Lewis was hot on my heels still waving the blonde wig and pleading with me.

"Kelly, please, just put the damned wig on, girl. Why you got to be so difficult?"

When I got to the front entrance of the hall, I saw what was written on the large marquee over the door and it all became clear. It read: "Welcome to The Distinguished Gents 15th Annual Pimp and Ho Ball". I watched as a steady stream of black people of every size, shape, age, and hue walked into the hall dressed in every color under the rainbow. Men wore suits, large brimmed hats with feathers, alligator shoes, and long fur coats. Women sported gold and silver sequined mini dresses, hot pants, tube tops, fishnet stockings, and sky-high heels and boots.

Hair that wasn't hidden under cheap and cheesy looking wigs was worn slicked back, teased out, spiked up, long and wavy, or bald. People smiled at me with mouths filled with gold and diamond studded teeth. The loud, pulsing music coming from the hall was old school funk from the seventies. I recognized the song playing as the Bar-Kays's "Shake Your Rump to the Funk". I could feel my own rump start to move. Lewis finally caught up with me at the door panting and holding out the wig.

But it was the smell of barbeque ribs, fried chicken, macaroni and cheese, collard greens, and peach cobbler wafting from the hall and tickling me under the nose that got me in the end. I took the wig from Lewis, who grinned. But instead of putting it on my head, I snatched the fur trimmed hat from his head, slapped the wig on him in its place, put the hat on my head, broke the brim down over one eye, and strutted into the hall to Lewis's shouts of outrage. He could scream and holler all he wanted. If I had to be here, then I was damned well gonna be the pimp. Kendra Clayton was nobody's ho.

Lewis dropped me off at my apartment at twenty to twelve. I was filled to the gills with good food, my feet were sore from all the dancing I'd done, and I had a slight buzz from all the fuzzy navels I'd downed in the course of the evening. Hell, I even posed for pictures sitting on Slinky Bledsoe's infamous Ducati. My wrist was feeling much better, too. Lewis looked at me and grinned. After taking first place in the Super Fly Best Dressed Contest, and second place in the pimp stroll, he forgave me for stealing his hat.

"I bet you'd rather cut yo' arm off then admit you had a good time," he said, laughing.

"I have to admit it was fun." I was laughing too. But inwardly hoping no one ever found out I actually went out with Lewis Watts.

"See, I knew there was a good time in you just dyin' to get out, Kelly." He put his arm around me and leaned in for a kiss. I wasn't that drunk.

"Don't press your luck." I hopped out of the car and slammed the door shut. I came around to the driver's side and leaned down into the window. Lewis puckered up thinking he was going to get a kiss after all.

"And for the millionth time, it's Kendra, not Kelly." I headed into my apartment.

A quick check of my voice mail showed no calls from Carl. Disappointed, I ran a hot bath and got undressed while humming the tune to George Clinton's "Atomic Dog". That song was one of the reasons my own dogs were aching. I'd danced to the entire twelve-minute club remix in three-inch heels. I was thinking about dogs chasing cats when it dawned on me that I'd forgotten to feed Mahalia.

"*Crap!*" I said aloud. I quickly put my robe and slippers on and hurried to Mrs. Carson's to feed her spoiled cat.

Mahalia was pacing impatiently next to me and shooting me reproachful looks with almond-shaped blue eyes as I filled her bowl with cat food. I didn't like the cat but felt bad that, no thanks to me, she'd gone all day without food. I wasn't much better than Stevie. No sooner had she bent her sleek head over the bowl than the loud sound of a dog barking from outside sent her jumping straight into my arms.

"It's okay, Mahalia. That bad dog can't get to you in here." I stroked her arched back and winced as she started to hiss and spit when the dog continued barking. She must not have found my words too comforting because she shot out of my arms and scrambled to the top of the refrigerator where she continued to hiss and spit. I walked over to the kitchen window and looked out. I saw a dog in the backyard. A large German Shepard. It continued to bark at the house like it knew Mahalia was inside. I shook my head and went back to my apartment and took a bath.

Afterwards, I lay in bed once again thinking about dogs and cats. I thought about the dream I'd had that I was Jeeves lying stiff and stuffed on Clair Easton's fireplace hearth, and about Ivy Flack's missing and probably dead cat, Tamsin, and Clair Easton walking Jeeves at all hours of the night and him digging up Ellis Kirby's azaleas. I wondered what Dennis was doing while Jeeves dug a hole in his father's flower bed not ten feet from his cottage?

I thought about Emma Kirby donating money to replace the missing reunion fund money and sat straight up in bed. I'd been so busy trying to find out if Clair Easton had seen Emma Kirby and Gerald together that I'd completely forgotten about what Emma had told me. She'd sent Dennis to tell Ms. Flack that she'd be willing to donate money to the reunion fund. Dennis never said one word about seeing Ms. Flack after that last committee meeting. Dennis loved reminding people that his parents had money. He'd have bragged about his mother saving the reunion but didn't. Why? Did he see Ms. Flack the day she died? And something else dawned on me as I thought about Dennis. His wrist was still bandaged, which I thought was strange at the time. But it wouldn't be strange if it were the opposite wrist from the one he sprained. What was underneath that bandage? I had a good idea and felt sick to my stomach because I realized that Jeeves hadn't just dug up flowers.

It was almost one thirty in the morning when I crept up the Kirby's steep driveway. All of the lights inside the house were off. There were no cars parked in the driveway. I walked under the arched portico, down the side of the house, towards the backyard, and prayed they didn't have some kind of motion sensored security system that was about to go off. I heard a car door slam somewhere off in the distance and instinctively pressed myself against the side of the house. Once I caught my breath, I continued on until I got to the fence that led to the backyard and garden. Unlike Clair Easton's gate, it was open and I walked through into the dark backyard. I pulled out my flashlight and turned it on.

The backyard was beautifully landscaped and filled with flowers and neatly trimmed bushes. I could smell honeysuckle and roses. Water trickled from a fountain in the middle of small pond filled with koi. All around the garden there were stone pavers that led to benches in what I assumed where the shadiest areas. The only light was coming from beyond the garden in the well-lit pool area. The area I was interested in was the bed of azaleas on the other side of the pool near Dennis's cottage.

I was headed towards the pool when I heard a splash of water and a woman's laugh. I ducked down behind a bush and shut off my flashlight. Then I heard a man's laugh and the woman squeal in delight as more loud splashes echoed through the garden. Someone was having a good time. Considering the bomb I'd dropped on Emma Kirby, I knew it couldn't be her and Gerald. I got up and crept over to hide behind a large stone urn to get a closer look. There were two people in the pool, a man and a woman. Though his thick silver hair was wet and looked darker, I recognized the man as Ellis Kirby. The woman was Emma Kirby's physical therapist, Ashley. Both of them were naked. Ashley was the only precious flower Ellis Kirby seemed to be interested in at the moment. I wondered if Emma had any idea?

"Stop, Mr. Kirby," said Ashley breathlessly, as she tried in vain to grab her bikini top away from the older man. She was laughing, or giggling to be more precise.

"If you want it, you'll have to go and get it," he said playfully and tossed the bikini top onto a lounge chair by the pool where it landed with a wet plop.

Ashley crossed her arms over her perky breasts and pretended to pout. Then she gave Ellis a sly look and very slowly—purely for effect I'm sure—got out of the pool and stood staring at him with her hands on her hips. Ellis stared at her lush, wet body glowing in the moonlight like he was in a trance and watched as she walked over to the lounge chair and bent over like she was going to retrieve her top.

Instead, she bent over with her legs spread wide and gave him an eager beaver shot. Even though I didn't have the view Mr. Kirby had, I looked away just the same. But it didn't take a genius to figure out that the splashing I heard next was Ellis Kirby scrambling out of the pool to take what Ashley was offering him. Dennis said his father had a bad heart. I hoped Ashley wasn't about to kill him with that lethal bod of hers.

I looked back and Ellis was lying on his back on the lounge chair with Ashley straddling him and trailing her long wet hair over his chest.

"Are you sure she won't be back tonight?" asked Ashley, flipping a lock of wet hair over her shoulder before sticking her tongue in his belly button. Ellis shuddered with pleasure. I assumed Ashley was referring to Emma.

"I told you she flew to our condo in Palm Springs. Said she needed a break." *I just bet she did*, I thought.

"And your son?"

"He won't be home until the bars close at three. We still have plenty of time."

And they didn't waste a minute of it.

For the next twenty minutes, I waited patiently by the urn and tried to block out the sounds of Ellis Kirby getting it on with his wife's physical therapist. It was almost impossible to drown out the sounds of Ashley's porn star worthy moaning, and Ellis Kirby's grunting and constantly asking her, "You like it, doncha? Is this what you want? Is it?"

To which she would reply, "Yes, Big Daddy! Yes!"

Big Daddy? Eew!

Every few minutes I would take a quick peek and see the two of them contorted into positions that I knew couldn't be conducive to real pleasure. It was like they were competing with each other to see who could come first, each one focused solely on their own pleasure. If I were a betting woman—and I'm not cause I'm usually broke—my money would have been on Ellis but he was hanging tough for a man his age. Ultimately, it was Ashley who threw her head back first and howled, closely followed by Ellis. They lay on the lounge chair panting and exhausted for about five minutes before Ashley jumped up.

"Race you to the shower, Mr. Kirby." Ashley took off like a shot—still naked—right past me for the house. I wonder what happened to Big Daddy?

"You can call me Ellis," he said, racing after her with his limp and spent ding-dong flopping with each step.

I was relieved they'd finally gone into the house, but I had to take a minute to shake the images of the two of them out of my head before I headed over to the flower bed. I looked at my watch. It was 2:15. I practically ran around the pool, careful not to slip on the slick mosaic tile, and headed straight for the bed of azaleas. The part I needed to see was the section that Jeeves had dug up that had been replanted with bright orange flowers. I looked around to make sure no one was watching. Dennis' cottage showed no signs of life. So, I carefully poked around in the dirt under and around the orange flowers, slightly uprooting them. When my fingers encountered plastic, I gently pushed the thick dark soil aside until I revealed a black trash bag.

I poked and pulled on the plastic until I made a large hole, then shone my flashlight inside. I was greeted by the sight of a dead black and white cat. Its face was frozen in a hissing death mask. Its fur was stiff and hard. It smelled really bad. It was Ms. Flack's missing cat, Tamsin. I could tell by the way the cat's neck flopped that it was broken. This had been what Jeeves had been after when he'd dug up the flowers. He'd smelled Tamsin. I noticed the cat's fur was smeared with dirt, meaning it had probably been buried without the benefit of its trash bag shroud the first time around. Dennis hadn't made that same mistake twice. And speaking of Dennis, I heard the unmistakable sound of a door opening behind me. I turned and saw Dennis standing in the doorway of his cottage smiling at me.

"I thought you were—" I began, not quite knowing what I was about to say. Dennis laughed.

"Out?" he said, coming closer. "And miss my old man's Saturday water therapy session with smokin' hot Ashley? Not on your life." He'd been home the whole time. *Crap!*

"You killed them both, didn't you?"

"I'm really sorry." He shook his head. I stood up slowly leaving the bag with the cat where it lay.

"Sorry for what?" I backed away, not taking my eyes off of him. "Sorry you killed Clair Easton, or sorry you killed Ivy Flack?"

"Naw, I'm not sorry I killed either one of those nosy bitches. Actually, I'm sorry for what I'm about to do to you." Then he lunged at me.

I threw my little flashlight at him and watched as it bounced off his big chest. I tried to jump back out of his reach and slipped on the grass, falling on my ass. Dennis grabbed one of my legs and I kicked out of his grasp and managed to get to my feet. I took off running towards the pool but didn't get far when something hard slammed into the back of my head. Everything went black.

Chapter Twenty-Three

I WOKE UP IN the dark. Confused and disoriented, I lay still for a few seconds and tried to get my bearings and figure out where I was. I tasted blood in my mouth. Tentatively, I touched my lower lip and discovered it was split. There was also an egg-sized knot on the back of my head causing pounding that made even thinking painful. Curled into a fetal position on my side, I slowly turned onto my back and reached out my hand hitting something hard and unyielding mere inched from my face. I tried to straighten out my cramped legs but couldn't. Where the hell was I and why was it so dark? Then another sensation cut its way through the mind numbing pain in my head. Movement. I was moving.

A familiar smell filled my nose. Exhaust fumes. Car exhaust fumes. I was in a moving car. Judging by the enclosed space I was in, I quickly realized I was in the trunk. Panic welled up inside me and I started screaming and frantically beating on the inside of the trunk. But the car didn't stop and after a few minutes both my throat and my hands were sore. I was feeling around the trunk for something to pry open the lock with when the car came to an abrupt stop. I heard the opening and closing of the car door and footsteps crunching on gravel.

Fumbling around in the dark, my hand came to rest on a hard, round, plastic cylinder. It was a large flashlight. I felt for the switch to the sound of a key being inserted into the trunk lock. When the trunk flew open, I flashed the light into my captor's face. When I saw who it was, memories suddenly came flooding into my head, jolting me back in time, making me remember how I came to be in the trunk of a car with Dennis Kirby staring down at me. He effortlessly knocked the flashlight out of my hands, grabbed me by the front of my shirt, hauled me out of the trunk, and shoved me onto the ground.

I frantically looked around and saw that we were in the gravel driveway of an old dilapidated white house that looked like it was in the process of being renovated. We were at the old Bridges place. The house that Dennis's cousin Julian had bought and was renovating when he fell to his death from the roof. I started screaming and then grabbed a handful of gravel and threw it in his face. Dennis was blinded briefly, then swore and came at me. I took off running towards a nail gun lying in the grass only to trip and go sprawling, scraping up my hands and forearms. I felt my head being tugged painfully back as Dennis

ANGELA HENRY

grabbed a handful of my hair. He started dragging me towards the cellar door on the side of the house. I struggled and kicked along the way to no avail as he wrestled one side of the heavy cellar doors open.

He proceeded to drag me backwards down the cellar steps. I could feel cool air and smell dank earth. I felt like I was being put into a grave. I started screaming louder and Dennis slung me hard against the cellar's far wall. I slid into a heap on the dirt floor and started to sob. My head already felt like a bomb hand gone off in it. So being dragged by my hair had only added to the agony.

"What the hell did you hit me with?" I clutched the back of my head. He was panting so hard that I thought he wouldn't answer me.

"Hey, I couldn't let you get away. I threw one of the flat rocks edging the flower bed at you. I'm still a pretty damned good pitcher, wouldn't you say?" he said between breaths.

"Why are you doing this to me?"

"It's nothing personal. I actually kinda like you. But I really don't have a choice. You're a big problem." He grabbed a nearby shovel and thinking he was about to hit me with it, I threw up my arms up to shield myself. Instead, he started digging a hole. Three guesses on who it was for.

"Like Clair Easton and her dog?" I looked around

335

wildly for a way out. I soon realized Dennis was between me and the only exit. The cellar was dimly lit. But I could see the floor was strewn with tools. There was a pick ax on the cellar floor. If I could get to it I might be able to use it as a weapon, but unfortunately I'd have to get past Dennis first as it was on the other side of him. Dennis didn't answer my last question. So I asked again.

"Were Claire and Jeeves problems, too?"

He sighed and stopped digging, running the back of his arm across his face to wipe sweat from his eyes.

"I'd just finished burying that stupid cat under a tree when Jeeves got into our backyard and dug it up again. What I didn't know at the time was that Jeeves hadn't been alone. Clair had been in the backyard, too, watching me when I chased Jeeves away and reburied what he'd dug up in the azalea bed. I didn't mean to kill my old man's stupid flowers in the process. I had to replace them with another color. Clair must've been out walking Jeeves and he got away from her again. She'd followed him into our backyard. When my old man asked me what happened to his flowers, I told him Jeeves did it, not knowing Clair had been there too. I never thought he'd actually go and confront the crazy old bitch about her dog and threaten to call the humane society to have him taken away."

"Then she came to see me and told me that she

saw me that night and if I didn't tell my father that I was the one who messed up his flowers, she would. So I killed her damned dog with rat poison thinking: no dog, no problem. But it sent her over the edge instead. She kept hanging around our house threatening me and saying she was going to call the police on me because she knew I was up to no good. Wanted to know what I had buried in my backyard, anyway."

"And you couldn't have that, could you?" I inched my way closer to the pick ax.

"I tried to reason with her. She wouldn't listen. I had to do something. Even if I moved the cat, I couldn't have the police snooping around our property and asking me questions. I had complaints against me in California for suspicion of distributing drugs that my folks didn't know about. Then my parents came home from their walk the other day and told me they saw her yelling and screaming at some woman who'd been at her house. I didn't know it had been you, but it gave me an idea.

"You killed Clair hoping the police would think it had been the woman Clair was screaming at?"

"It was easy. I snuck into her backyard through that back gate. Her door was unlocked. I went inside and saw her walking into her living room. There were hedge clippers on the floor by the front door. I just grabbed them, waited, and stuck them in the side of her neck when she came back out of the living room. She never even knew what hit her. Didn't even scream."

"Was it that easy with Ms. Flack?"

Dennis laughed out loud. "Now, that was one crafty bitch. Acting like she was a victim like the rest of us when she was the one behind it all. She deserved what she got."

"How'd you find out it was her?" Dennis wasn't paying any attention to anything but the hole he was digging. I was almost poised to make a lunge for the pick ax but wanted to keep him talking and distracted.

"My mother sent me to tell her she'd be willing to donate money so we could still have our reunion. I went to her office. She was busy talking to her secretary and I started flipping through a magazine on her desk and noticed it was cut up and had letters missing just like that threatening note she claimed she found in the cafeteria. But it wasn't until I went to her house to give her the check that I realized she was the blackmailer. All her bags were packed. She was ready to skip town with our money. She'd be out there somewhere free to blackmail me for the rest of my life."

"What did you do?"

"She was running bath water when I got there. Told me to wait while she turned it off. I followed her

338

into the bathroom and knocked her out then turned off the water and put her in the tub. Then I plugged in her blow dryer and dropped it in. You should have seen the way she twitched." He laughed again. I inched closer to the pick ax while he continued to talk.

"Then her damned cat attacked me when I came out of the bathroom." He pulled the bandage off his wrist revealing several long deep-looking scratches. "I wrung its neck good."

"And you couldn't leave it behind because then everyone would know she'd been murdered," I said. He grinned and I took that as a yes.

"But one thing I could never figure out is how she found out about what I did," he shook his head in confusion.

"All anyone would have to do is call your former employer to find out about the allegations about you giving steroids to the student athletes you worked with. It wouldn't be hard to find out at all," I pointed out.

Dennis stopped digging and looked at me strangely. He immediately realized I wasn't against the wall where he threw me. He followed my gaze to the pick ax and we both dove towards it at the same time. I got there first, grabbed the handle, and swung out wildly, missing him by a mile. He knocked the ax effortlessly out of my hands with one vicious chop to my sprained wrist and backhanded me across my face, sending me flying back against the wall. Then he picked up the pick ax and drove it hard into the ground in a corner out of my reach

I felt something warm trickling down my face and put a hand to the wetness. My nose was bleeding. Dennis picked up the shovel again and continued to dig. How was I going to get out of this? No one would ever find me down here. I'd go missing, never to be found again.

"She wasn't in on it alone. She had a partner. If you let me go, I'll tell you who it is," I said, desperate now.

"You'd say anything right about now, wouldn't you? I'm not that stupid. You were probably the one in on it with her. But, don't worry, babe. You won't be down here in the dark all by yourself. You'll be in excellent company."

I looked around the small dank cellar trying to figure out whom he could be talking about. We were the only two people down there. Was he hallucinating?

"Dennis, what are you talking about?" I asked slowly. "Who else do you think is down here?"

"Shut up! I gotta get this hole dug. I don't like being down here any longer than I have to. Brings back bad memories."

"What bad memories?" I asked. But clarity was

beginning to dawn on me. This wasn't about steroids or being fired from his last job. He'd done something else, something much worse, and that's what he'd thought Ivy Flack had found out about.

He didn't know that Cherisse had been the one making the phone calls to the reunion committee telling them how much they needed to pay to keep their secrets buried. Only Dennis's secret was buried in this cellar—literally—and that's what he thought he was being blackmailed about. That's why he'd killed Ivy Flack.

"Dennis, my God, what did you do? Who else is buried down here?"

Dennis turned abruptly and came at me with the shovel. "I told you to shut up!"

Before he had a chance to get to me, however, I heard a loud clicking noise, followed by a soft thud, like someone pounding a steak. Dennis screamed and dropped the shovel. He twirled around desperately grabbing at his back. When he turned I saw a large nail sticking out of his back just above his shoulder blade. He grabbed the nail and pulled it out with a loud grunt and threw it against the wall. I looked beyond Dennis and saw Cherisse Craig standing at the bottom of the cellar steps holding the nail gun in her badly trembling hands. She was sobbing.

"He killed my sister, Kendra. He killed Serena.

Didn't you, you sorry motherfucker?" Cherisse squeezed the trigger on the nail gun again firing another nail, this time deep into Dennis' left shinbone. He fell to the floor of the cellar screaming.

"She's lying! She's crazy!" Dennis said, sobbing and clutching his leg. I doubted he'd be able to pull this nail out.

"I knew something wasn't right about what you said about Serena at Estelle's the other night and it didn't hit me until yesterday what it was. Serena told me the last time I talked to her, the day she took off for California, that she was getting a tattoo of her and her girlfriend's names in a heart. Her girlfriend was having second thoughts about going to California with her. She was going to do it to prove her love. But I never saw the tattoo because she hadn't gotten it yet. You must have seen her right after she got it done. How did you see it, Dennis? She wouldn't have shown it to you. You two weren't friends. She couldn't stand you because of the way you treated me. How did you know about the tattoo?" she screamed. When Dennis didn't answer her, she raised the nail gun again.

"Wait a minute!" he said, throwing up a hand.

"Tell me!" She started to squeeze the handle slightly.

"Okay, okay! I was in love with Serena! Are you

342

ANGELA HENRY

satisfied? But, she never gave me the time of day. I sent her flowers with an anonymous note telling her to meet me here at the house. Julian and I used to come here and chill and get high all the time."

"Then what happened," I asked him. I had to go past Dennis to reach the safety of Cherisse and the nail gun but I was afraid Dennis would grab me. I stayed put.

"I had a candlelight dinner waiting for her. But when she got here, I could tell I wasn't who she was expecting. I told her how I felt anyway and she...she...just laughed at me!" Dennis moaned like the memory of that rejection hurt him more than the nail sticking out of his shin.

"Go on!" Cherisse took a step closer.

"At first I thought it was because of the way I treated you. I told her I would apologize to you and get my friends to do the same. But she called me a stupid asshole and said she could never love me because she was gay. I didn't believe her. Thought she was just making it up to scare me away. That's when she pulled down her pants and showed me the tattoo on her hip. It was still fresh and had a bandage over it. It was a heart and inside it said Audrey and Serena Forever. She told me she and Audrey were in love and running away to

343

California together. That's when I knew she wasn't lying. I realized that's why Audrey was so hot to pass that science final so she could graduate on time, and that's why she broke up with Julian. She was in love with Serena. I couldn't believe it."

"So, you figured if you couldn't have her, no one would?" Cherisse's hands were still trembling. I was praying she wouldn't drop the nail gun.

"No! It wasn't like that! I thought I could change her mind. I tried to kiss her but she slapped my face. I got mad and shoved her but her pants were still down around her hips and her legs got tangled up and she fell and hit her head on the corner of the table! I swear I never meant to kill her! I swear!" Both Dennis and Cherisse were sobbing now.

"And that's why Audrey tried to kill herself, isn't it? She thought Serena took off without her and it broke her heart." I stood up slowly. Dennis just nodded.

"What did you do with my sister? I've been following you since yesterday hoping you'd lead me to her grave. Is she down here? Tell me!" She placed the nail gun against Dennis's forehead.

As I watched the two of them, it occurred to me that I may not have been the only one to realize

ANGELA HENRY

someone was buried in the cellar.

"Dennis, did Julian find out what you'd done? Did you push him off the roof?"

Dennis buried his face in his hands and howled. "I am such a fuck up! My parents have been telling me that all my life and it's true. I had no idea Julian had bought this place. I was still living in San Diego. I came home for a visit and he told me he had a surprise for me. Brought me out here and told me he'd bought the place and was going to renovate and sell it. Make a huge profit. Said he was almost finished with the roof and would be working on the cellar next. I couldn't let him find her. I came out here while he was working and threw a brick at him. I was just hoping he'd fall off the roof and break an arm or leg and not be able to work for a while. I just wanted to buy some time so I could dig her up and rebury her someplace else. I never meant for him to land on the fence. Julian was the only person who loved me."

"Where is she? Where's my sister?" Cherisse screamed in his face. Dennis flinched and timidly pointed near the place where he'd sunk the pick ax into the cellar floor. Cherisse turned to look, and in that instant Dennis knocked the nail gun out of her hand and shoved her to the floor. He got to his feet and

345

started kicking her with his uninjured leg. She curled into a ball and started whimpering.

I ran over and kicked the nail protruding from his shin, probably sending it another half inch into the bone. He stopped kicking Cherisse and his face went white. The sound that came out of his mouth was inhuman. He stumbled backward, tripping over the same shovel he'd been digging my grave with, and fell impaling himself on the pick ax sticking out of the dirt floor. Damn. That karma's a bitch.

Epilogue

WHEN I GOT HOME early the next morning, after giving my statement to the police, and being checked over in the emergency room, there was a message on my answering machine from Carl. It said:

Kendra, by the time you hear this, I'll be on my way to Atlanta. I came by to reason with you and what did I see? You all dressed up getting into another man's big, fancy car. Guess your paranoia over me and Vanessa was a reflection of your own guilty conscious, huh? I guess I never really knew you at all, did I? Well, I hope you find whatever it is you're looking for, but I now know it's not me. Goodbye.

Carl was gone. I couldn't believe it. And I didn't know what was worse, the fact he thought I'd been cheating on him, or the fact that he thought I'd been cheating on him with Lewis Watts! I sat down on my couch and cried myself to sleep.

I went to four funerals that next week: Ivy Flack's, Dennis Kirby's, Serena Craig's, and Clair Easton's. The first two I attended purely out of a need for closure more than anything else. Ms. Flack's funeral was well attended by students and staff at Springmont High. They'd loved her. Despite everything I'd found out about her, she'd been an excellent principal. I tried to think about the Ivy Flack I'd known before I found out about Alice Ivy Rivers. I mostly succeeded.

Dennis's funeral was attended by his parents, Gerald, and a few of his coworkers at the college bookstore. I was also surprised to see Ashley, the physical therapist, there. I stood well away from the small group and just observed. Dennis's parents looked numb with shock and clung to each other. Gerald kept sneaking peeks at Emma Kirby, who totally ignored him. I couldn't tell if it was because of grief over her son's death or anger over Gerald's baby with Sunny. Mostly likely it was both. Ashley and Ellis Kirby also didn't make much eye contact. I watched Ellis and Emma leave their son's gravesite to go put flowers on Julian's grave. Seems Dennis couldn't even have his parent's undivided attention at his own funeral. Unnoticed by the Kirbys, Gerald and Ashley left together.

Serena's funeral was also sparsely attended by Audrey and her girlfriend, Janice, Cherisse, and me. Audrey had left her husband and was now living with Janice, the woman I'd seen her with at Estelle's, and was preparing to fight for custody of her children. Audrey's grief over Serena's murder was tempered with a certain amount of joy. Audrey had been waiting for Serena at the bus station the night she died. She was heartbroken when she never showed up. Now she knew the love of her life hadn't run off and left her eleven years ago like she'd thought. Audrey was at peace and felt free to be who she really was.

Cherisse was also at peace. She planned to change her major to psychology and become a high school guidance counselor like Ms. Flack. I didn't have the heart to tell her the truth about Ivy Flack. There was nothing to be gained from shattering her illusions about a woman who was her only high school friend. Cherisse had also stopped seeing Gerald and had let go of a lot of the anger and hurt from high school. I told her I'd never tell a soul about her helping Ms. Flack blackmail the reunion committee and I meant it. I was hoping we could finally be friends. She seemed to want that, too.

Clair Easton's funeral was by far the saddest. Mr. Diaz, the landscaper, and I were the only ones who came. None of her neighbors bothered showing up. There were no flowers, and the only music was provided by the church's minimally talented organist, who must have thought she was performing on Star Search the way she kept cheesing and winking at us.

The service was brief and rushed because a christening had been scheduled for immediately after the funeral. So Clair Easton's fifty-eight years on earth were hurriedly summed up in fifteen minutes by a lisping minister who kept mispronouncing her last name as Eastman and clearly hadn't known her. Afterwards, I made awkward small talk with Mr. Diaz, who seemed to have had genuine affection for his eccentric client.

I felt restless after leaving Claire's funeral. I drove around for a while to think. I had tried to call Carl to explain what had really happened the night he came over and saw me getting into Lewis Watt's car. But I when I dialed his cell phone number, I found out it had been changed. I even tried to get his new number from his mother. No such luck. She basically told me I'd fucked up and it was my loss. Her son was better off and I needed to leave him alone so he could find happiness with someone else. So, I did. His mother was right. He wanted marriage and babies and needed to find someone who wanted those things, too, because that person wasn't me. And I didn't know if it ever would be.

Hours later, I found myself parked in front of Rollins's house. If nothing else, I always had a friend in him. At least I thought I did. I hadn't seen him since our dinner at Estelle's. Even after my latest caper hit the papers, I hadn't heard a peep out of him, which was strange. I noticed the car parked in the driveway behind his gold Mercedes and figured it was his daughter Inez's car. As far as I knew, she was still living in the apartment over his garage.

I let myself into his backyard and walked up on his deck, my hand poised to knock on the sliding glass door. But the lights were down low. I cupped my hands and looked in. Rollins was inside and he wasn't alone. I could hear music playing. It sounded like Ray, Goodman, and Brown's "Special Lady". Rollins was slow dancing with someone I couldn't see at first. Her head was resting against his shoulder. I couldn't move. All I could do was watch. Finally, the woman lifted her head and I saw her face and wanted to scream. It was Detective Trish Harmon.

Now all of the new clothes, hairdo, and attitude were understandable. She was in love…with Rollins! I watched as he leaned down to give her a kiss, then they turned and left the room hand in hand, heading for the bedroom, I assumed. Was this what he meant when he asked me to let him move on? He'd met Trish Harmon and wanted to be with her? I felt dizzy and had to sit down on the deck steps. Well, what did I expect? He had every right to be happy. But with Trish Harmon? This was not happening.

Later, I was sitting in Frisch's devouring a mountain of hot fudge cake when my cell phone rang.

It was my best friend, Lynette.

"Did you hear?" she asked, sounding highly agitated.

"Hear what?" I was not in the mood for any more bad news.

"Stephanie Preston's gone."

"She died?" I said, not at all surprised since last I'd heard she was on death's door. I was relieved I wouldn't have to testify against her.

"No, Kendra, she escaped from custody."

"What?" I sat straight up in my chair. "How? I thought she was dying?"

"Everyone did. They found out the prison doctor treating her was one of her ex-johns from back in the day when she was hooking in Vegas. He purposefully got assigned to the prison she was in to be near her. He'd been lying to everyone about her condition so he could help her escape. She wasn't dying. She was getting better. Now they're both in the wind. Nobody knows where they went. I'm scared. What if she comes after us and tries to kill us again?"

I was speechless.

"Kendra, you there? Aren't you scared?" she asked when I didn't answer her.

I was scared to death all right. And what's more, I'd never felt more alone in my life.

About the Author

Angela Henry lives in Ohio and works in the library field. She is also the founder of the award-winning MystNoir Website, which promotes African-American mysteries. This is her fourth Kendra Clayton mystery.

Discussion Questions for Schooled in Lies

1. Did you enjoy high school? Why or why not?

2. Do you go to your high school reunions? Why or why not?

3. Are you surprised that Kendra wasn't popular in high school?

4. Have you ever been bullied or been a bully?

5 Do you think Kendra was right to be worried about all the time Carl was spending with his ex wife?

6. Do you think Ivy Flack was right when she said everyone has secrets?

7. Do you think Kendra was wrong not to go to the police when she found out who was behind the accidents and threats to the reunion committee?

8. Do you think people who committed serious crimes as teenagers can change?

9. Were you surprised that Kendra was so conflicted about marriage? Can you relate to her feelings?

10. What surprised you the most at the end of the novel?

Made in the USA
Coppell, TX
13 February 2020